Erminie

Patricia Lee

Copyright © 2020 Patricia Lee

All rights reserved.

ISBN: 9798650689904

DEDICATION

To my husband Rick, who allowed me to dig into his family tree and discover the fascinating woman that is Erminie

ERMINIE

AUTHOR'S NOTE

The inspiration for this book began with research into my husband's family tree. It was inspired by scant but tantalizing tidbits of oral history as told by a grandfather and great uncle who immigrated to Canada from Vermont in the early 20th century. Birth, death and census records gave me a glimpse of a large French Canadian family living in Vermont then, later, Montreal. One member of that family stood out. Erminie, a third generation American girl with French Canadian roots. I felt compelled to tell Erminie's story and give her a voice. This is a work of fiction, but hiding within these pages is a real girl, living a difficult life in an unforgiving time.

ACKNOWLEDGMENTS

I would like to express my gratitude to the many people who offered feedback and helped in the production of this novel. Without the help of so many, this book would not have been possible. Many thanks to Lynn McKenna, Debbie Malone, Linda Mosley, Iona Glabus, Bonnie Schaffer, Troy Radke, Jo Anne Lauder (cover design) and Dianne Shannon (editing).

CHAPTER ONE

I stand, eyes glued to my boots, fingers in a tight wet knot behind my back. I know Papa sits in one of the chairs behind me, but I don't dare turn to look. I'm grateful for his support but mortified he's seeing me here, in this place, in this predicament. It was brave of him to come.

"My name is Erminie Menard, from Pittsford," I mumble in the direction of Justice Boehm. My voice has a husky piece to it I hardly recognize. Boehm is asking all of us our names and where we're from. He sits at the front of the room, not nearly as important looking as I imagined a justice would be. In fact, I've seen him before. He owns a motor car and drives around town scaring the horses. I've seen children laughing at him on the street, probably while scheming to get a ride in the noisy thing. Now Justice Boehm sits suffering in the heat with the rest of us, beads of sweat oozing from the freckled pink of his scalp. The window is open and the air is thick with the smell of lilac, but no breeze finds its way to where we stand. I feel a drop of sweat creeping down the small of my back. I pray this is over quickly.

Justice Boehm has collected names from the boys who stand to my left. He returns to me now. He wants details. I lift my head but find I can't quite bring myself to look square at him. Instead I focus on a spot just behind his ear, on the portrait of our new president. I can't even remember this new president's name. It's lost to me. Justice Boehm asks me questions about that evening. It seems like another life but it's only been a week or so.

I answer the questions. Minimal words. My throat feels all dry and tight. Yes, I stole the money from Loveland's Mercantile. No. No one was with me. This is a lie and I feel my face flood with color. I wonder if Justice Boehm notices. But he goes on with his questions. Why did I steal the money? I'm intensely aware of my father behind me. I wanted to buy a new dress. Another lie, this one easier. He nods as if this is something one

1

would expect from a girl, and moves on to question the boy beside me.

There are four of us in all but the others are there for different reasons. The boy beside me hasn't yet spoken. He's small, dirty and barefoot. I've never seen him around town before. Earlier, when asked his name, he kept his eyes on the floor and remained silent. A small gray woman, an official of some kind, stepped forward and spoke to the justice on his behalf. "He does not speak, your honor. His name is Daniel Bedford. He is eight years old and he is alone. His mother has recently been committed to the insane asylum in Brattleboro. His father was killed in the quarry shortly after his birth. There are no other siblings or relatives to care for him." The justice nodded, made a note in his book and moved on to the other two boys. Their faces are familiar, though I don't know them. I learn their names are Oscar and Will. They're boys Maman would forbid me to talk to if she saw them in the street. Both are dark and swarthy. Together, it's revealed, they set a series of fires around Pittsford. Neither gives a reason and neither seems to give a fig. Justice Boehm, frowning, scribbles more notes in his big book.

It's over quickly. Justice Boehm sentences me to one year at the Wells Industrial School in Vergennes. The two older boys are sentenced to two years, and little Daniel is to be held there until he completes his schooling or until his sixteenth birthday. We're ushered out by Tanner, the town constable.

Constable Tanner has been kind to me. There's no jail in Pittsford but he has a room on the upper floor of his house where he keeps prisoners until they can be transported elsewhere. He keeps the three boys there, but his wife puts me in a different bedroom in their house. "It wouldn't be proper for you to stay in there with the boys," she clucks as she takes me up to the room. I've spent the last week here eating meals brought to me in my room. Despite their kindness, I cried when I first heard Mrs. Tanner turn the key in the lock. Kindness or no, I was a prisoner, no different than the three boys upstairs.

Now, Tanner takes us all back to his house. The two older boys are shackled to a rusted metal ring in the back of Tanner's buckboard. Daniel sits silently in the back with them and I sit up front with Tanner. It makes me feel conspicuous, being singled out like that. But, truthfully, I'm afraid of the two dark sullen boys and glad to have some distance between us.

HENRY

My eldest has gotten herself into a bit of trouble. Jenny didn't want me to come. She was afraid someone would see me coming into the courthouse and it would just make things worse. For once she didn't get her way. Minnie needs me now. She shouldn't have to face this alone. I'd hoped I could take my girl home with me but the judge is sending her to Wells Industrial School for a year! There's two separate laws for the rich and the poor.

She's a good girl, my Min. I know she'll get past this all right. Maybe it will even be good for her. Her ma pulled her out of the French school years ago but, if I'd had a say, I would have let her go longer, so maybe she could be a teacher. She's good with the little ones. She would be a great teacher.

CHAPTER TWO

Early the next morning Mrs. Tanner wakes us for breakfast; she serves it in the kitchen this time. After our biscuit and ham, Tanner loads us into his wagon for the trip to Vergennes. It's a hot, dusty, dirty, sullen trip. Tanner isn't much for talking. Mrs. Tanner has packed some food and water. Tanner doles it out and we eat as we travel, stopping only to water Brownie, Tanner's old mare. At one point during the trip Tanner addresses us, the four of us. It sounds like a rehearsed speech, like something he's said a million times before. He tells us how lucky we are to be going to Wells, how it's a modern school, how it will change our lives. "Set us on the right path," he says. One of the older boys snickers. The rest of us hold quiet. It will be what it will be. I quit school four years ago. Not my choice but Maman said she needed me at home. It seems funny that I was made to quit school and now I'm being forced to attend one. After all this time the idea of any school is terrifying, let alone a reform school. And there's no doubt, for all its airs about being a progressive school, Wells is a reform school. People don't go there because they want to.

I haven't seen Vergennes before. It's bigger and noisier than Pittsford. People, horses and streetcars crowd the streets. A few motor cars sputter down the main street weaving in amongst the wagons and carts. I hear Tanner mutter under his breath about "this godforsaken town," but he always speaks in soothing tones to a jittery Brownie.

We come to a stop in front of a large double wrought iron gate. The metal winds around to form the letters "WIS" and the two gates meet right in the middle of that big letter I. A uniformed man is standing in a box inside that gate and when we stop he steps down from his box, unlocks the gate and swings it open for us. "Afternoon Mr. Tanner," he says. "While since I saw you."

"Four from Pittsford," Tanner says, pushing his hat back on his head and wiping his forehead with the back of his hand. He leaves a white streak in the dust that coats his face.

"You got a crime wave down there in Pitts?" the man smirks.

Tanner just shakes his head tiredly and hands the reins to a boy who has run up to meet us. "Come on you lot. This is the end of the road. Get your sorry asses down here and let's go get you checked in." He moves to the back of the wagon and unchains Oscar and Will from the wagon. He leaves the chain that connects them to each other though. I guess it's so if they try to run they'd have to do it as a team.

Our little party shuffles down a walkway edged with beautiful flowers and shrubs. At the end of the walk is a grand brick building with Vermont marble steps and huge oak doors. I've been imagining snarling guard dogs and a lot of bars, so I'm pleasantly surprised. Even so, the impressive architecture and pretty surroundings do little to calm the butterflies in my stomach. Tanner hustles us up the steps in front of us and instructs a scowling Oscar to get the door. We file into a large airy room. One entire wall consists of windows. Dappled sunlight dances across the floor. The two side walls are lined with chairs. Just inside the door a tall, lean uniformed guard tips his hat to Tanner. A woman sits behind a desk on the fourth wall, beside a closed door. She and the guard are the only occupants of the room. Tanner gestures for us to approach the desk and line up. Oscar and Will shuffle awkwardly in their leg shackles, getting in each other's way and snickering about it. The woman ignores their insolence and asks each of us our names, checking them off, without comment, in a large ledger laid open on her desk. When she has that all written down, she tells us to have a seat. Thinking it's maybe smart to put some distance between myself and the Oscar and Will duo, I sit on the wall opposite them, beside Daniel. Tanner leans over and speaks quietly to the woman at the desk. He turns to Oscar and Will and unlocks their leg shackles, pocketing the key and draping the chains over his arm. He turns to address us all.

"I'm leaving you four here. Mind your manners and do your studies and if I see you back in Pittsford I expect to get no trouble out of you, hear?" Without waiting for an answer he's gone with only a nod to the guard at the door. We're now in the charge of the solemn woman at the desk and the guard. Tanner's leaving gives me a sick feeling in my stomach. I suddenly feel alone, as though the last link with Pittford and home is gone. Odd I should feel any sort of connection to the man who arrested me and held me prisoner in his house, but there it is.

As the heavy door closes behind Tanner, the woman calls Oscar's name. He rises slowly and saunters toward the desk. Every step oozes insolence. I see, or more like sense, the guard at the door tense, his hand moving almost imperceptibly closer to his sidearm. The woman at the desk seems unfazed. She gestures toward the door on her right and Oscar pushes it open and disappears into the room on the other side. The rest of us sit in silence. Will looks less cocky without Oscar by his side and I know right away who the boss is. Beside me, little Daniel wipes his nose on his sleeve and I wonder if he's crying. I haven't heard a sound from him the entire trip to Vergennes except for the occasional sniffle or cough. I chance a sideways look at him but his head is forward and his greasy hair covers most of his face. I feel bad for him anyway. He's so little. Without thinking much about it, I drape my arm around him and give him a little squeeze. The thought crosses my mind that maybe the boy has lice and maybe touching him isn't such a good idea. But right then the lady at the desk calls my name. I get up and head to the door through which Oscar has just returned, a crooked grin on his face. The lady at the desk hands him a sheet of paper. He hesitates a beat, then turns and shoves the paper into his pocket without looking at it. I wonder if he's really that confident or if he's as scared inside as I am. I wonder if I can manufacture that kind of courage but I don't think I have it in me.

I cross the threshold into an office such as I've never seen before. Heavy green velvet draperies frame the windows and a massive oak desk dominates the room. Behind the desk sits a plain thin man dwarfed by the grandness of his surroundings. His hair is parted in the middle and pomaded onto his little skull. Round gold-rimmed spectacles perch on his nose making his eyes look outsized and watery. He's wearing a dark striped waistcoat over a white high-collared shirt. A large mustache, waxed to curl up at each end, dwarfs his face. Everything seems too big for him. He leans forward as I enter and gestures at a chair just in front of his desk.

"Sit, young lady." he commands. I do as I'm told. Even the chair is big. My feet barely reach the floor.

"I am Mr. Wyre, the headmaster here at Wells. It's my duty to welcome you here and to ensure that you know the rules that will govern your life for the next," here he quickly checks a paper laid out in front of him, "one year." Not knowing what to say or do, I nod. He continues. "We have high expectations for our students, and a low tolerance for discipline problems. You will be assigned a work detail which will change every six weeks or so at the discretion of the staff. In addition, you will attend classes. We have an academic stream but I think you might be better off in the Home Management Program. You will learn the practical skills that will make you both a good employment prospect and a good wife and mother." He sits back in his chair and steeples his fingers under his chin before continuing. "Mrs. Partridge, the woman you met in the waiting area, will give you a schedule with your classes and your work detail. Pick that up from her when you leave. As for the rest, you're expected to stay within the limits of the walls unless you have specific permission to leave and are accompanied by one of the staff. You will be assigned a room in the girls' dorm. You're expected to sign in and out each time you leave and enter the dormitory building. We must know where you are at all times. The staff are in charge here, and what they say goes. Smoking, drinking, fighting, fraternizing and disobedience are expressly forbidden and may result in a longer stay here at Wells. Is this all clear Miss Menard?" Again I nod. "Good. You may go. Don't forget to pick up your schedule from Mrs. Partridge."

I rise, and turn toward the door. I have yet to utter a single word. As I reach for the door knob Mr. Wyre adds, "Welcome to Wells, Miss Menard. I'm sure we'll be seeing a lot of you." I don't know what he means but I know I don't like his tone. Hand still on the knob, and without turning my head, I mutter a thank you and let myself out of the room.

Mrs. Partridge hands me my paper. At the top is the stylized Wells "W". "This is your schedule, dear." she says kindly. "I've put you on the cleaning detail for the first six weeks. You'll work with Mr. Dinardi and his crew. You can meet him in the basement of this building tomorrow morning. Make sure you are here at quarter to seven so he can assign you to your work area. You will clean each morning from seven to ten o'clock. Calisthenics are in the square at half past ten for one hour. You have some time to get cleaned up before lunch. In the afternoon you will attend your various classes. Your class schedule is here," she points at a chart midway down the sheet. "It's too late today to get you started but I'll have one of the girls show you to your room and help you get settled."

Daniel and Will both have their turn with headmaster Wyre. Daniel is the last. Wyre actually walks him out and wordlessly turns him over to Mrs. Partridge, looking a little disgusted. Daniel is now definitely crying, streams of snot are running down his dirty face. I feel so bad for him. I wonder if he was even able to climb up onto the enormous chair in Wyre's office. Mrs. Partridge takes a handkerchief from a desk drawer and wipes Daniel's nose. Then she balls the thing up and dabs at his eyes. Even from where I sit I can see that the handkerchief has come away black from the road dust and whatever else Daniel has on him. I see her take the handkerchief and toss it in her waste basket. She hands Daniel his schedule, same as mine, but she doesn't even try to explain it to him. I wonder how he's going to get on in this place.

Now that we've all seen Wyre, Mrs. Partridge says something to the guard who pokes his head out the door and gestures to someone. A boy and a girl come in. Mrs. Partridge tells me that the girl will show me to the girls' dormitory. Daniel, Will and Oscar are to go with the boy to their rooms. The guard follows them out.

CHAPTER THREE

The girl summoned to collect me is Ada. She's painfully thin, round shouldered with deeply pockmarked skin. Dishwater blond hair falls in greasy strings around her face but she smiles brightly and I like her right off. Mrs. Partridge introduces her as one of the senior girls. She asks her to take me to the girls' house and locate a bed for me in the Oak Room. On the walk over Ada explains there are several rooms within the girl's house, each named after a species of Vermont tree. She rolls her eyes as she tells me this, clearly believing the naming system is more cringe-worthy than patriotic.

As we walk I see almost no one on the vast grounds. Those that are about are moving purposefully, like they have some real important place to be. According to Ada most everyone is in their afternoon classes.

The girls' house is a solid three-story brick building some way from the administration building we've just left. Beds of flowers line the walkway and creep around the foundation. A veranda wraps around two sides of the building. I later learn only female staff can enjoy the shade here. Like the administration building, the entrance is by way of a series of Vermont marble stairs and the door is a heavy oak double affair. Ada pushes this open with what looks like every ounce of strength her skinny frame can produce. Inside we find ourselves in a foyer of sorts. It's dark; no windows, gloomy and airless. Seated at a desk beside the door is a uniformed female guard.

"Sign in please," she barks, with no trace of warmth in her voice. "And make sure you return my pen."

Something about the woman sets my teeth on edge but Ada dutifully picks up the pen and writes her name on one line of a large book lying open on the table. She glances up at a large wall clock behind the woman, then enters the time-"3:20". Beside that, in a column marked "purpose" she writes "orientation". Handing me the pen she instructs me to put my name, the time and to write "check-in". I do as she says and set the pen, meaningfully, on the table above the book. The woman remains silent and expressionless. Ada points me toward a set of stairs.

"Oak Room is on the second floor."

We climb the stairs without conversation but once on the second floor Ada leans in conspiratorially. "That was Mrs. Letourneau. She's got the personality of a prune but she's pretty harmless. Some of the girls say that her husband left her and that's why she's such a grump. But you didn't hear that from me. Personally if I was married to her I'd be on the first train to Boston too." She chuckles at her own joke and pushes open a door to the left of the hallway. I wonder that this tiny girl doesn't have arms like a man.

"Welcome to the Oak Room" she says, sweeping her arm in a grand gesture, bidding me to enter.

The room is long and narrow with a row of beds down either side. Beside each bed is a small, three-drawer desk with a chair. Tall windows line the outer wall, each with an ironwork grating on the outside.

"There are eight beds in this room. Three of them are empty right now. All the ones on the window side are taken, I think, so don't bother looking at those. Just make sure you don't take one that belongs to someone. They'll have their stuff on the bed or in the drawers. No touching other girls' stuff," she warns. "No surer way to make an enemy around here than to touch their stuff. There are extra uniforms in that closet down there at the end. There should be a few sizes so find one that fits-but they all fit like gunny sacks so don't expect a miracle." Ada tugs at the waist of her own over-sized dress. "You have to wear the uniform all the time, shoes too. The only thing of your own that you wear is your underwear. The lavatory is down the hall on the left. Dinner bell is at five o'clock. I don't think you need to do anything until then except get yourself settled and put on your uniform. The other girls are all in class right now but they'll start coming in soon." With that Ada says her goodbyes and leaves me to find a bed.

It isn't hard to figure which beds are taken. Most of the girls have dolls or stuffed animals perched on their pillows. Some have colorful quilts draped over the beds. Occupied desks hold brushes and combs, mirrors, school books and the paraphernalia of any girl's room. The beds that aren't occupied stand out in their austerity. Plain chipped iron frames, the mattresses covered by a sickly green cotton spread. I find a bed about midway down the row, across from the windows. I sit down and give a little bounce. The springs protest but the mattress feels comfortable enough. It doesn't take me long to unpack. I've brought next to nothing with me, only the tired old valise that Maman packed up with a few essentials. Papa delivered it to Tanner's the night I was arrested. He was only allowed to stay for a few minutes so we had an awkward conversation in Tanner's kitchen. Papa told me he'd try to come to the hearing. He never asked any questions about my arrest or the money, though he must have been burning to ask. Now I tuck the valise under my bed, suddenly feeling a surge of affection for its dusty and battered self.

    I stow my few articles of clothing in the drawers. I won't get to wear them anyway but that's no real loss. Most of my things are mended and more than gently worn. I actually like the idea of a uniform, though when I check them out in the closet, I realize Ada has been generous in her description. They're faded and soft from washing. Most have patches. None look like they will fit me properly. They are gray pin-striped dresses, each with a white pinafore whose purpose seems to be to cinch the whole thing together. I pick one that seems least likely to drown me. I find a pair of black lace-up boots at least a size too big for my feet. There's no private area in the room to change so I quickly wiggle out of my dress and put the uniform on, hoping no one will come in and catch me in my tattered gray underwear. I put on the boots and lace them as tightly as I can to get a decent fit. I wander down to a communal lavatory that seems to serve our room, along with others on the floor. Here there are several private stalls and a line of sinks under a long mirror. I'm used to sharing washing facilities with my siblings but this is a lavatory of industrial proportions. I do my business and freshen up a bit. There are no towels. I later learn I should have claimed one from the upper shelf of the closet. I use my apron to wipe my face and dry my hands, leaving the cotton crumpled and streaked with dirt. I am not off to a good start in the clothing department.

    When I get back to the room it's still empty. I lay down on my bed and close my eyes. Sharing a room with five other girls, I have a feeling the quiet won't last.

CHAPTER FOUR

It all came about because Harry Loveland had a grand plan. Harry was a blond-haired, blue-eyed god. He befriended me shortly after we moved to Pittsford at a time when I was very lonely. My family had moved several times in the last few years, following the quarry jobs and my father's restless nature. First it was to Pittsford from Proctor, where I was born. Then from Pittsford we moved to Danby, then Rutland. But after just over a year in Rutland it was back to Pittsford. With my father it was a need to climb out of the quarries and do some of the more creative marble carving, where the pay was better and where Papa thought his talents would be better used. So far, he never got beyond etching cherubs onto tombstones. Maman was a social climber. She wanted to be that woman that everyone in town looked up to and admired, but Papa always disappointed her. So we moved, always searching for a better job, a higher station, a more understanding employer. But mostly, Maman wanted to stay far away from Rutland and my Grand-mère, Papa's mother, who she considered arrogant and overbearing.

I never really had a chance to make friends, so when Harry started talking to me at church every Sunday I felt like maybe I had a friend at last. Aside from his considerable male beauty, Harry was rich, at least when using my family as a measure. His father owned the Mercantile in Pitts where Harry worked after school and on weekends. His family had been in Pitts since before Adam. There was a whole section of the town named after some great-great-grandfather of his. Maman wasn't as crazy then. When she saw me talking to this boy she hoped it would be a way to marry me off and maybe elevate her station at the same time. What she didn't know was that Harry would be my undoing.

It turned out Harry and I had the same dream, or at least our dreams shared certain elements. We both wanted to escape our suffocating families and move to Boston. Once in Boston our dreams parted ways. I wanted to buy a beautiful home overlooking the Charles River and have a passel of kids. I wanted to do this with Harry, though I knew right from the start his dream was very different. Getting married was way down his list. Still, I thought we could make it work. I thought, somehow, things would come together for us if we just got the process started. When Harry suggested a scheme to get money to fund our escape from Pittsford, he made it sound so easy. He assured me nothing could go wrong. He even managed to make it sound like the right thing to do.

The plan was that Harry would take a small amount of money from the Mercantile's cash each week. Not so much that it would be missed, he assured me. He would pass the money to me at a pre-determined time each week. I would come into the store under the pretense of looking for some thread or a bit of fabric or to admire some shoes that had arrived. Harry would come by and slip the envelope of money into my bag while making small talk. I'd take the money home, and hide it. This is where things got more complicated for me. My family rented a two-story house on the east side of town and I shared a room with my three little sisters, Ethel, Viola and Leona. Privacy was non-existent and I lived in fear that someone would discover my trove. I'd sewn an inner pocket into my winter coat and kept the money there, in the closet I shared with the little ones.

I had four envelopes of money hidden away when Tanner came to get me. It turned out Harry Loveland's father was a better book keeper than Harry gave him credit for. He noticed sums of money missing. It didn't help that Harry's greed had gotten the better of him and each reach into the cash drawer had extracted a greater sum than the time before. Mr. Loveland knew who, among the staff, was the likely culprit. He also knew his family's good name was in jeopardy. He took Harry aside and made him tell where the money was. Looking back, it probably didn't take much for Harry to spill the beans. In the end, Harry got off free and clear, while I, who had done nothing more than store the money, received the visit from Tanner.

When he arrived at our door there was no point in denying anything. He knew everything, right down to the extra pocket sewn into my winter coat. My father was silent. My mother made much noise, protesting that Tanner had the wrong house, the wrong person. We had no good family name to protect, really, but my mother didn't understand that. I knew she could feel her grip on the social ladder slipping because of me.

Tanner escorted me up the stairs to my bedroom and I showed him where the money was hidden. Downstairs, I could hear the little ones peppering Maman with questions she had no answers for.

That was when Tanner took me to his house for what, in Pittsford, passed for my incarceration. I waited eight days for Justice Boehm to arrive from Rutland for his regular court date. It was during this time that Mrs. Tanner gave me some gossip about Harry and his father. The Lovelands were insisting they would "handle" Harry themselves. The fact that Harry was not facing Justice Boehm with me was a bee in Mrs. Tanner's bonnet, no question. It wasn't her decision though. As for Mr. Tanner, he either couldn't, or wouldn't go against the Loveland's wishes.

    I never saw Harry Loveland again. By the time I returned from Wells he'd left town. He hadn't gone to Boston as he hoped, but to Rutland, which wasn't nearly as grand. I never bothered telling anyone that Harry had masterminded the plan. It seemed pretty obvious that everyone already knew. It's just that no one seemed to care.

CHAPTER FIVE

I surprise myself by dozing a bit, exhausted by the hot dusty ride from Pittsford. I must be sleeping pretty sound because I startle when the door crashes open and two girls bump into the room, laughing at some shared joke. I quickly sit up, swinging my feet down to the floor. For some reason I feel guilty, like they've caught me dead to rights in their room. Of course, it's not like I have any say in being here. The pair stop when they see me. The shorter of the two approaches the bed.

"What have we got here?" She extends her hand and I rise to take it. "Name is Boxer," she says, shaking my hand firmly, like a man would do. "This one is Cora," she indicates the taller girl who hangs back, clutching a bundle of books to her chest. "The others'll be here right quick but you're lucky to be meeting the best first." Boxer chuckles and swings around to Cora. "Cora here is the smartest girl in the school and I'm the toughest. We all gotta be good at somethin'. What's your name, hon?"

I stammer my name, a little intimidated by the girl, elf-sized but able to fill the entire room with her presence. She's well under five feet, not even reaching my chin. But she's solidly built like she's all muscle. Her hair is far and away her most striking feature. It's coal black and bobbed to just below her chin. There it billows out in a tangle of curls that frame her face. I saw a cartoon once called Mutt and Jeff. I can't remember now which one was Mutt and which one was Jeff but it seems to me that these two girls are the female equivalent. Cora is tall, very tall, and lean as a beanpole. Her long, tired-blond hair is perched up on her head adding to her already considerable height. Where Boxer fills the room, Cora looks like she wants to disappear in it. I like them both.

"What kind of a name is Boxer?" I ask, then quickly remember my manners. "That is if I'm not being too nosy."

"Nah," she dismisses my concern with a toss of her hand. "Everybody asks that. It's easy though. It's because I'm a boxer. Or I was before I came here. I used to do exhibition matches in Rutland, the southern parts of the state and sometimes over into Massachusetts. I even boxed in Boston, she adds with obvious pride. I could beat any female out there, and some of the men too. Trouble is I got too good. Threw a punch at a girl in Brattleboro and sent her flying clear out of the ring. They needed to call a doctor for her and word got out that we was fightin'. They came and arrested me and here I am. Men can knock the hell out of each other and nobody cares, but let a girl try it!" Boxer shrugs. "Anyways, that's my story. Cora here killed her pa. What brings you here?"

I struggle to keep my jaw from dropping right down into my boots. Cora killed someone? In all my life I've never met anyone who killed a human, at least not that I know of. Yet here I am standing face to face with a killer who looks like she would run away from a goodly sized kitten. But Boxer is impatient.

"C'mon you can tell us. What got you in here?"

"I stole some money. From a store." I decide there's no point in going into the whole story of being duped by Harry. That part was my own damned fault and I know nobody is going to give me any sympathy over it.

"Well, you are welcome in our little coven Erminie. The others will be here directly. It's not such a bad place. The other girls are no real problem, most of them anyways. It's the staff you have to watch out for. Especially Wyre. You met him?"

I nod. "He seems nice," I lie.

Boxer snorts. "The son-of-a-bitch can't keep his pecker in his pants. You do what you can to stay away from him. If you can't stay away then you do what you gotta do and nobody's gonna hold it against you." As if she's realized some private and very funny joke, Boxer bursts out laughing. Even Cora offers a smile that doesn't quite reach her eyes. Before I can ask what's so funny the door bursts open and three more girls flounce into the room, all giggles and chatter.

The first of the girls, a busty brunette, pulls up short at the sight of me, standing there with Boxer and Cora.

"Christ on the cross, look what they've dumped on us. Another cow turd from the sticks." She swishes over to one of the beds near the windows and throws an armful of books on her bed. The second girl, a heavy girl with red-blond hair, wordlessly follows her, flopping down on the adjacent bed. The third girl hangs back near the door, nervously fingering a ripe pimple on her chin.

"And here we have the rest of our happy group," Boxer announces, theatrically. "The princess there is Jessie. She's a real sweetheart as you can see. Her friend there is Margaret. And the one there by the door is Mathilda-Matty to most of us. Come in Matty and meet Erminie."

Shyly, Matty steps forward and offers a limp hand. I shake it as best as I can but it's like squeezing a dead perch.

Boxer leans in a little closer. "Don't mind Jessie. She likes to put on airs but she's mostly harmless. And Margaret just does what Jessie does. No mind of her own that one. We go down to supper in a few minutes. Sit with us. We'll help get you off on the right foot."

I nod thankfully. I don't really believe I need to "get off on the right foot", but I have to admit Jesse's bitchiness has unnerved me.

A while later, we all file out to the dining hall, which Boxer affectionately refers to as the "grub club". It's a long narrow building on one end of the grounds. Young people of all ages and sizes are filing in from different directions. It's the first inkling I have of how many are housed at this school. I see little Daniel, walking alone, dragging his toes in the dust.

"Hold on," I say to Boxer and the others. I dash over and put a hand on Daniel's thin shoulder. He flinches like I've smacked him, but when he sees it's me he gives me a shy little smile. Good, at least he knows who I am, I think.

"Would you like to eat with me and some of the girls from my room?" I ask. The thought occurs to me that I might not be doing him any favors by singling him out and inviting him to sit with a bunch of girls. Still, he looks so small and forlorn I can't bear to leave him on his own. I try to imagine little Ethel here on her own, and how I sure would want someone to take care of her. Of course, I chuckle to myself, Ethel would have organized a revolt and broken through the walls by now. Not Daniel. He simply bobs his head and allows me to move him along with my hand on his back.

When we rejoin Boxer and the other girls, Jessie and Margaret have gone on ahead. I'm glad. I can imagine what Jesse would have to say about the little waif. Boxer just looks at Daniel curiously. "Friend of yours?" she asks.

"We came in together. He doesn't speak. Seems like he might need a friend."

Boxer nods. "They don't let boys and girls sit together at meals but I think because he's little no one will raise a stink." And that's that. Daniel becomes part of our group. Though I only hear about it much later, Boxer will defend him with her tiny efficient fists on more than one occasion.

CHAPTER SIX

Sleep is slow to come my first night at Wells. There's a lot to get used to. Except for my time at the Tanner's, I've never been away from home. I miss my family-my three little sisters and the boys, Henry Jr. and Martin. I even miss my parents, though things have been very strained with my mother, and Papa frustrates me the way he always lets Maman have her way.

Then I have to process all the new people I've met, and all the new sounds that nighttime brings. The other girls in the room sigh, snore, moan and sometimes just flop around in their beds like they can't get comfortable. All of that makes the aging springs squeak and squeal. Sharing a room is no new thing to me, of course. Back home, baby Leona shared my bed. I miss her chubby, grubby little arms wrapping round my neck for a goodnight hug. I even miss the weight of her little body beside me at night, though truthfully it's very hot and I do enjoy not having the extra body heat.

In the morning my hard-won sleep comes to an abrupt end with pounding at the door. It's six o'clock and the knocking at the door is the girl whose current work detail involves making sure everyone is up. I wonder who wakes her every morning.

Everyone hurries to dress. There's much grumbling and bitching. I'm shy about changing and dressing in front of the others. The night before I went through an elaborate process, pulling my nightgown on over my head then wriggling out of my clothes under its cover. Now I see that everyone is hurrying to get their own clothing on and don't seem overly concerned with me and my worn underthings.

According to the schedule Mrs. Partridge gave me, my first work detail is cleaning. As we hurry over for breakfast, Boxer assures me that Dinardi, the staff member who heads the cleaning crew, is a pussy cat with a bulldog exterior.

After a breakfast of gooey-gray porridge I scurry down to the basement of the administration building. I'm determined to get through my year at Wells with as little fuss as possible. I've never been afraid of hard work and Maman had me in charge of most of the cleaning back home. This seems like it should be an easy go.

I find Dinardi in his musty kingdom at one end of the administration building's lowest level. He's sitting at an ancient desk lit by a single bare electric bulb hanging from the ceiling. Other students are lined up, doing some sort of check-in. I take my place at the end of the line and use the time to study the man who will be my first real contact with a Wells staff member. My first impression, aside from his enormous girth, is that Dinardi is a very hairy man. Dark hair snakes up out of the collar of his shirt. He reminds me of a troll from one of Viola's story books. I'm not crossing his bridge.

When I get to the front of the line, Dinardi demands my name without looking up. "Menard. Erminie," I respond. His eyes quickly scan the sheet in front of him then rise, finally, to look at me. "I'm new," I say in response to his quizzical look.

"Umph," he grunts. "Forgot I had a new girl starting today. Wait over there 'til I get through with this lot." His English is heavily accented. He waves me impatiently over to the side of his desk. Beside me is a large store room filled with pails, mops and brooms. Shelves line the walls filled with bottles, jars and boxes of what appear to be cleaning potions of various kinds. The center of the room holds several wheeled wooden carts. Some students are now claiming carts, stocking them with rags and various cleaning supplies, and wheeling them away. There is clearly a routine here I know nothing about.

Finally the last of the other students has checked in, collected their supplies and moved off. Those with carts are being taken, one by one, to the upper levels of the building by way of a creaking, shuddering lift. I can hear it chunking up to the upper floors. There are no carts left so I suppose I'm going to avoid that particular pleasure, at least for now.

"I'm going to put you today in the girls' residence. You will know where most things are already, yes?" I nod, not at all sure that I know where anything is other than my room and the toilets.

"Come, I will walk with you there." Dinardi is an unusually spry man for his size. I struggle to keep up as he pistons up the stairs and across the square to the girls' dorm. We check in with Letourneau, and Dinardi tells me to write "cleaning detail" as my reason for being there. He takes me to a storage room on the main floor and produces a key. "You keep this key and return it to me at the end of your shift. There is a room just like this on each floor. The key works the same in all those rooms, yes?" I nod. He opens the room to reveal a cart like the ones I saw before, as well as a smaller, yet still extensive supply of cleaning supplies. "Make sure you have a mop, a broom, two rags, for the dusting and for the washing up. Also a bottle of cleaner, here." He grabs an unmarked jar from the shelf. "No need to move the cart up the stairs, there is one for each floor." With that nugget of information, I breathe a sigh of relief. I've been visualizing trying to wrestle the heavy wooden cart from floor to floor.

"You will mop all floors, dust all surfaces and clean sinks and toilets. This floor and second floor only. No third floor. Another young lady has third floor. It is for staff and you need a special key." I nod.

"I will be back to check on you. Remember you have to have everything done and report back to my office by ten o'clock so there is no time for napping, capisce? Listen for the bell, it will tell you when you must return to my office. But you have to have everything put away and locked up before then so keep your eye on the clock in the foyer. Most importantly, don't touch any personal items in the rooms. Just do the floors there. If anything goes missing they will come to you. Very important to remember."

I have the sense Dinardi has delivered these warnings many times before and really doesn't think I'm going to listen. Or maybe he thinks I'm just stupider than most. I resolve that I won't mess up my first day "on the job" or give Dinardi any reason to be disappointed.

I enjoy that first morning. The girls' dorm is empty except for the odd girl slipping in for a forgotten item or a staff member roaming through on a security check. I go into all of the girls' rooms, but only to mop, each girl being expected to keep their own desk and personal area clean and tidy. The hallway and the lavatories are the biggest job. Dinardi comes twice, once to check on my progress and no doubt the quality of my work. The second time he reminds me to start packing up in preparation for the bell. The rest of the time I'm on my own with my mop and my pail and my dust rag. I enjoy the quiet and the time to think. As for the cleaning, it's soothing to me. Familiar. And Dinardi's exacting standards are no different from Maman's so I feel I've nothing to fear there. If all my time with the cleaning detail consists of working in the girls' dorm I'll breeze through the next few weeks.

When the bell rings I've already finished my cleaning and am half way across the square to the administration building to check out. From there I join the other students in the main square for half an hour of calisthenics, girls at one end of the square and boys at the other. The girls' group is led by a very young teacher named Ms. Brierly whose curvaceous body and enormous bosom is only partially disguised by her staff uniform. As we march and squat and circle our arms at our sides I see several of the boys at the other end of the square looking our way, some snickering, some making rude gestures. The male teacher in charge makes some attempts to stop them. Finally though, he gives up and turns the whole group of boys to face the opposite way. I believe a few of the girls think they might be the focus of this attention but the realists among us know it's Miss Brierly drawing the looks. For her part she seems not to notice.

Hot and sweaty we return to our rooms for a few minutes before lunch. It's considered unseemly for students, especially the girls, to arrive at the dining hall in disarray so there's chaos as we queue for time at the sinks to wipe sweat-streaked faces and tidy our hair.

The afternoon is taken up with classes. Because I dropped out of school after four years, some administrator has decided I'm not suitable for the academic classes. I resent this. I was always at the top of my class. Dropping out had nothing to do with brains and everything to do with Maman. No matter. I'm put in the Home Management program where it's expected I'll learn "useful and marketable skills that will assure me of a successful marriage or, failing that, gainful employment," on my release. I know I can handle the academic classes as well as any of the girls, but Home Management will be easy. It was my life before I came here. I've been in charge of my younger siblings since I was old enough to change a diaper and most of the cooking and cleaning was my responsibility. Fact is, my desire to escape the boredom that went with that life is what has gotten me here. So here I am, in my first class, Cooking, learning to properly boil an egg and be a good wife.

CHAPTER SEVEN

My problems begin during my second month at Wells. I've been happy. Truly happy. Of course I miss my family, especially my siblings. Among the students are the usual collection of bullies and thieves and liars who make life difficult, but I'm also making good friends. I've not had friends in a such a long time. I've forgotten the simple pleasure of sitting on a bed and gossiping about a handsome boy, or trying out different hairstyles while sharing giggles with other girls. Even prickly Princess Jessie, with her condescending ways, has become nothing more than an annoyance. There's even a kind of unity among we girls in our dislike of Jessie.

In spite of the constant signing in and out and the rigid routine, I feel, almost unbelievably, more independent than I ever have in my life. In angry moments back home I screamed at Maman that life with her was like living in a prison. I'm beginning to think life in a prison is better.

Then Dinardi changes my work area. I don't think this is cruelty on his part. There's a normal rotation that people on the cleaning crews move through. Supposedly it's meant to help us become familiar with all areas of the school. If someone is sick or discharged we should be able to take over that area seamlessly. For the rest of my life, though, I'll wonder if Dinardi knew what he was sending me to. If he did know, could he have prevented it?

The day, and the week, begin like all the others. Colleen, who wakes us each morning, hammers on our door and we all scramble to get where we need to go. I hurry over for breakfast, wiping sleep from my eyes and straightening my uniform. When I check in with Dinardi he tells me I'm being shifted to the administration building crew for the next while. My heart drops. I'll need to get my cart on the dreaded lift and up to the other floors. I don't realize that lift is going to be the least of my worries.

I pick a cart, check my supplies, add a couple of missing items and wrestle the brute into line at the lift. My work area is the main floor so at least I have only to go up one floor. Directly in front of me in line is Will, the boy who came in with me from Pitts. I've seen him from time to time at meals and across the square but we haven't spoken. I know from the rumor mill that Oscar ran away our first week in. I wondered at the time if Will chose not to go or if Oscar hadn't asked him. In any case, Oscar hasn't been located, or if he has we haven't heard it. Oscar was a second timer at Wells and there are no third chances here. If he was captured he would be sent straight to the state prison. In Oscar's absence, Will seems to have lost the chip on his shoulder. He nods at me and comes round to help me get my wonky-wheeled cart onto the lift with his. Once on the lift there's silence while I imagine my body hurtling down the elevator shaft amid a shower of cleaning products. As the lift shudders to a stop on the main floor I realize that Will is looking at me with an amused smile.

"First time?" he asks. I nod, surprised and pleased to have made it alive. "It's not so bad once you've done it a few times. I'm heading up to three, but I'll give you a hand. You got the cart with the crooked wheel. Try to get a different one next time. This one only goes right. You'll take a chunk out of a wall and Dinardi will call you on the carpet."

Together we ease the cart out into the hallway. I thank Will and wave stupidly as he pulls the door closed and continues on his way. Well here I am, safely on the main floor with my bad news cart and all my limbs intact. Other than acting crazy as a bedbug in front of Will, my day is going just swell.

Dinardi has given me a list of things that need to be done. He seems to feel I know what I'm doing now and doesn't give me a personal tour of the area. I set to work. This building is busier than the girls' residence. Staff, uniformed and not, hurry back and forth, most not acknowledging me in any way. I keep my head down and do my work. I have no desire to have anyone reporting back to Dinardi that I was slacking. About an hour into my shift Mr. Wyre comes by. Unlike the other staff, he stops, putting a proprietary hand on my cart.

"What's your name young lady?"

"Menard, Erminie," I respond.

"Oh yes, quite. Strange name. Pittsford." He moves on without further comment and I continue my work. He passes by again a few minutes later, appears to hesitate briefly, then moves on without comment. I don't see him again that day.

The following day Will helps me with my cart again, though I arrived early and secured a different cart, one with wheels that all roll in the same direction at the same time. I don't really need his help but I enjoy the feeling that someone is looking after me. Looking back I wonder if I might have overplayed the damsel in distress.

I get myself set up in the main hall and begin my mopping. It's only a few minutes before Wyre appears. He motions for me to follow him, muttering something about a mess in his office that needs attention. Dinardi's original instructions were that I would occasionally be asked by staff to clean things beyond the usual floors, desks and toilets. I envision a spilled drink or a broken glass. I ask Wyre what I should bring with me but he waves me off impatiently and heads toward a back hallway. I mopped here yesterday and I know this is a second entrance to his office that saves him from crossing through the waiting area. His actual office is off limits to any unaccompanied students, including cleaning detail. He ushers me in and quietly closes the door behind me. I feel an odd prickling up and down my spine. The room looks in perfect order.

No sooner has the door clicked shut than Wyre's hand is over my mouth. His other pushes me against the wall. "Not a sound", he hisses. "Understand?" I try to nod to the extent my head will move but he keeps his hand over my mouth and partially over my nose. I'm having trouble breathing. I feel his free hand undo the topmost buttons of my dress and reach in to squeeze my breast. It hurts and I try to move to the side but he shoves me roughly into the wall. "That's right. I like a little spirit. Sadly I have some things that need attending to, but I've enjoyed this very much. You have lovely little titties. Now go and finish your work." He releases his hand from my face. "You don't want to disappoint Mr. Dinardi, do you?"

With that he opens the door to the hall and gestures grandly with his hand indicating that I should leave. I'm stunned. It's all happened so fast I feel I might have dreamed it, except I feel my upper lip swelling where it has ground against my teeth. And my breast is sore. I look down and realize that the buttons of my dress are still undone. I refasten them. Wyre has already closed the door. I don't know what to do with myself. Should I tell someone? Dinardi? Boxer? I'm too embarrassed to tell Boxer and I doubt Dinardi will believe me. After all, I'm not even really sure I believe it myself.

I go back to my cart and stand there for a few numb moments. I'm ashamed that someone has touched me in so intimate a place, and I feel angry that it was no less than the school headmaster. Above all I feel very alone. Eventually I collect myself and finish up my work. I drop the cart off in the basement and avoid eye contact with Will as I leave to go to calisthenics.

The rest of the day passes in a haze. I attend to my Household Management classes as best I can but get a dressing down for daydreaming from Miss Granger, the tired old biddy who teaches the Cooking class. At the end of the day I settle into my room with the other girls. Boxer has nudged up the window and is smoking a cigarette, blowing the smoke out the narrow opening to avoid getting us all in trouble. She looks so confident, so brazen, I feel sure she would know what to do. In the end though, I can't tell her. After all, what could she do? March into Wyre's office and punch him in the face? It's a pleasant thought but not a practical one. I don't even bring the subject up.

CHAPTER EIGHT

The next day I'm a jumble of nerves. I slog through my cleaning routine, wondering when-or if-Wyre will come by. When I hear footsteps I duck into one of the offices or down a hallway. It's always someone else though, and Wyre doesn't appear by the end of my shift. I'm even more convinced that my experience was some weird sort of dream. I decide the best thing is just to forget about it. While my conscious mind believes forgetting is a worthy idea, my unconscious mind isn't convinced. My dreams are filled with a leering Wyre, part man, part monster, who stalks me through a huge maze-like house. At one point in the dream I leap from a second story window to escape his clawed hand, waking just before I hit the lawn below.

I wake tired and tense. I consider pretending I'm sick. Or dead. Minor illness is not a reason to get out of work at Wells, though, and I don't know how to fake-or contract-something truly serious in the next few minutes. I can't eat my porridge so I go without breakfast. It's the first time I remember anything interfering with my appetite. I'm what my mother often called a hearty eater. This was said in such a way that I knew it really meant my appetite would prevent me from ever finding a suitable husband.

Again, I avoid Will as I get my cart and supplies and head to the main floor. I know I must look impolite after his kindness to me on that first day, but I feel I can't have him look at me.

I've no sooner parked my cart at its usual spot on main than Wyre appears. It occurs to me that he has been waiting in a side corridor because he is suddenly just there. "Come with me," he orders, grabbing my upper arm roughly.

"Sir, I have to get my work done here," I protest.

"I have other work for you in my office," he says, tightening his grip painfully on my upper arm. I will later find a line of four tiny bruises along the inside of my arm where his fingers have dug into my flesh.

He half drags me to his office and pushes me inside, closing the door behind us. With the door closed he rounds on me. He's angry. Points of color have risen in his pasty cheeks and his eyes have a dangerous glint that frightens me. Anger, but something else is smoldering there as well.

"I am the head of this school and I demand obedience. Absolute obedience. Are you clear on that?" He takes a threatening step toward me. I take an involuntary step back. That seems to infuriate him even more. His hand comes up as if to hit me but he apparently thinks better of that. Instead he turns to the desk and pulls the big oak wheeled chair around to the side of the desk. He sits down and beckons me to come to him. I think about running for the door but I know he'll be on me before I can make it into the hall. I could scream, I think, and get the attention of Mrs. Partridge at her desk just outside the door. But, like running, screaming will only make things worse. I move toward Wyre suddenly feeling strange and lightheaded. He pulls me down into his lap. I don't resist. His hands unbutton my dress and are suddenly all over my breasts, pressing and pinching and twisting. Then one hand moves up under my dress, probing and rubbing my most private place. When I try to squirm away he clutches me tighter with his free arm around my chest.

"Always remember who's in charge," he hisses in my ear. "It is my duty to teach you, and teach you I will. You will learn things in this office that the other instructors won't teach you. In fact, you should thank me for my kindness," he laughs. I feel a finger move up inside me, probing painfully. Just when I'm positive he has degraded me in every way possible he pushes me off his lap, spins me around to face him and forces me down to my knees in front of him. He unbuttons his pants exposing a huge pink thing. I've seen male parts before, when my brothers were young, but nothing like this. I try to pull away and now I do scream. He's unfazed. He grabs handfuls of hair on either side of my head and pulls my head down. "Take me in your mouth. If you hurt me in any way I'll return the favor," he hisses.

I resist as best I can. It seems inconceivable that I can get that in my mouth and I have no idea what to do. But he's strong and I have no choice but to open my mouth and take him in. It bumps up against the back of my throat and I gag and choke. He seems oblivious, though, like he's forgotten the me that is me is even there. He pushes into me rhythmically and painfully, grunting and moaning. Suddenly I feel like I am drowning. Something fills my mouth. With a groan, Wyre releases me and pushes me away. I gasp for air and retch. I have nothing in my stomach but my body keeps heaving as if trying to get rid of the last of Wyre.

"Don't make a mess on my carpet," he says, devoid of sympathy.

Getting my stomach under control, I wipe my mouth and my eyes with my apron.

"Get out of here. Don't bother telling anyone about this. It won't help you. Everyone here works for me. Always remember that. Everyone here is mine."

    I lunge for the door, sobbing, still wiping my mouth. I leave my cart where it is and run. I don't really know where to run, but I end up back at the girl's dorm. Letourneau looks up at me curiously from the book she's reading but makes no comment. I write 'sick' as my reason for entering the building and she doesn't question me. I expect I'm quite a sight. I haven't done up my dress, my hair is mostly down around my shoulders and my face is swollen, wet with tears and God knows what else. I go to my room for a towel and soap and head to the lavatory. There is one tub that all the girls share. There are all sorts of rules about its use but I don't care. At this time of day no one is around so I fill it, pull the privacy curtain around the tub and submerge myself in the warm water. I scrub myself with the course soap, inside and out, until my skin is raw. I soap a corner of my towel and scrub my tongue and the inside of my cheeks. When I can do no more I lay back in the water and let it swallow me up. I have no idea what I am going to do.

CHAPTER NINE

I Eventually I drain the bath, pad back to my room and climb into bed, wrapping myself into the thin blanket. Mid-afternoon Letourneau comes into the room. She's been dispatched by the head of the Home Management program to check on me. I've been missed at my classes. Dinardi is also pissed because I left my cart and didn't check out. It seems I'm in a heap of trouble.

I explain to Letourneau that I'm ill; that I think maybe my breakfast has not agreed with me. I tell her I'm sorry but I didn't want to stay in the admin building and make a mess. She studies me carefully and runs a not-unkind hand over my forehead. "Stay here then. I'll tell them you're sick. But you'd better be back to work in the morning or you'll have to go to the infirmary." I nod gratefully. I've at least bought myself some time.

The other girls return in the afternoon. I pretend to sleep. They leave to go to supper and I stay in bed. When they return for the evening I still pretend to sleep. Boxer isn't fooled. She sits on my bed. Ignoring my closed eyes and feigned deep-sleep breathing, she asks me what's wrong. The kindness in her voice causes a surprising and overwhelming flood of emotion. I begin to cry. Not quiet crying. Not the dainty way ladies weep. I whoop and hiccup as wave after wave of anger and fear and self-loathing come out of me. I cry so hard I can't form words, let alone sentences. The other girls all crowd around my bed in alarm. Except Jessie and Margaret who seem more curious than concerned.

Finally, when I get the worst of it under control, Boxer takes me by the arm, dragging me from my bed. She leads me down the hall and into the lavatory. She sits down on the cold stone floor with her back against the door and indicates I should sit in front of her. I do.

I've planned on not telling anyone, but the whole thing comes rolling out of me. I sit there like a spectator, watching the words spill out of my mouth. Boxer listens, just listens. She doesn't seem shocked. She doesn't seem repulsed. I'm grateful to her-have never felt more grateful in my life.

But when she finally speaks, it isn't what I want to hear. "Min, love. He does this to all the girls. Most of them anyway. I should have told you but I guess I hoped he wouldn't take a fancy to you. Listen. He runs this show. The staff all know, or at least most of them. The best thing you can do is stick it out until Dinardi moves you to a different spot. Or, I guess you could ask Dinardi to move you sooner. He's a decent man and he might do it. The problem is, if Wyre figures Dinardi has crossed him, then Dinardi will be in dutch. Dinardi usually moves people around about once a month. That's all. You just have to stick it out for a month. Do what he tells you. You'll soon be done with him and once you are out of that building he won't bother you again." What Boxer doesn't say, but what I now understand, is that a new girl will take my place.

The next morning I tell everyone I'm too sick to work. Letourneau comes and marches me over to the infirmary where the weasel-faced, foul-breathed school doctor pronounces me fit as a fiddle. By then I've missed breakfast and part of my shift but Letourneau walks me over to Dinardi to explain that I've been ill but am ready to go back to work. He's already sent someone else to admin to cover for me, so he has me tidy the storage room by his office. He's quiet and kind and I don't know whether he feels sorry because I'm sick, or if he understands what happened. I know now I'm not the first and I wonder if everyone knows. I can't work up the courage to ask him to move me.

The next day is Saturday. I'm back on Main but don't see Wyre. I'm weak-kneed with relief when my shift ends and I can turn my cart in and head over to the exercise square. We don't clean on Sundays so I have a day's respite from the worry of Wyre's office. It's the end of my good luck though.

The next week Wyre is there. Every day. And every day he comes to get me. Every day is more shameful and degrading than the one before. He has me take off my clothes for him, even dance naked for him. And always it ends with me taking him in my mouth until he's done with me. To make things worse, Dinardi begins to grouse at me because I'm not getting my work done. He writes me up one day when he finds my cart unattended and me nowhere to be seen. I explain that I was in Wyre's office at the time. He nails me with a look I can only describe as disgust, like he knows what I was up to in that office. I feel sick all the time. I'm not sleeping and I have no appetite. My already shapeless uniform starts to hang off my shoulders. I know I can't continue like this.

Wells is run by a board of directors. On the wall in Mrs. Partridge's waiting room is a framed photo with names of all the board members. The chairman, right up at the top, is Thomas O'Connell. I don't know if Wyre has a *boss* but I think maybe this O'Connell might be able to help me. And it isn't just me I'm worried about. I know without a doubt this isn't just about me-that any girl who works on the floor will be prey for Wyre and his own peculiar brand of "education".

In my room at night, I craft a letter to O'Connell, at first in my head, then later I put it down on paper. I write and rewrite it, trying to get the right amount of urgency in my words, but leaving out anything that might identify me. Before I'm able to send it though, I receive a surprise visitor.

CHAPTER TEN

Visitors are allowed on the last Sunday of each month. I've not had any visitors. I'm disappointed but not surprised. It's a long trip from Pittsford to Vergennes. Sunday is the only day that Papa doesn't work at the quarry and so he needs to help Maman with things around the house. As for Maman, well, I know that she won't come to see me. She would never set foot in this place and I can practically smell her disappointment in me wafting up from Pittsford.

So I'm surprised when one of the younger girls comes to the open door of our room on the final Sunday of August, my second full month at Wells. Elsie bounces outside our door, excited to share the news that I have a visitor. For some girls, visitors are a normal thing, but it's always exciting for everyone. Not only do visitors bring news from the outside but also gifts that can be shared among room-mates. Strictly speaking visitors aren't allowed to bring in food from the outside. Generally, though, the guards turn a blind eye to things like sweets and home baking, drawing the line at alcohol and cigarettes.

So I thank Elsie, who skips off to give someone else a similar happy message. I head off to the dining hall. While I'm signing out I tell Mrs. Letourneau's Sunday replacement that I have a visitor. She looks bored and unimpressed and I feel silly. On visitor Sunday the dining hall is converted to a visiting area for the afternoon. One end is for the boys and the other end for the girls. Visitors sit across the tables from the student they are visiting and guards circulate, keeping an eye that no contraband is being exchanged. A few children sit on knees or play in and around the tables. These are younger siblings and sometimes children of students, being raised by a grandparent or an aunt. I walk into the visiting area and stand for a few moments, surveying the crowded room for a familiar face. I am not sure who I should be looking for.

Finally I see her. Grand-mère is perched imperiously at the edge of a chair, pushed well away from the table. She seems reluctant to touch any more of Wells than absolutely necessary. I hurry over to her, weaving through the tables. She stays seated but offers both her elegantly gloved hands as I approach. I see a warmth in her eyes that brings tears to mine. I'm grateful that the family matriarch has taken time to visit me, but I confess to also being ashamed; ashamed that she should see me here with guards and an assorted crew of thieves and murderers. Grand-mère is in her late sixties, I suppose. Ancient in my eyes. She's a woman who has seen her husband march off to fight the rebs and nursed him when he came home with a lame leg and a broken mind. She's carried ten children and buried three of them, as well as grand-père. I suppose there isn't much she hasn't seen.

"Mémère, thank you for coming. How did you get here?"

"I came with Father O'Hennesy. He was coming to Vergennes to attend to some business and agreed to give me a ride." Father O'Hennesy is the priest at Grand-mère's church in Rutland. Chalk up another person who knows of my problems. "How are you my dear? You look so thin. Do they feed you in this place?" She casts a doubtful look around the dining room. As if that reminds her of something she suddenly reaches down and picks up a cloth bag at her feet. "I brought a few things you might enjoy. You can look at them later. There are a few things there that the guards might not approve of, so best we keep it to ourselves for now, oui?"

I nod and tuck the bag underneath my chair, wondering what sort of contraband Grand-mère has smuggled past the guards. She has a way of looking at you that makes you feel small and insignificant and I wonder if she used it on the guards as she came in. I like to think so. Today though, with me, she's all warmth and kindness. I've always been her favorite, the oldest of her many grandchildren. It seems my misfortunes haven't turned her from me as I feared.

"You really are very thin, Minnie. Are you well?" I wonder, just for a second, if I should tell her about Wyre. But I can think of no way to tell this grand lady about the terrible things I've done. Surely she couldn't forgive me for that! Instead I tell her that the food isn't as good as at home and we exercise every day so I don't have a chance to get fat. In truth I was "pleasingly plump" (another of Maman's sayings) before I came to Wells. I can now feel my collarbones and hip bones protruding from under my dress. I know I must look shockingly thin to Grand-mère.

"Your father wanted to come but your mother is keeping him busy," she says with a hint of the special kind of distaste she reserves for my mother. "The children all sent notes for you. They are in the bag. Leona drew you some pictures, I think. She is a firecracker that one." Grand-mère chuckles at some memory of my baby sister. "Ethel is being a big help while you are away. She is a good girl, that one. But she is young, still. I know they are looking forward to having you home in a few months. Your mother is," here she pauses, as if looking for the right words without being ungenerous, "having some difficulty getting on."

I nod. I know what she means. Maman is crazy and getting crazier, but no one in my family ever says it. No one is happy about the younger children being with her and the boys are always busy with school and work. No one really expects them to care for three little girls except in the most basic sense of making sure the house doesn't burn down around them. I've always been the one to brush their hair and mend their clothes and make sure they're clean and presentable. Maman has become more distant with time.

Grand-mère goes on. "When you left your Maman probably didn't know, but she is expecting another child." This catches me off guard and I guess it shows on my face. "Oui. In November, I believe." All I can think to do is nod.

"We help where we can Minnie. You know that. But with Henry packing you all up and moving to Pittsford, we're limited to how we can help. I visit as often as I can but Jenny doesn't want me there. She's a cold fish when I go. I'm sorry. I shouldn't be saying these things. She is your mother."

I nod. "I know what she's like, Mémère. None of this is a surprise to me. How is Papa?"

"Oh," she tosses her gloved hand dismissively. "You know your papa. He is here. He is there. He is everywhere." She chuckles. "I wish he would stand up to your mother, but I also know he isn't an easy man to live with. Always trying to catch that dream. But a few more months and you will be home and things will go more smoothly."

I nod. I don't have the heart to tell Grand-mère that I only plan on sticking around home until I save enough money to head to Boston. If I have to take the younger children with me then I'll figure out how to do that. Living in the same house with my mother long term isn't an option.

We make small talk and, despite more poking into my weight loss, I don't tell her about Wyre. When she rises to leave she kisses me on both cheeks amid a cloud of face powder and lavender. "You are a good girl, Minnie. I know that. We all have problems from time to time and sometimes we make mistakes. But that family back in Pittsford needs you. I hope you will remember that. I will ask the Blessed Mary to see you home safely."

I feel tears squeezing out of my eyes in spite of my best efforts. Now that Grand-mère is leaving I feel overcome with emotion. I wish I could tell my terrible secret. I wish I could believe she would understand.

When I get back to my room I'm relieved to find all the other girls are out somewhere. I drop onto my bed and excitedly reach into the bag from grand-mère. I pull out the items one by one like I am handling holy relics.

First is my old doll, named Betty Lou after my first real friend in Danby. A note is pinned to her dress. It's in Ethel's big sprawling hand.

I thought you would like to have Betty Lou with you for company. She misses you terribly. Also she is a terrible bed hog so you should have her. I miss you and look forward to having you home. School is hard. Sister Therese is a witch and gave me the strap for talking. Papa is fine. Maman has been having a lot of her headaches. The little ones miss you and cry for you.

I confess to still more tears as I read Ethel's note. I set it aside and dig a little deeper into the bag. Beneath Betty Lou is a tin filled with peppermint candies. There's also a bag of peach blossoms and some sugar cookies. These last must have been baked by grand-mère. Finally, under the cookies, is an envelope. Inside are five, one-dollar bills and two other wrinkled pieces of paper torn from a school notebook.

I set the money beside me and greedily open the first of the folded papers. It's from six-year-old Viola. She's just learning her letters and I can imagine her struggling with the pencil, tongue stuck out the corner of her mouth, trying to get things just so. She has written "Min" across the top of her paper, then beneath that "I mis yoo." She has crossed out yoo and written "you" above it. I can see Ethel leaning over her, insisting she correct the error. I wonder if Maman was there when these notes were written. Did she help or did the girls do them on their own? In any case, there's nothing from Maman or Papa, nor from either of my brothers. The last paper is a drawing done by little Leona. In it a stick girl with spikey hair stands beside what looks like an enormous dog. One of the little girl's hands is raised as if waving or making to pet the animal. I don't know what the picture means and it makes me sad that I can't hug Leona and tell her what a clever little artist she is.

My first task is to hide the money before the other girls arrive. It's an enormous amount. Though I mostly trust the girls from my room, I don't mean to tempt them. I decide to split the money up, hiding each bill in a different location among my clothes, in my old valise and beneath my mattress. That done, I prop Betty Lou on my pillow. Then I lie down beside her and cry.

JENNY

I've struggled so much. Even as a child I was plagued with these blasted headaches. They draw on my resources and steal my energy. Losing baby Louis added another misery. He was so tiny and helpless and I couldn't protect him. I found him one afternoon in his cradle, blue-lipped and lifeless. Henry found me curled up with his little body in our bed. I'd lain there, wrapped around his little body for hours, though I had no sense of the passing of time. I was only seventeen, a child myself, really. Losing my first born should have made me appreciate my living children more, but each successive birth deepened the dark hole in which I find myself. I tried. I tried so hard. And now another is on the way. I know this is God's blessing but I just don't know if I can do it.

CHAPTER ELEVEN

Cora is the first to arrive back in the room. Naturally shy, she hangs back when she realizes I've been crying. "I'm okay. Sorry. Just being silly here. Did you have a visitor?"

"Mmmmm...yeah," she responds. "My mum and my baby sister were here." I nod.

Cora's mom comes every visitors' day. I eventually had to ask Boxer why a mother would visit a daughter who murdered her husband. Truthfully I'm jealous. My own mother hasn't sent me so much as a note in the three months I've been at Wells, and I didn't even kill anyone. Boxer finally told me Cora's story. She was beaten by her father for as long as she could remember-way back to when she was a little girl. Worse, as she got older, he made her perform sexual acts, sometimes right in front of her mother. Any attempt by Cora's mother to intercede meant a beating for mother and daughter. Cora saw only one way out. When her father began to fondle her younger sister, Cora took a poker from the stove, approached her father from behind while he dozed in his chair and beat him to death. When the court heard about the things that had been going on in the home, they sentenced Cora to Wells rather than to a prison. Boxer tells me this story in her unique, matter-of-fact way but none of the horror of it is lost on me, especially after the things with Wyre begin to happen. I dream about beating him to death but I also realize what a huge amount of courage such a thing would take. Above all, I understand I'm already an inmate. Killing the man would, at best, result in being moved to the state prison for God knows how long. It might even get me executed, like that Mary Rogers after she killed her husband down near Bennington a few years ago.

No, the solution to my problem has to be legal. Eventually I settle on a final copy of my letter, seal it up and address it to Thomas O'Connell, the chairman of Wells' Board of Directors. While I don't go into the details of the acts committed by Wyre, I hope it will be enough to have someone look more closely at Wyre's conduct. It's clear many people on the Wells staff know something is going on, but are afraid to put their job on the line. I give the unsigned letter, along with one of my one dollar bills, to Brand Hillier, a boy I've gotten to know on the work detail. He's being released, and agrees to find an address for O'Connell and mail the letter for me. Once it's out of my hands I feel both a sense of release and suffocating dread. The dread part begins to take over when Brand leaves the grounds the next day. I fervently pray Brand will take my money and throw the letter in the garbage. But there's no going back now. The letter is unsigned so it can't be directly linked back to me, but I still feel everyone will know it was me through some sort of Well's grapevine.

Several days pass. I'm still pulled into Wyre's office regularly, though he seems to be tiring of me and his requests for "extra work" are less frequent. I'm nearing the end of my cleaning work detail and know that I'll soon be moved into another area away from Wyre. I begin to hope, then believe, nothing will come of the letter. Even so, its existence is a cloud over my head.

One day, Wyre steps from his office and beckons me to follow him. As usual he leads me the back way into his office and closes the door behind him. Today is different though. Today a very round man with a red misshapen nose and pockmarked skin sits in front of Wyre's desk. I'm confused and my face must show it. Wyre gestures toward the man.

"Allow me to introduce Chairman O'Connell, Miss Menard."

I nod at the man, struggling to keep my face blank. "Pleased to meet you Mr. O'Connell." I feel my legs turning to rubber and have to will them to keep me vertical.

"I believe you sent a letter to Mr. O'Connell regarding our lessons here?"

I shake my head, probably too vigorously. "I never sent a letter." I struggle to stay calm. They can't prove anything. I even printed the letter so no one could match it to my handwriting. In the end, it doesn't matter. Common sense tells Wyre who sent the letter and that's all the justification he needs. Both men use me that day. Unlike Wyre, who never put his thing inside me, O'Connell shoves me onto the desk, pulling my underthings down around my ankles, forcing my legs apart and pushing himself in. I scream and thrash but neither man pays any heed. Nor does anyone come from the outside to help me. Wyre sits to the side and reads a paper, his lack of interest adding to my humiliation. When O'Connell finishes, Wyre has his turn. He forces himself into my mouth, telling O'Connell that this is how you keep them quiet. They both laugh. O'Connell moves behind me, reaches his hands into my dress and rubs my breasts, getting himself all worked up again. When Wyre is done with me, O'Connell takes another turn though he can't quite make his thing work and keeps fiddling with it. By the end, all I can do is lay there on the floor where I eventually end up. I gaze up at the ceiling and imagine I'm safe in my bedroom back home, counting the cracks in the ceiling. There's no point in fighting. There's no point in screaming. There's no one to help me. The best I can hope is that it will be over quickly.

When they're done, Wyre tells me to get my clothing in order. He opens the office door and tells Mrs. Partridge to have a guard come to his office. He sits down at his desk, folds his hand primly and looks at me almost sadly.

"We have a job to do here, Miss Menard. We deal with youth, like you, who have no regard for the law. To do that we must have complete obedience to all staff, and particularly to me as headmaster. Without that obedience no learning can happen and we have failed in our job. I hope you have learned that. We can have no questioning, no complaining, no disobedience. I am sentencing you to a week in segregation and am adding an additional month to your sentence. This is a kindness. I could send you to the state prison for your infractions, but I'm hoping you'll learn from this and become a productive member of our student body for the rest of your stay." He's interrupted by a tap at the door and one of the male guards enters. "Please take Menard to segregation." I'll bring the paperwork down shortly. The guard nods and takes my arm.

And that is that. I'm marched across the square to a separate cottage I've not visited before. I know it by reputation though. It's the place where troublemakers are sent to cool off. Outside is a guard who turns to unlock the door as we approach. Inside are four windowless concrete cells down one side of a long room. Across from the cells is a desk where another guard is seated. From his position he can see into all four of the barred cells. The cells are empty and they put me into one of the middle ones. There's nothing in the cell except a dirty mattress on the floor with a moth-eaten gray blanket and a commode housing a five gallon pail. Though the day is hot, the cell is cold and damp and I have nothing but my dress. I sit on the mattress, back propped against the wall, and wrap the smelly blanket around me for warmth. The guard who brought me over is gone. The new guard has closed and locked the cell door. I can still hear the echo of it slamming shut in my head. I can hardly believe all this is happening to me. I've asked for none of it. The letter has been my downfall, but surely I'm not the evil doer here? How could everyone (for it now seems obvious that all staff must know some of what Wyre is up to) think it's all right to treat people this way? Wyre seemed genuinely hurt that I've disappointed him which confuses me even more. I've led a sheltered life, educated by nuns and hidden away by a suffocating mother. Maybe I just don't understand how the world works?

As depressing as the cell is, I feel a sense of relief. I have one week here and presumably even Wyre can't take advantage of me here. I watch the guard carefully but he's gone back to reading and seems absorbed in his newspaper, hunching over it in the gloom. Eventually I lie down and sleep a bit but wake up when I hear Wyre come into the cottage. I tense, but he delivers some papers to the guard, exchanges a few words with him, and leaves without as much as a look in my direction. I doze a while longer but come awake again quite suddenly, realizing I need to use the commode. It's in plain sight of the guard who's finished his newspaper and is playing a game of solitaire. I don't know what to do. Should I ask him to turn around? I'm embarrassed to ask such a thing but as the urgency grows I know I have to do something. Finally I stand and walk to the door.

"Excuse me," I say, as politely as I can. "I need to use the commode. Is there a way...." my voice trails off. The guard looks at me curiously. I start again. "Could I have some privacy for just a minute? I'll be really quick," I finish, lamely.

"Should have thought of that, princess. You just have to go. Doesn't interest me in the least."

I haven't used the facilities in front of anyone since I outgrew diapers. I don't think I can make my body do it. The guard shows no signs of turning around or leaving. He's gone back to his card game. In the end, pure animal need overcomes my shyness, or at least it almost does. I strategically drape my blanket over the front of my body, holding it in place with my teeth while I get my underwear down and sit on the commode. The sound of it hitting the bottom of the pail sounds like cannon fire to me but there's nothing I can do about that except let it go. After I finish, I quickly rearrange myself, using the blanket as cover, and return to the mattress. I'm horrified about what will happen when I have to do the other. I wonder if I can go a week without moving my bowels.

I've been in the cell for three days. I've not moved my bowels in that time but I have gotten pretty good at manipulating the blanket to shield me from the guard while doing the other. No one has emptied the pail so it's stinking pretty high. A boy has been moved into the cell next to me and I'm sure he can smell my pail. But, after a day of hearing the noises and smelling the smells that come out of that boy, I stop worrying about it. Finally in that third day the guard escorts me while I empty my pail in the trees behind the cottage. That's the only time I leave the cell.

Three guards rotate through eight hour shifts. The first one, the one I've already told you about, is Stan. Stan is older than the other two. I think of him as "Grumpy Stan". He never smiles, never talks but leaves me alone. He's always hunched over his paper or his cards. He slides my food tray under the door and always says "grubs on". He says it in a kind of grunt like making actual words is too much work. The second guard is the one who walked me over to the segregation cottage and the one who took me to empty my commode. His name is Robert and he is the nicest of the three.

He was all business when he brought me over here, but has turned out to be pretty kind. He always greets me when he arrives and tells me what the weather is doing outside. We chat for a few minutes then he opens a book he's reading. It's called *Golden Bowl*. Once I ask him what it's about.

"I'm not sure," he laughs. "An old bowl I guess. My sister gave it to me. She is..." he waves his hand over his head as if birds are fluttering up there. Then he laughs and goes back to his book. I decide I like his sister.

The third guard is Myron. He comes on at eleven o'clock and is there the whole night. I don't like Myron. I sometimes catch him watching me and I make an extra special effort not to use the facilities when he's on duty. I make sure I'm just a lump under the covers when he comes in. I feel better when they move the boy into the cell next door. Although I can't see him and we aren't allowed to speak, at least I know I'm not alone with Myron. My nerves reach their peak when I hear a strange noise on the third night; a kind of a huffing sound. Trying not to move I peek out from under my blanket. Myron is standing against the bars of my cell. The light is bad and I can't see real well but he looks like he is rubbing himself there in front of my cell. I shrink down and stay really still. I know he has a key and I'm afraid he might come into my cell to finish the job. He doesn't, but I know not to trust him.

I'm feeling a little achy and, about noon on the fourth day, my absolute worst fear comes true. I drape the blanket over me and have a look and sure enough, there is blood on my underwear. I don't know what to do. I'm mortified. It's beyond embarrassing. My uniform dress has an apron over it. I took this off when I first got into the cell. After some thought (ripping my uniform will probably come with it's own punishment), I tear the apron into three pieces. Stan is on duty at the time. He looks up when he hears the tearing sound. It's actually the most lively I've seen him in the four days. Looking back I think maybe he was worried I was doing something to harm myself-like hang myself or something. But I tell him my ankle is hurting me and I want to wrap it. This seems to satisfy him and he goes back to his card game. I don't think he ever even looked to see if I had a bandage on my ankle after that. I roll the three pieces of cloth up into narrow bandages and, using the blanket for cover, I get one of them up into my underwear. I have three days left in my stay and I don't know how I am going to make those three pieces of cloth last that long. It's a whole new thing to worry about but at least I'm good for today. I hope I can share this story with Boxer when I get out of here, and laugh about it. Right now though, nothing is feeling very funny.

The more I think about it, the more I believe maybe I can work this to my advantage. It's going to take a boatload of courage though. In the evening, when Myron comes on duty, I crawl out from under the covers, swish over to the cell door and lean against it in what I hope is a provocative way. Wyre had me pretend to be a street walker from time to time. It seemed to excite him when he was in a certain mood. Now I think maybe I did learn a useful skill from Wyre because Myron looks at me with a sly grin on his face. He's missing most of his front teeth.

"I need to ask you for a favor," I say, all charming-like. Flirting with Myron is beyond repulsive, but these are desperate times.

His grin gets even bigger and he moves in closer so I can smell his breath. "Favors cost," he says back.

I suck in my breath and go for it. "I'm having my monthly visitor," I blurt. "I don't have anything…you know? I need for you to get me some rags or some towels or something or I'm going to get blood all over everything in here." He pulls back from the cell door like he's afraid he might catch something.

"I don't know anything about that stuff," he says, going a little pale.

"You don't have to know anything about it, you just have to know how to get me some towels." I'm beginning to enjoy myself. I'm thinking that Boxer would be proud of me.

"I can't leave my post. I'll get fired if I leave."

"Well I've made up a couple of emergency ones, but I'll have to give them to you to take and get washed then," I say, looking out at him with my best puppy dog eyes. I am only just discovering the power of being a woman.

By this time poor Myron looks fit to faint. "Listen, when I leave here in the morning I'll talk to one of the women and get them to bring you something. That's all I'm gonna do. Now go to sleep."

I do go to sleep, with a piece of my apron tucked into my underpants, secure knowing that Myron isn't going to come into my cell in the middle of the night. Or ever. The next day, sure enough, one of the women guards comes with some special pads and a belt to hold them on. The pads are coarse and hard and have been laundered a million times but they will do the job all right. I give her the story about how I couldn't get any help and had to use my apron to keep things clean. I figure maybe I won't get into trouble about the apron if I own up to it right away. I never hear one more word about that apron.

I finish up my last three days in segregation without anything else happening. Robert smuggles me in a magazine even though he isn't supposed to. That helps pass the time. It's his sister's-a Time magazine from March. It's full of a lot of Irish stuff because of St. Patrick's Day, and some old news like Taft taking over as president. But it's something to do and I like looking at the advertisements. There's even one for a Thomas Flyer Motor Car. In the picture, a well-dressed man sits inside holding the wheel. Beside him a woman in furs rests a gloved hand delicately on the door. I close my eyes and pretend the fellow driving is my husband and we're getting ready to go driving. Perhaps we'll pick up some of our wealthy friends and go for dinner. In the picture, the background is of mountains, but my motor car is going to be a city car.

At the end of the week a female guard comes to get me. I quickly stick the magazine under the mattress. Robert isn't there so I can't give it back to him. I hope he'll know to look for it, or that the next guest will find it and have something to read. I've already put all the used towels into the same paper bag that the clean ones came in. I take them with me because I don't want anyone else to see the dirty things. I don't know what will happen to my stinking pail but at least I won't be there to see the look on the face of the person who has to empty it.

The guard takes me back to the girl's dorm and stays with me while I sign in. When she leaves, I run as fast as I can up to my room. I feel dirty. I haven't even had a chance to wash the stink of Wyre and O'Connell off my body, let alone the blood and stink of the segregation cell. It's the middle of the morning so I know I should be on a work detail somewhere but I don't know where. The room is empty so I grab my towel and hurry to the lavatory. I climb into the shower and scrub and scrub until my skin feels raw. I dry off and dress in a clean uniform. I rinse out the soiled pads in the sink. That's the rule. After they dry a bit they go into a separate box to be properly laundered. Only girls do this job for which I'm thankful. Back in the room I put my soiled clothes in the laundry box and the remains of my apron in the garbage. I tuck the unused pads in my drawer for next time and hang the damp ones on the back of my chair to dry. Just when I'm feeling like maybe I'm human again the bells sound for calisthenics. I hate to get all sweaty again but I actually find I want to get outside in the sun after being cooped up in that cell for a whole week. Besides, I know I'll get in dutch if someone catches me hanging around the sleeping quarters in the middle of the day. I quickly pin up my damp hair as best I can and run out to the square to line up with the other girls.

After calisthenics we go back to the dorm to freshen for lunch. Boxer and the other girls all walk with me. The girls are excited I'm back and anxious to hear all about my time in segregation. There isn't much time for talking, but I promise to fill them in later. Once we get to the dining hall I join Boxer and Cora at their table. Little Daniel is there too. He eats with Boxer because she looks after him and doesn't let the bigger boys thrash him or smear food on him. Everybody is still crazy to hear all about segregation and why I was put there and what it was like. We aren't really supposed to talk at lunch, so I spout out as much as I can when the guards are turned the other way. Of course there's a lot I'm not about to tell them with Daniel sitting right there!

After lunch I do a quick calculation about what day of the week it is and figure out I should be in Home Accounting class. That's the one where we learn all about budgeting and record keeping and such. In my estimation it's the most useful class we have. I've missed a few classes but Mrs. Charter, the teacher, doesn't comment. Before I leave for the day she passes me a sheet with some chapters written down. "Read these before next class. It will get you caught up to the others." I smile at her and thank her. Mostly I'm thankful she hasn't made a big deal about me being away.

Of course, come evening, I need to tell my room-mates all about my week in segregation and what got me sent there. I'm not sure how much to tell them. In the end I tell them most everything, leaving out the really bad details. I tell them how Wyre has been tormenting me and that I finally had enough. I tell them about the letter but leave out the part about Brand since I don't want to get him in dutch, even though he's away from this place. I tell them about O'Connor and Wyre being in the office together but don't go into the details of what they did. Boxer, of course, wants to hear it all. She paces the room and swears like a sailor. Wyre and Wells get all kinds of imaginative names. Her language colors the room. Cora sits beside me on the bed and holds my hand. I cry and talk and snot something fierce. Little Matty seems horrified. She hangs back away from me and I worry she might think less of me. Margaret and Jessie lean forward, interested but not in a shocked kind of way. I get the sense they know all about Wyre. I wonder if either of them has been in his office…for that, I mean.

When I'm about done talking Jessie pipes up, bold as you please. "Did you like it? Those things that Wyre and O'Connell were doing, I mean?" She says it with such a nasty look on her face. I truly hate her at that moment. It's Boxer who wipes the smirk off her face though. She comes out of nowhere and smacks Jessie across the face, not with a closed fist but with enough force to split her lip. Then she grabs Jessie by both shoulders and leans in real close so their faces are nearly touching.

"You shut the fuck up. Do you hear me?" She shakes Jessie so hard I can hear her pretty white teeth rattle. "Nobody should have to do those things. Wyre is a prick and you're a stupid bitch." Boxer's spit is flying into Jessie's face, she's that mad. "We have to stick together, not pick at each other like a bunch of old crows." Boxer releases Jessie and storms over to the window. She lifts the sash a couple of inches (it's fixed so it won't go any higher). She rolls herself a smoke, strikes the match on her bedpost and lights the cigarette. She releases a stream of smoke out through the window and mutters a few more curse words to herself. Meanwhile Jessie runs her arm over her face to wipe away Boxer's spit. She doesn't say anything much, just curses a bit under her breath and moves over to her bed at the end of the room. I hope the yelling and the smoke won't draw the attention of whoever is on guard duty, because I really don't want any more trouble. I'm wishing I'd kept my big mouth shut about the whole sorry mess.

Lights must be out by ten, but Boxer comes and sits on the floor by my bed in the dark. "I'm sorry I couldn't help you Min. Before, when you told me about Wyre, I mean. I already got extra time in here for telling him what I think. I just want to finish here and get out and maybe head to New York City."

This is the first I've heard about Boxer pulling extra time. She never mentioned it before. I'm not really surprised though. She's broken every rule there is and isn't choosy about what she says or who she says it to.

"It's not your fault, Boxer. I don't see there's anything anyone could do. Wyre and his cronies just see the girls in this school as their property. If the Chairman of the board is in on it too, then it goes deeper than what you or I can handle. Thanks for being my friend though. I can really use a friend right now." I'm right on the edge of getting weepy again so I change the subject. "Will you and Jessie be OK?" I whisper.

"Oh yeah. She and I go at it from time to time. We'll be square again in a couple of days. Some people just need reminding. I'm off to bed." Boxer starts to get up but I stop her.

"Do you know who's cleaning admin main right now?"

"A girl named Clara. She's that one from the Birch room, downstairs. She's homely as a barn door so maybe she won't be to Wyre's taste. I think maybe Dinardi put her there on purpose after hearing what happened to you."

"Does everybody know?"

"Well, they don't know *exactly*. But everybody knows mostly what goes on around Wyre's office. There was a lot of chatter after they locked you up. People figure things out, you know…but I never said anything," she adds quickly. I believe her.

Boxer shuffles off to bed in the dark. She bumps her knee or her toe or something on one of the beds and lets loose a frightful stream of curse words in a hoarse whisper. Then it's quiet as she finally climbs into bed.

I don't think I'll be able to sleep but strong emotions are tiring for me and I'm out before I have time to think much about homely Clara from the main floor and whether she's Wyre's newest victim.

MRS. PARTRIDGE

I don't know how much longer I can do this. The sounds that I hear from that man's office make me physically sick. It's not even just the girls. Wyre's depravity knows no bounds. Even the younger staff members aren't safe. What I didn't know was that O'Connell was in on it too. He's always seemed a decent sort when he's been by the office. I had no idea the sickness at this school went so deep.

If my Ben wasn't so sick I'd leave this job, but at my age, another job will be hard to come by. We need to eat and we need to buy his medicines, so I stay. Some nights when I get home I feel dirty; sometimes I cry. My Ben tells me that the students are lucky to have at least one kind person at the school. But I don't know what good I can do for any of them. I feel so helpless.

The one thing I can do is write down the things I see and hear. I don't know yet who I am writing it for, but I keep a journal of all the ugliness going on in this school. At least the things I know about because I'm sure there is plenty I don't hear of. The children who "disappear," or who die of mysterious diseases. Those who run away because they don't feel like they have any other option. The ones who take their own precious lives. I write it all down. One day, I hope, I can use this journal to make them pay. For now, though, all I can do is watch and listen and write.

CHAPTER TWELVE

I get my new work detail the next day-gardens. After not seeing the light of day for a week, it's heaven to pull weeds and water flowers. I even welcome the heavier work, though that's mostly given to the boys. The gardening crew is less closely supervised so there's more visiting back and forth. It's a much better location for learning school gossip (though I later learn that the kitchen is the absolute best for knowing everything going on in the school). Best of all, from most of the flower beds you can see the front gate. You can see who's coming in, whether for deliveries or to visit. You can also see who's being discharged. Most fairly bounce to the gate carrying whatever possessions they own. A few trudge to the gate, head down, like they didn't really want to leave. I wonder about those. I wonder why they don't seem happy and figure maybe they don't have a home to go to. Or maybe they have the kind of home where they get beat every day like Cora. It gets me thinking that maybe it isn't so bad having a crazy smothering mother. At least I have my brothers and sisters and papa. But then, maybe I'm not welcome back home now either. I haven't heard from anyone since Granmère's visit.

The back of the grounds is a huge vegetable garden that provides produce for the school. The view isn't as good back here. You can't see the gate. What you do see is the school's cemetery. It's tucked into a corner of the grounds, surrounded by a high page wire fence. It's small because I guess most kids who die here at Wells are sent back to their home towns. There are still plenty of graves, though. Most are just wooden crosses without any names or anything. I get a creepy feeling when I get too close to that graveyard. I can't help but wonder what happened to them all. My friend Will and I work in the garden together from time to time. One day I ask him what he thinks happened to the kids in those graves. He heard there was a big outbreak of some kind of sickness many years ago. Some of the graves were from then. Others? He just shrugs. "Who knows?" Two boys are sent in every day to tidy it up. I'm never asked to do that and I'm glad. It feels like a very bad place to me.

I work in gardens through what's left of summer and into the fall and get as brown as a wild Indian. True to his word Wyre extends my sentence by one month so I know I'll be here until the end of July. It doesn't seem so bad though, and nobody bothers me out here. I rarely see Wyre during this time and if I do it's from a distance as he struts across the grounds like he's real full of himself. The whole ordeal seems like maybe it was a nightmare, except it was a nightmare that keeps coming back to me. Some nights I wake up and feel hands on me and I'm so sure it's real that I sit up in bed, my nightgown and hair wet with sweat. A couple of times I even scream, scaring the other girls who tell me to hush. One time Jessie was so mad she flung her hairbrush at me in the dark. It hit me in the shoulder and rattled off onto the floor. That girl has pretty good aim or maybe she just got really lucky. Whatever the case, I had a bruise on that shoulder for a week.

In mid-October I get reassigned to the kitchens. Kitchen staff start out with the grunt jobs like mopping the floor, scrubbing the grease off the big industrial cook stove and washing the dishes. After doing that a while you get to help with food preparation-cutting up vegetables and sometimes serving the students- and by serving I mean slopping food onto their plate as they file past. The students that are in the kitchen the longest and show the most promise got involved in planning meals and preparing the food. There's nothing fancy served at Wells and they get cheap meats and spin them out as far as they can. But the gardens offer up free vegetables so there are always lots of potatoes and carrots. The most common dish is a vegetable stew. If you're lucky you might find one or two pieces of stringy meat in your bowl. Sometimes you can't even recognize what that meat is. But none of that is the fault of Miss Bette who runs the kitchen like a military general. It isn't uncommon to see her fling off her apron and stomp off to the administration office to complain about the quality of this or that, or to question a shipment of meat that hasn't arrived. Delivery men cower when they see her sailing toward them. God help the man who brings his delivery of eggs or milk, or whatever, too late for the meal she's preparing. That means a quick change of plans in the cooking and, if there's one thing that drives Miss Bette wild, it's changing plans. With the students, Miss Bette keeps high standards and is quick to temper. She's harshest with the boys she's required to train but who, she loudly proclaims, have no business in a woman's kitchen.

My room-mate Jessie is on the kitchen crew and so is little Daniel. He's so small that Miss Bette keeps him mostly in the back peeling potatoes and wiping down the counters, but I like having him where I can keep an eye on him at least part of the day. He still doesn't talk but he's attached himself to Boxer and me. One time, when we were walking across the square on our way back to our rooms, he slipped his grubby little hand into mine. It made me cry a little bit, but I didn't say a word. It just made me think how lonely he must be with his mother locked up in an asylum and no other family to care for him.

As for Jessie, she's generally disagreeable. She doesn't think she should have to work in the kitchen. But then, she doesn't think she should have to work anywhere. When I first met Jessie with all of her airs I thought she must have come from money. But it turns out her folks were just as poor as mine-poorer maybe. I've never figured out why she acts all high and mighty like she does.

I've been cooking most of my life so Miss Bette brings me up through the ranks pretty quickly. She calls me a quick study. It isn't long before she puts me in charge of certain jobs, meaning I have to tell others what to do. Some of them don't like taking orders from me but I try to be as fair as I can and still get them to do what needs doing.

One day Miss Bette asks me to go into town with her on a shopping trip. Most things are delivered to the school but once a month Miss Bette has one of the guards drive her into the shops so she can pick up special things that she thinks no one else knows how to buy. When she asks me if I want to go with her I'm to the moon happy. I've only been outside of the walls of Wells once since I arrived. It was actually right after I got here and we were all herded out onto the street in front of the school to watch a parade. Vergenne was having a big celebration, it being 300 years since Champlain came and named the big lake that separates Vermont from New York. It was a grand parade with horses and floats and Indians dressed up in their war paint. Everything was muck and mud from the rain the night before, but nothing could spoil that day for me. Because it happened right after I got there I thought maybe outings like that were a regular occurrence but I was dead wrong. I haven't left the grounds since. Besides that parade, my only glimpse of Vergennes has been from the seat of Constable Tanner's wagon when he brought us in on that hot dusty day in June. Almost six months ago that was. It seems like that was some other girl rattling along beside Constable Tanner in that wagon.

A trip into town with Miss Bette is a special thing to do and I can tell some of the other girls are mad when they hear about it. Everyone is wishing it was them. Jessie especially has her little snub nose out of joint. She figures she's been in the kitchen longer so she should be the one to go into town. I know Miss Bette would never take her though, because she complains constantly and Miss Bette doesn't much care for whining. In any case, I don't worry too much about Jessie and her problems.

On the morning of our trip to town we finish up with serving breakfast and Miss Bette gets the others set with the washing up. The guard that drives us is Robert, the friendly guard from when I was in segregation. I'm happy it's him and he seems pretty pleased to see me. Mostly he talks to

Miss Bette though. He's a pretty chatty fellow and he and Miss Bette seem to get on well. In fact I start to wonder if it's a coincidence that he's driving us or maybe he signed up for the job because he's sweet on Miss Bette. She seems different with him too. She giggles a lot with him. A giggling Miss Bette isn't something I've seen before.

It's really cold and there's a lot of snow so Robert has brought a cutter. He helps us up and, once we get settled, he drapes a big buffalo robe over our laps. It weighs a ton and smells pretty bad but the cold is nothing after he lays that hide over us. The trip into town is short. Wells is really just on the edge of town and we have to drive into the center of town where the shops are. Robert drops us off and says he'll meet us at that same spot in one hour. I swear I see him wink at Miss Bette as he helps her down from the cutter.

I'm mostly along to carry things for Miss Bette but I don't mind. We start in the general store where Miss Bette picks up some cleaning things-- she doesn't let Dinardi or any of his crew anywhere near her kitchen- as well as some salt and some spices in little jars. She picks up some material remnants to make drying towels for dishes. We go to the grocers and buy some things that I think must be for Miss Bette's private dinner because it isn't anything that we students get at the school. She has some cheese and some fancy olives soaked in oil. She even buys me a banana to eat right there in the store. I haven't had one of those in years!

By the time Robert picks us up we're weighed down with packages. He has to tuck them behind the seat to make room. When we get back to the school I have to hurry off to my classes. Miss Bette gives me a note to give to anyone who has questions about where I was, particularly Miss Brierly since I've missed calisthenics. In the winter the exercises are a grim cold affair. I'm more than pleased to have avoided them for the day.

After classes I race back to the dining hall to help prepare the evening meal. As soon as I walk into the work area I sense something is up. Eyes are deliberately nailed to whatever work each person is involved in. A room usually buzzing with voices is suddenly quiet as a grave. When talk resumes, it's about odd things that seem contrived. Miss Bette is, at that moment, in the storeroom searching for some missing canned goods. Daniel smiles as I come in but the reception is otherwise pretty chilly. Jessie glares.

I know something is up, probably having to do with my trip into town. No sense in fretting about it though. I go to my work station and set about my chores. Soon after Miss Bette comes back into the kitchen, barking orders and muttering to herself and things return to normal.

After supper is served to the other students, and the kitchen crew has their meal, Jessie quickly disappears, leaving me to walk back to our room alone. At least I'm alone until little Daniel trots up behind me and slips his hand into mine. We walk together until we have to part ways. I chat to him, asking him about his day. As usual he answers with grunts and nods and a peculiar hunching of his shoulders. When we part he wraps his thin arms around me and gives me a hug before scampering off. Whatever was going on in the kitchen hasn't affected Daniel's affection for me. Maybe I should ask him about it.

Back in the room Jessie has already retreated to her bed with some school books. She doesn't seem inclined to talk to me and I decide to leave things alone for now.

The chill in the kitchen continues over the next few days, though, until I feel the need to get to the bottom of things. The kitchen is a hub of gossip for the entire school so whatever is being said in the kitchen will most probably have spread among the other students, and maybe through the whole darned state. I make a point of walking back to the residences with Daniel a few days later. Because Daniel doesn't speak, people forget he's there. Maybe they have a sense that if he doesn't speak, he also doesn't hear. I know otherwise, of course. Daniel may be a mute but he has perfectly good hearing and a clever mind.

"Daniel," I say, tucking his mittened hand into mine as we walk. "Are people in the kitchen mad at me?" He looks at me, puzzled. Realizing he's inclined to take things very literally I change my approach. "I mean, are they saying things about me when I'm not listening." He nods eagerly, happy that he understands what I'm asking. "Is it about going into town with Miss Bette?" He shrugs, then shakes his head. Suddenly he stops, squats down and writes with his mitten in the snow. I lean over to see what he's writing. "Hore" it says in big childish letters. Four letters but it's clear that the gossip is about more than picking up spices with Miss Bette. I hurry to wipe the letters from the snow before anyone else comes along the path. Daniel looks alarmed, like maybe he's done something wrong so I quickly assure him we're fine, but the word is bad and we can't leave it in the snow. He nods obligingly. I can't tell if he even knows what the word means.

After I leave Daniel to make his way to his room, I think about how best to handle the situation. Jessie is likely behind the gossip. If she didn't start it, I know she'll have been in thick. Honestly, what I want to do is tell Boxer and let her handle it in her blunt way. But I know if I don't confront Jessie myself, she'll just try to get under my skin in other ways. I have to make her respect me. Still, I think maybe I should speak to someone else, to get the whole story before I confront Jessie. In my mind it's better to go into battle fully armed. Maybe this whole thing has been confined to the kitchen and isn't as big as I think.

The next morning, while running an errand for Miss Bette, I see Will. Will is still working with the garden crew. These days their work consists mostly of clearing the walkways. I often see him as I walk back and forth from the kitchens, bundled in a heavy worn jacket and scarf, shoveling or sweeping the unending snow. It's a particularly cold winter and I feel bad that he has to spend so much time outside. But, considering the chill in the kitchen these days, maybe he has it lucky. I'm not supposed to talk to him while he's working, not supposed to talk to him at all, really. They are pretty good at keeping the older boys and girls separate so there can be no "fraternization". It's next to impossible to get time alone unless you're in the same work crew or in the same classes. Will and I are neither. It's especially hard now that I'm either in my afternoon classes or in the dining hall getting ready for the next meal. I fling a nervous look over my shoulder to make sure no one is watching and ask if he'll meet me outside the school building before afternoon classes. I'm sure I catch just a flash of worry in his eyes, but he smiles, makes a mock bow and says, real formal-like, that he would be delighted. I marvel that the scary sullen boy who rode in from Pittsford with me in Constable Tanner's wagon has changed so much in just six months. Maybe good things do come from being in Wells, if one can keep away from its headmaster. More likely it was Oscar's bad influence that made him so unlikeable in the first place.

I get away from the kitchen a little early after the noon meal and hurry over to the school building. I see Will heading slowly up the steps. He stops and looks back and I catch his eye. He steps inside the building and I hurry to catch up. When I get inside the door I pause. I see him up ahead leaning casually against the wall. When he knows I've spotted him he ducks inside the open door beside him. I follow. He's in a cloakroom connecting two of the classrooms. Some younger students are filing in and hanging up their overcoats, looking at us curiously. I know we have to be quick.

Will grins. "This is Jacobsen's classroom. He's always late. The other room is empty. We have a couple of minutes."

"OK, well this is hard for me." But, I hurry on, "Have you heard any rumors about me?"

Will shifts uncomfortably. He drops his head and looks at the floor somewhere near my feet. "I was afraid it might be about that."

"You have then?"

He nods. Finally he lifts his eyes to meet mine. "But I don't believe them. And even if they were true it wouldn't matter. I think you're a great gal no matter what people say." He throws this last bit out at me like a challenge, like he expects me to slap him for being forward. Instead I smile. He's a true friend and I'm grateful.

"What are they saying? Is Jessie behind it?"

He nods, dropping his chin again. Not looking at me. "Yeah. It's Jessie. She's saying that you," he pauses, glancing around at the younger children now pouring into the room, "that you did things with Wyre. That you did stuff for him so he would cut your time." My blood is beginning to boil but I can tell Will has more to say, he's just having trouble spitting it out. I wait.

"She's telling people that the week you were away you were with Wyre and some of the guards, together like." Will trails off. He shrugs his shoulders helplessly. I feel sorry for him.

I reach for his hands to reassure him but realize touching him will only generate more interest among the young students who are already curious about us. They now fill the cloakroom, stepping around us, struggling to pull off their outerwear, smelling of snow and damp wool. "Thank you Will. Thank you for being honest with me. None of it's true," I add, "I hope you believe me."

"Of course," he says. "I believe you. That girl's just trouble. There some's that believe it, but most people know she's full of it. She said you told all the girls in your room this stuff, and that you have dreams at night and wake up all excited like, thinking about it."

I shake my head. "I have to get to class but thank you again." He nods. I head to the door knowing he'll follow me out in a bit.

I spend the afternoon in a black haze. My body is in the classroom but my mind is finding creative ways to kill Jessie. Murder would get me sent to the state prison but I think it might be worth it. I have sewing class and I'm finishing the stitching on a dress that I can take with me when I'm released. But my mind isn't on the stitching and I keep having to take it out. This earns me a scolding from the teacher that makes my mood even darker.

After classes I go back to the kitchen to help with the evening meal. Jessie is there, of course, but I ignore her. Things are still frosty in the work area but I wonder now if people believe Jessie, or are just afraid to cross her up. She's not well liked and has a tongue like a fishwife. Besides, I know the other girls in my room will have heard the rumors and most will stick up for me; at least Boxer and Cora will, and probably Mattie too.

At the end of the day I'm tired beyond words. Jessie has hurried ahead and is already plopped on her bed reading. She doesn't say anything when I come in. I signal for Boxer to come to the lavatory with me. I ask her if she's heard the stories and she says she has. "Didn't believe 'em though. Jessie is full of shit and everyone knows it. I wouldn't put an ounce of worry into what she says."

"I talked to Will. I wanted to know who all has heard her story. If Will has heard it everyone has. Why didn't you tell me?" Truth told I'm feeling a little bit betrayed by Boxer right now. Why didn't she put a stop to it?

"Jessie is the kind who'll dig her own grave. She'll keep talking until she talks herself into a hole. You just have to give her time to do it."

"Give her time! Holy Mother Mary, give her time to ruin my reputation?"

"Relax Min. You're in jail, or next to it. Your reputation is already shit. Jessie's too. Ain't it good to know that the worst has already been done?"

I don't share her sense of humor on the subject and she knows it. She shrugs. "Can you write like Jessie?" she asks, abruptly.

CHAPTER THIRTEEN

Over the next couple of days, Boxer and I spend a lot of our evenings together in the lavatory. So much so that I worry Jessie will be making up even more rumors about me. Boxer and I are cooking up a plot that makes me alternately squirm with fear and grin with delight.

Boxer has stolen an English assignment tucked into one of Jessie's notebooks-an old one she's not likely to miss. Together Boxer and I have studied the handwriting; small, round, flowery. I've practiced it, every curve, every swoop and swirl. I can recreate it with some confidence but we're missing one thing. We don't have Jessie's signature. We've been through her papers and nothing has a signature. There are returned assignments but she has printed her name at the top of those. We hope for an unsent letter or a scrap where she has doodled her name but nothing. Not one to be stopped by a detail, Boxer formulates a plan within our plan. She'll get Letourneau to leave her desk for a few minutes. My job is to look in the right hand drawer of Letourneau's desk where, Boxer assures me, she keeps the sign-in books that have been filled. I wait around the bend in the stairs and listen as Boxer tells Letourneau she's seen a boy prowling in the bushes under our lavatory. With a snort, Letourneau is out of her chair and out the door, trailed by Boxer. I rush down and pull on the drawer-upper right, Boxer has assured me, though I have no idea how she knows these things. It won't open and, at first, I'm afraid it's locked. However, with another jerk it flies open. I grab a book, not the one on top since that's the most recent one and so more likely to be missed. Instead I take the third one down. Jessie has been around long enough that it will contain her signature. I have no idea how we'll return the book. Boxer and I haven't got that far in our planning. I'm beside myself that Letourneau, or someone else, will come in the door or down the stairs and catch me. Fortunately there isn't much traffic this time of night when everyone is supposed to be in their rooms. I stuff the book under my apron and hurry to the lavatory on our floor. There I tuck the book into the back of my underwear before going back to the room. Boxer comes in some time later, looking a little flushed but otherwise calm. She tells everyone she saw a boy under the window of the lavatory and reported it to Mrs. Letourneau but when they went to the area all they found were a few tracks (which, I know, Boxer has cleverly laid down there earlier in the day).

There's a flutter of excited chatter about the Peeping Tom. Jessie wants to know if Boxer recognized him, Margaret asks if he was cute and Mattie looks plain terrified. I put my arm around her and assure her no one can climb up to that second-floor window, let alone see inside and that no harm will come to her. I feel bad scaring the poor thing like that.

Whenever we can find a free minute Boxer and I work on that letter. We do a few practice ones until we have it just right, then we tear a blank page from one of Jessie's notebooks-deliberately leaving a jagged edge that can easily be used to match the paper with the notebook. We even use one of Jessie's pencils for good measure. Our tools assembled, I write the letter:

Dear Mr. Wyre (no my love, I will call you Abraham),

Dearest, I lay awake each night thinking of you, reliving the brief minutes we have stolen together. I yearn to be lying next to you. I think of the things you have done to my body, how you have made me feel like a real woman for the first time. I ache for your touch. I hope when I am released we can finally be together forever. You are my everything.

Forever your love,

Here at the bottom I painstakingly copy Jessie's signature. I've done this so often now it feels quite natural in spite of my sweaty palms. When it's done I fold it many times until it's a small wad of paper, maybe an inch square.

The next morning, during breakfast preparations, I give the paper to Daniel. I've already told him what to do and he's a willing accomplice. He makes a show of bending to pick up the paper from the floor-right near the foot of Agnes Arnot. Agnes has been specially selected because she's the biggest gossip in the kitchen next to Jessie herself. Daniel picks up the paper and makes like he's reading it, making sure to catch Agnes' eye while he does it.

"What have you got there you little dwarf? A love letter? Hand it over." Daniel hands the note to Agnes, pretending reluctance. He's playing his role perfectly and I love the little guy even more. Agnes reads the note. I hope she doesn't become too bold otherwise Ms. Bette will hear her and take the note before Agnes can do her fine work. But no, we've judged Agnes just right. I watch as she sidles over to one of the other girls and slides the note along the counter so she can read it. The girl titters but Agnes shushes her and they slide the note down the line. In this way it makes its way through the kitchen crew. When it gets to me I press my hand over my mouth like someone who feels they might be sick just with the reading of it. Part of me feels sad as I watch Jessie become a laughing stock, but I know for sure that no one is going to be talking about me after this.

CHAPTER FOURTEEN

As spring comes to Wells, I'm counting down the days until my release. I feel like nothing bad can happen to me if I just keep my head down and stay out of trouble. But, one day in early May, Daniel doesn't show up for breakfast. As the day wears on, we learn from some of the boys that he's dead. There's no official word from the school. Daniel simply disappears from our lives. The school rumor mill says he's been beaten to death. Some of the rumors have it he was beaten by a group of older boys for sport. The more sinister versions involve guards and gun barrels. I think of Myron leering into my segregation cell and think he could do that.

I am numb with grief for my little friend. Boxer and I sneak over to the cemetery one evening on our way to the dining hall for supper. The gate is closed and locked so we can't go in, but there's a mound of fresh earth marking a new grave. There's no way of knowing for sure if it's Daniel's since there's no marker, not even a wooden cross to mark who lies there, but we don't know of anyone else who has died. We lean on each other and sob. I've never seen Boxer cry before and it makes me weep even harder for the small boy who had nobody in the world except for us. I cry because he's gone and we couldn't save him. I cry because he will be forgotten here in this cemetery and no one will ever come and lay flowers on his grave. I cry because I live in a world where people will beat a small boy to death just because they can. I cry because I want to go home.

The day of my discharge finally comes at the end of July. I've received three letters from my father. One of these was to tell me that Maman had a baby boy they called Donald. The most recent note said he'll be by to pick me up and take me home. On my last day I say goodbye to all my friends. The girls in my room-Margaret and Mattie have moved on and new girls have moved in-the girls in my classes and girls I have gotten to know on my work details. I find Will and say a quick goodbye. He even gives me a forbidden kiss on my forehead.

My longest goodbye is saved for Boxer-tough, smart and kind-a true friend. I'll miss her dearly. We promise to write, to not lose track of each other, but in my heart I know I'll likely never see her again. I know she knows it too. We hug, I cry and she makes me swear to eat a juicy steak on the outside and think of her. She'll be released in two months and has vowed to go back to boxing. She makes me swear to come and see her fight in Boston sometime. She doesn't cry.

I pack my few things in my battle-worn valise, including a few new things made in sewing class. Miss Bette has given me a jar of preserves and I tuck that in among my clothes to keep it safe. I include a hand- made Christmas card that Daniel gave me; the only thing I have to remember him by. Tucked on top is Betty Lou the doll, who has graced my pillow since Grand-mère delivered her months ago. I sign out one last time and Mrs.Letourneau wishes me well in her own cranky way. I stop at the Admin building to pick up my paperwork from Mrs. Partridge who comes around her desk to give me a warm hug. I'm surprised. I rarely see her and she's always very businesslike. I always feel uncomfortable around her because, to my shame, I know she must have heard some of the things that went on in Wyre's office. Today though she's kind and soft and I think that there are some things about Wells I will miss very much.

My warm feelings continue when I see that Robert is the guard on duty at the gate. He makes a grand show of checking my papers before opening the gate to release me back into the world.

"I'm sorry to see you go Erminie," he says quietly, following me part way out the gate. "I heard you were leaving today so I brought a little parting gift for you." He slides the book, *A Little Princess* it's called, from under his jacket. "My sister helped me pick it for you. She said it's very good. I haven't read it," he adds apologetically.

I take the book from him quickly, knowing this is something that can get him in a heap of trouble. Tears prick at my eyelids. "Goodbye Robert." And then because I can think of nothing else to say I add, "Thank you for being kind." He smiles warmly and, just for fun, I lean in and say "I'm sure you and Miss Bette will be very happy." He blushes right down to the roots of his fair hair and waves me out to the street with a sheepish grin.

My first steps outside the walls feel strange. I feel like I'm floating-like my feet might actually leave the ground. But I'm brought back to earth quickly enough. There's no one there. I'm expecting Papa but the dusty street is empty save for a delivery cart or two. I set my valise down and prepare to wait. It's obvious he's been delayed by work or by some whim of Maman's. He'll be here. The minutes drag by. I feel foolish standing here on the street. I worry what men passing by will think of a single girl standing alone outside a reform school. A couple of the men slow and look me over but keep their horses moving. Two more stop to ask me if I need a ride. One, I'm sure, has black thoughts, the other seems genuinely to want to help. I turn them both down, saying my papa is on his way. I try with my voice to make "my papa" sound bigger and more fearsome than he is.

Robert comes to the gate. He can't stay there he says, but he does for a couple of minutes, just to keep me company. No men stop while he stands there. What he does is point in the direction of the train station. "Maybe something has happened to your pa," he says. "Might be you need to take the train. I can give you the fare," he adds.

"No. Thank you Robert. I have some money. Enough, I think. I'll start walking to the station but if my Papa comes, can you tell him what direction I've gone?"

Robert smiles. "Of course I will. Mind you, don't talk to any of these degenerates that wants to give you a ride. There's none of them that mean you well."

I nod, pick up my valise, thank him again for his kindness and set out in the direction he's indicated. I've walked perhaps five minutes when I hear a cart approaching fast from behind. I keep moving purposely forward until I hear my name called. I stop and turn. Relief makes me weak-kneed. It's Papa in a buckboard. He's urging a tired looking old horse along at a trot. Over his shoulder peer my brothers Henry Jr. and Martin. Their faces are dusty and streaked with sweat but they all look happy to see me, if a little stressed.

Papa reins the horse to a stop beside me and jumps down, throwing his arms around me in a great bear hug. All the while he's apologizing for being late. Henry Jr. hops down, punches me in the arm and grabs my valise, throwing it up into the buckboard like a sack of grain. I have a moment of fear for Miss Bette's glass jar of preserves tucked in amongst my underthings; but any damage is already done and I don't want to spoil the moment. Martin waits beside me and, when Papa releases me, gives me an awkward brotherly hug.

Papa helps me up onto the buckboard, climbs aboard, takes the reins and urges the old nag forward.

"Where's Queenie?" I ask, Queenie being the horse my father has owned since I was a child.

"Had to sell her," he says tersely. "Rented this one in Pittsford. Hope she makes it home."

"You sold Queenie?" I'm shocked. Queenie was a part of the family.

"No place to stable her, no feed. It didn't make sense to keep her. Little Leona took it real hard, though."

My mind wanders back to the picture Leona sent me of a stick figure, hand raised, beside a giant dog. Not a dog then, but Queenie. She was waving goodbye to Queenie. Poor Leona. I wonder if Maman took the trouble to comfort her or if that job fell to Ethel.

We're quiet for a while, like we are all having a moment of silence for our dear Queenie. But boys can't be quiet long and soon Henry Jr. and Martin are arguing and wrestling in the back. Papa doesn't seem too pleased with the fuss but I think about how much I've missed these two.

"How is everyone back home?" I ask. "The girls? The baby? Maman?" I add this last so as not to seem disrespectful but to my own ears it sounds like an afterthought.

"Oh, you know. We're doing good. The girls are growing like weeds. I expect you'll be surprised when you see them. Your Ma, well it's a lot for her to manage on her own."

"Mmmm. How is she feeling?"

"She's tired. The headaches are worse. She sleeps a lot. She had a difficult time delivering wee Donny and she's not been able to spring back. It'll be good to have you back home to help out."

I feel a little stab of annoyance. So good to know I was missed. But I tuck that thought way down deep out of the way. "It'll be good to be home. I missed everyone."

"We missed you too Minnie. Listen. I'm sorry I didn't get up to visit. Your grand-mère said the place is clean?"

Clean, I thought. Yes, it is clean. Why wouldn't it be clean with an entire population of slave labor to clean it. But I say nothing.

Papa goes on. "She told us you were not looking well. Was the food not good?"

"The cook was very good. Miss Bette was her name. She did the best she could. I was on the cooking crew for a while."

"Mmmmm," Papa nods. "You always were a fine cook."

We drive on. Papa seems to have run out of conversation and the boys are having a heated argument about baseball and the best stance when batting. Apparently Pittsford has a team and both have signed on, making them both experts.

What with the late start from Vergenne, and the age and condition of our horse, we don't get to Pittsford until evening. While I'm excited about seeing the girls and the new baby and being home in my own bed, I'm nervous about Maman and how she'll be. Papa has offered no clues on the trip home about how I should expect to be received.

Papa drops me and the boys off at the door and leaves to return the horse and buggy to the livery. I brush the dust off my clothes as best I can and straighten my hair. I want to tap on the door first to announce myself, but Martin bursts through the door, excited to be the one to bring me in.

My reception is not what I expect. Not from Maman, at least. Predictably the girls swarm me before I'm even through the door. Ethel and Viola pepper me with questions, while little Leona hangs onto my leg like a giant leech refusing to let go. Maman tries, half-heartedly, to make them mind, but eventually leans in over them to give me a kiss on each cheek.

She seems cordial. She also looks very tired. All the commotion wakes baby Donny who lets loose with a powerful howling. Ethel runs to fetch him to show him to me, proud as punch.

Amid the mayhem we finally sit down at the kitchen table where someone, possibly Maman but more likely Ethel, has prepared a pot roast. I know the meat is very dear and I begin to feel, not like a criminal returned home, but like a long lost and most-loved daughter. Papa has returned and joins us at the table saying the blessing. He thanks God for the pot roast and my return, in that order.

With food to keep them busy and their initial excitement abated, the little girls settle. Over our supper Maman asks me questions about school, about my classes and my teachers. There are no tears, no recriminations. She treats me as if I've returned for the summer from a private boarding school somewhere. It dawns on me that this might be how she represents the situation to others. Papa looks a little uncomfortable but doesn't say much. He never does. I hold baby Donny on my knee and bounce him while I eat. It all feels very much like the perfect family. The thing is, I know it's not likely to last.

CHAPTER FIFTEEN

We settle into a routine. Maman sleeps late most days. Once school starts, it's me who gets Ethel and Viola fed and off to school. I tend to Leona and Donny and look after the cooking and cleaning. When Maman gets up she's one of two people. On good days she dresses, greets me cordially, and goes out of the house to shop or visit friends. On bad days she remains in her darkened room, snapping at anyone who ventures too close. On these bad days I keep Leona and Donny away from her, sometimes taking them out into the yard to play to make sure the house is quiet. Me leaving the house makes Maman even more crazy though. She's been kind, loving even, on some days. But she's made it clear I'm not to leave the house without her permission "in case I'm needed."

I'm happy to be home. I've missed the little ones so much. Still, in many ways, I feel more confined here at home than at Wells. I feel Maman's almost constant scrutiny of my cooking and my cleaning and treasure the times when she's asleep. Through it all though, she doesn't mention my crime. I think I'm right that she has told her friends, those few she has, that I've "been away at school". If they wonder how a family who can hardly feed their children can send someone away to school, they probably don't say anything. Maman has always liked to play the grand woman and I feel I've become a cast member in the play that is her life. In it I play both the role of loyal housekeeper and brilliant, devoted daughter. I don't know how to get off her stage.

Each Sunday we pack up the family and walk to mass at St. Alphonsus. Even on her worst days Maman does not miss church. It's the time when she shines. She walks arm in arm with Papa, back ramrod straight, long golden hair tightly pulled up and held in place by an impossible array of pins, hat perched fetchingly atop it all. The rest of us trail behind Maman and Papa, hoping not to be noticed.

In the church hierarchy we are near the bottom. New to the town and poor besides, we don't dare take those sacred seats near the front of the church. Still, Maman brazens herself up as close as she dares and we all squeeze onto a bench about half way down the aisle, Maman to the inside, Papa on the outside and the rest of us arrayed in between.

Today I'm seated beside Papa, holding Donny on my knee. As we wait for the service to begin I reach over to straighten Leona's collar. In the process I spot a face in the row behind me-one I've not seen before because I know I would remember that face, or, more particularly, that hair. One eye is covered by a tumbling mass of waving dark hair. The other dark eye is directed at me. I nod my head vaguely by way of greeting and turn quickly back to the front of the church. I'm unsettled by the intensity of the boy's gaze. It seems very unchurchlike. I'm distracted for the rest of mass, afraid to turn my head and catch his eye again, but very much wanting to. After the service, as we all stand to file out, I risk another peek. He's moving to the end of his row. A casual hand sweeps the hair out of his eyes and away from a very handsome face. He doesn't look my way. I feel vaguely disappointed. It's a fine day and everyone congregates outside the church door to exchange greetings and discuss politics, the weather, illnesses and any scandalous news that might be about town. Maman stops to visit with a neighbor. I keep an eye on the little ones and use the opportunity to scan the crowd for my mystery boy. He's nowhere to be seen. I feel a twinge of disappointment, then give myself an internal scolding for being such a silly girl.

By the following Sunday, I've almost forgotten about the dark-haired stranger. Yet, when I idly scan the congregation, I realize he's sitting behind me again, in almost the exact same position, just over my left shoulder. His eye catches mine again and this time a tiny trace of a smile touches his mouth. I smile back and turn away. Thirty minutes into the mass I realize I'm still smiling. Again, I scan the crowd after the service but he's nowhere to be seen. It becomes a sort of game. I vary where I sit; sometimes nearer to Maman and sometimes closer to Papa, sometimes in the middle of our family group. Almost always he appears over my left shoulder. This is no accident. In fact, I wonder how he manages it, short of asking people to move. His church attendance record is such that even Maman would approve. He's not missed a day since that first.

One Sunday, as the days grow shorter and crisper, there's an announcement about a church harvest supper and dance. The following week my secret crush waits for me at the end of his aisle, something he has never done before. As I pass him he takes my wrist, lifts my hand and presses something into my palm. I glance quickly at my family. Maman has marched on ahead and Papa is bending to pick up Leona. Nobody has noticed. I nod at him and keep moving, aware that tongues will wag if we have been noticed by anyone else. I drop the paper, for it's a wee scrap crumpled to the size of the spitballs the boys shoot at the girls in school, into the pocket of my coat. By the time we get out the door of the church he's gone, but the high color in my cheeks remains until well after we are home. I'm thankful for the chilly wind that covers my giddiness.

When I get home I change into my everyday clothes and cautiously transfer the note into a new pocket. I dare not read it yet for fear the girls will notice and make a fuss about it. Thankfully though, they're busy scrambling out of scratchy church petticoats and into their more comfortable everyday clothes. Finally, on a visit to the outhouse, I carefully pick apart the paper ball and read the note. It's printed in pencil on a scrap of lined paper torn from a school notebook. In the dimness of the privy I have to squint to read the tiny faint letters.

"Would you like to sit with me at the harvest supper?" the note reads. "I would be pleased to see you home after the dance." This is followed by a scrawled signature that I can't make out. I turn the note every which way but can't make out the name of my admirer. Perfect. I'll have to ask Maman and Papa for permission to go to the supper with a boy, but I don't know the boy's name.

I look at the note again later when I get some time alone in our room. The light is better here, but I still can't make out the name of my dark-haired suitor. Still, I'll have to give him an answer at church on Sunday because the supper is the following Saturday. There won't be another chance.

I've seen Papa nod absently to the boy in church so I decide to approach him first. Perhaps he knows the boy's name, which would save me at least one embarrassment. I get Papa alone and, casual like, ask him if he knows the name of the boy who sits behind us in church. He plays dumb, but does it in a way that tells me he's teasing. Eventually he confesses that the boy works at the quarry and everyone calls him Jonesy. "He seems like a nice young man," he adds. Perfect. Jones must be his last name and I still don't know his first.

"He's asked me to the harvest supper. May I go?"

A look of surprise crosses Papa's face. He's probably wondering how and when anyone got close enough to ask me out. The surprise is followed by concern and my heart drops. "I don't think your maman will think much of that idea Min. She'll be needing you here to look after the girls."

"But you're going to the supper. I heard you say so. Why can't we all go? I can keep an eye on the girls there?" I hear a whiny note in my voice that even I find annoying. I take a breath and start again. "There's going to be a fish pond and games for the children. The girls will have fun and I haven't been out anywhere since I got home."

Papa shifts uncomfortably in his chair and reaches for his paper, signaling that his part of the discussion is about to end. "You'll have to work that out with your mother. It's not my place to say one way or the other." He shakes out his paper in a very businesslike way to announce the end of our conversation. I know that's the end of that. Once again my future rests in my mother's hands and my happiness has never been topmost in her mind. I return to our room to get the girls ready for bed.

Though my path is by no means certain, I write my own note. I leave the salutation blank since Jonesy sounds strange and is most certainly not the name he signed on the note. I'm not even sure Papa was thinking of the right boy when he gave me the name. In the note I tell him I'll be happy to join him at the supper and dance-that I will meet him there and will be with my family. I very carefully print my own name so at least one of us will know what to call the other. I've decided to give him the note at church and use the following week to convince Maman she should take the girls to the supper and take me to help look after them.

At church on Sunday, the boy waits casually at the end of his row while my family files out. He pretends to be replacing one of the hymnals. I see my father glance at him with a new sort of look in his eye, but he says nothing, nods his usual abstracted greeting and follows Maman down the center aisle, Leona perched sleepily on his hip. Ethel and Viola are behind me. I pause and encourage them to go past me, then slip the note into his open hand. He smiles and we move on, not exactly side by side, but close enough that I can smell tobacco smoke and something that might be hair pomade. I feel like my heart is about to explode in my chest.

My approach with Maman is not to tell her about the boy from church. I just need to get to the harvest supper and deal with the rest later. At first there's no problem. Maman has already considered taking the little ones, so having me offer to care for them is just a nice footnote in her plan. It's Papa who spoils it all. At some point, not in my presence, he must have told Maman about the boy. Now she stands before me in full sail. How dare I arrange to meet a boy on the pretense of a family night out. What kind of sinful girl must I be to do such a thing? She goes on in that vein but I drift off, thinking, instead, about how it will look when I don't show up to the supper. What will Mr. No Name think of me? I want to die.

And so, on Saturday night, the entire family stays home. Maman makes it clear to the girls they are missing a wonderful adventure because their older sister has lied. I want to point out that I didn't lie, I just withheld a bit of information. But it will make no difference. Maman is in a snit and feels a headache coming on. The girls are in tears and furious with me. Papa slinks out to his tiny dark workshop to get away from the lot of us. He, at least, is probably relieved that he can stay home. More and more he seems to be withdrawing from the family and really, I can't blame him.

Sunday morning we go to church as usual but Maman is vigilant. She stays by my side the entire time. The best I can manage is a small shrug at the boy, trying to tell him it wasn't my fault. He nods slightly and leaves ahead of our little parade. I'm sick that he is slipping away and I still don't know his name. My life and my world are closing in around me. Suddenly all I can see in my future is a life waiting on my mother and never having a life of my own. I want to cry but I refuse to let Maman know how much she's hurt me.

CHAPTER SIXTEEN

Our house is located at the end of a street-small family homes, most of them rented like ours. During the day it's busy with children playing and adults coming and going. At night it's usually quiet. Children sleep. Adults rest after long days of hard work, most in the quarry. The evening silence is usually only broken by the barking of dogs or, sometimes, by a drunken fight in one of the houses.

Wednesday night, four days after the supper and three days after I last saw "Jonesy" in church, I wake up to a strange sound outside on the street. My first thought is some sort of night bird, but none that I've ever heard before. I ignore it, wrench a few precious inches of blanket away from Leona, and flip over. The sound persists. The window of our room faces the street and eventually I'm driven to get up and see who, or what, is making the sound-a sort of strangling raven croak. I slip carefully out of bed, not wanting to wake any of the girls. Outside I see nothing. But then a shadow moves near one of the large red maples that line our street. As I watch, the shadow moves from behind the tree to the side, still staying close to the trunk. I watch fascinated. It doesn't occur to me to be afraid, though that would be a normal reaction. Instead I watch the figure finally move away from the trunk of the tree. Now that the shadow has disentangled itself from that of the tree I can see details of height and shape. It's Jonesy, faintly lit by a slash of moonlight and a distant streetlight. I lay a finger over my lips to keep him silent, not even sure if he can see me. He gestures for me to come down. I shake my head. Ethel is muttering restlessly on her mattress on the floor. Even supposing I can sneak out of the house without my parents hearing, any one of the girls could wake up to find me gone. He persists though, gesturing insistently. Finally I hold up two fingers-two minutes. Wait. He nods.

I move to the dresser in the corner of the room. One of the girls' notebooks is there. Quietly I tear a scrap off one of the back pages, fumble for a pencil and hurriedly scratch a note, hardly able to see the marks I'm making in the darkened room.

"I can't come down. I'm sorry I couldn't come to the supper. Maman made us all stay home."

I start to fold the note, then quickly flatten it out again on the desk and add *"What is your name?"*

I fold the note into fourths and go to the window. It's closed because the fall air has become chilly. I inch the window open and hold the folded note outside to make sure he sees it. Then I drop it. I can't see its progress but I can see the shadow boy move quickly forward. He goes out of sight briefly near the wall of our house, then he steps back and waves the note at me. Then he blows me a kiss! I watch him hurry off down the street and don't go back to bed until several minutes after he disappears. I spend the rest of the night tossing and turning and remembering that kiss floating up to my window.

The next night I stay awake hoping the boy will come. He doesn't disappoint me. Around midnight I hear that strange bird call again. I smile because the sound bears no resemblance to any bird that ever flew the skies over Vermont. I believe my boy fancies himself a red Indian. I've prepared for his arrival hoping it doesn't make me seem too forward or jinx things. I've tied a string onto a small woven basket that I made at school when I was younger. Dried reeds poke out in all directions making it look like a porcupine but it's small and light and has a handle woven into it to which I've attached the string. I've also written a note, this time in the light so I can see what I've written.

"Thank you for coming to see me. I'm so sorry I can't come down but I share a room with my three younger sisters. I hope we can talk in person soon but my mother is very strict and thinks it improper for me to talk to a boy. Erminie."

I tuck this note into the tiny basket, crack the window a few inches and lower the basket down on the string. As I lower it I see the boy move forward into the shadow of the house. I suddenly worry that the string isn't long enough. With the window mostly closed I can't get my head out to see. I have to hope he can reach the basket. I lower it until I run out of string then keep a tight hold on my end so as not to lose it altogether. I feel a gentle tugging on the string. He has reached it then. My heart is thundering. I feel like I'm connected to him somehow through that string. That, and the terror that one of the girls will wake up, or that a neighbor will see him prowling under my window, makes me feel faint.

After a few seconds I feel a more substantial tug on the string, intentional this time. I reel the rope in through the window and grab the basket hungrily when it arrives. Inside is a note. He's obviously written it before he came. I pull it out and unfold it, leaning close to the window for a bit of light. There's cloud cover tonight though, and it's very dark. I can't make out what he's written. I hold it up to show him I have it and point at my eyes to say I can't see. He nods and blows me another kiss. Then he turns and strolls away, pausing once to turn back and wave. I watch until he disappears into the darkness.

CHAPTER SEVENTEEN

I'm up at first light, pulling the note from its hiding place inside my pillow case. I roll away from Leona into a fetal position, opening the note against my thighs, out of sight of Ethel and Viola. Both appear to be asleep on their mattress on the floor. I love them to death but keeping secrets is not something either of them is good at so I use great caution.

Unwrapping the note is exciting and feels a little dangerous. My fingers tremble and there's a small tight knot of excitement below my breast bone. Finally I have it spread out against the fabric of my nightgown. I see the same careful printing-in pencil-as the first note.

Erminie,

Thank you for your note. My name is Wingham. That is my mother's family name. Mostly people call by my middle name, Owen. My last name is Jones so the men at the quarry call me Jonesy. You can call me any of those. Erminie is a strange name but not half so strange as Wingham. I hope we can be friends and maybe step out together some time, once your parents get to know me.

The note is signed with the scrawling signature of the first one, with what I now recognize as Wingham. Wingham. Such an unusual and mysterious name. I whisper it to myself. I imagine naming our son after his father, Wingham. Then decide Owen will likely get him less kidding in school. I read the note through again, and yet again, before tucking it back into my pillow case. It's time to get the girls up for school.

That exchange begins many such 'dates' at my window. Owen comes by at least once each week. Every other night I watch for him until midnight, since I can never be sure what night he'll show up. I'm in constant fear we'll be found out. How can it be that no neighbors see him, or that his tracks under my window go undetected? Sometimes I wonder if I'm dreaming the whole thing. But I see the tracks-and more importantly I have an ever-growing cache of notes written in his careful hand.

My initial fear begins to fade. Twice one of the little ones wakes to see me at the window but I tell them I'm too warm and need to open the window a crack. Neither asks why I'm too warm when the room is frigid with the chill of early winter. They simply go back to sleep in the way of small children. I keep every one of Owen's notes. I tuck them, and the string I use to raise and lower the basket, into the toe of my dress shoes. I see him at church and we smile and nod and murmur an occasional hello but Maman still keeps a close watch on me and often takes me by the arm to make sure I don't dawdle too long. I can't imagine how we'll ever go on a real date when she won't even let me speak to him. It's so unfair I want to scream. I want to scream at Maman and I want to scream at the whole world that seems determined to keep me a prisoner.

Owen's notes often beg me to come down to see him. At first I can't even imagine having that kind of daring. But, as winter turns to early spring and we continue to be undetected, my courage grows. The fact that we seem to be making no progress with our relationship also goads me on. I want to talk to Owen, touch him, get to know him in a way our hurried notes never allow. Finally, I make my decision. I prepare a note that says simply "Wait for me. I will be right down." I tuck it away for the next time he comes and every night I wait.

He finally comes, as I know he will. It's mid-week, just before midnight. I'm keeping my usual vigil near the window. I sense that he'll come, long before he materializes out of the starless night. I lower the basket, and my note, quickly and silently. Practice has made me stealthy and efficient. Even as I feel the tug on the rope telling me he has the basket, I've slipped on my shoes and pulled a blanket around my shoulders. I've rehearsed this in my mind a hundred times over the last few evenings.

The door to our bedroom is open to draw warmth from the oil stove on the main floor. It's easy to slip past the mattress where Ethel and Viola are sleeping and out into the hallway. I've memorized the creaks and cracks of each step and avoid them where I can, staying close to the edge of the staircase. I tiptoe through the living room where I can hear Papa snoring in the bedroom. Last is the kitchen, which suddenly seems huge and threatening with its shadows and the sheer amount of territory I'm forced to cover. No chance to avoid the cracks and creaks here, but I do what I can. Finally I reach the door, pausing only briefly to listen before stepping out into the porch. I instantly feel the cold rush up under my nightgown and the blanket and for the first time it occurs to me that I'm going to meet my love in my nightgown, bare-legged and with hardly a care for my appearance. Too late to worry now. I'm committed. I hurry down the last four steps and out of the porch. As I do so, Owen steps around the corner and takes my upper arms firmly in his hands to keep me from crashing into him. I'm momentarily startled then suddenly find myself melting into his arms. It seems my body has a will of its own and what it wants is physical contact with Owen. We stand motionless in each other's arms for several seconds. My heart is hammering so hard I'm sure he must be able to feel it, but he says nothing. His face is buried in my hair and my cheek is pressed against the coarse wool of his jacket.

Eventually he takes my arms again and pulls me around the corner where we're out of range of both the raw March wind and the eyes of any neighbors who might still be up.

"I want to kiss you," he whispers with an appealing hint of desperation. I say nothing, just nod. With surprising speed his lips were on mine. I kissed Harry Lovelace, of course, but it was always a messy clumsy event accompanied by roving hands that always made me push him away almost before we'd begun. Owen's kiss is different. Tender and gentle, he makes no other demands. His arms pull me firmly into the warmth of his body but a kiss is all he asks. When he releases me I want more but he steps back, hands on my forearms again, as if to look at me. I'm suddenly aware of my tousled hair and the ratty blanket hanging half off my shoulders. I must be a sight.

"You are so beautiful," he says. I chalk this up to idle flattery but still I feel the color rising in my cheeks and look down involuntarily at my toes. He lifts my chin with his forefinger, making me look at him. "Thank you for coming out tonight. You have made me the happiest man in Vermont." I hear no touch of sarcasm, no suppressed laughter. He sounds genuine and my color rises even higher. "You should go back inside, he says, I don't want you get in trouble and you'll be freezing."

I nod absently. He steals one last quick kiss, then turns me and points me back towards the door. With quaking knees I retrace my steps, quietly easing the door open, then closed, gliding over the creaky kitchen floor, negotiating the noisy staircase and finally crawling back into bed beside Leona's warm little body. It's only when I'm safely back in my own bed I realize I didn't say a single word to Owen.

ERMINIE

OWEN

She is beautiful, this girl with the beautiful blue-gray eyes. I spotted her in church with her family and couldn't stop looking. Back then I sat at the back, when I bothered to go to church at all. But after I spotted Erminie my church attendance increased dramatically. One day I got to church early and sat right behind her. My reward was the prettiest little smile and a little blush. Right then I made up my mind that I was going to marry that girl.

Her family hasn't made it easy. The mother keeps a firm grip on all her girls and I'm not the boy who's going to impress that woman. Erminie noticed me though, and I can tell she's interested. I hoped I would get a chance to see her at the church supper and dance but her ma wouldn't let her come. Right then I got to thinking that maybe I could work on her pa. He works at the quarry and seems like a decent guy. If I could get him to like me, to be on my side, maybe he could work on the mother. He's polite enough but it's not like he's ready to write me a letter of recommendation.

I finally got up the gumption to go to her house one night. I thought I might get her to come down but she didn't that night. She did send me a note, though-lowered it down in a little basket. She's creative that one. All winter that's the best we've been able to do is exchange notes, until tonight. Tonight she came down. You could have knocked me over with a feather. Between the time she left the window and the time she showed up outside the door felt like an eternity. I was sure that mother of hers had caught her sneaking out and I'd for sure never see her again if that happened. Suddenly she was there, though, wrapped in a blanket and so lovely she took my breath away. I held her in my arms and kissed her beautiful lips. She's sweet and gentle and passionate. But she was scared too. I could tell. So was I if you want the truth. Being scared adds a little something to a rendezvous like that, but I didn't want her to fret too much. I was scared she might not come down again.

CHAPTER EIGHTEEN

I lay awake and restless the rest of the night. My body is still quaking with left-over excitement, but I'm also horrified. I didn't even speak to him! Our whole relationship is based on a few nods, the occasional muttered greeting in church and about a dozen notes passed back in forth in a stupid basket. And what do I do when I finally see him and have a chance to talk to him? I forget to say anything. What he must think of me I don't even want to guess.

But of course I do guess. How can I help it? I spend hours replaying the whole scene in my mind, imagining what witty things I might have said and trying to work out what he must have been thinking. But that kiss! Oh, he must have meant that. It was such a perfect kiss. Could someone kiss like that if they were busy laughing on the inside? Maman always says that boys only want one thing. Maybe that's it. Maybe Owen just wants that one thing and doesn't care about small talk or witty conversation. How can I know what he's thinking?

The rest of the week I'm moody and distracted. Of course there's no one to notice. Papa is away all day and Maman only pops her head out of her room to give me some new set of orders or to make sure I'm doing a respectable job of my chores. The older of my siblings are off to school every day, arriving home in a flurry of questions about supper, teasing, pushing and shoving and general mayhem. In the evenings everyone goes their own way. The boys are usually off with their friends doing God knows what. The little girls play house or do homework. No one has the least concern that I'm dying right there in front of them.

On Sunday I consider pleading illness to get out of church. How can I face Owen now that he's discovered I'm a witless doorknob? Still, I know that would be cowardly and, try as I might, I can't believe that kiss was the kiss of a boy who was either mocking me or wanting to lay me down in the snow and have his way with me. No. When I replay the kiss it's always tender and beautiful and heartfelt. It's only me I find lacking in my reenactment.

I prepare another note to Owen to pass to him at church. In it I apologize for being tongue tied. I consider writing some tripe about being under his spell (which is kind of true but sounds really sappy). Instead I tell him I hope he'll come again and maybe we can talk a bit and learn about each other. I realize as I write I'm agreeing to come down to meet him again and the idea excites and terrifies me.

I do go down to meet him again the next time he visits. And the time after that. In fact I sneak outside almost every time he visits unless one of the girls is awake or restless. I learn to sidestep every squeaky board in the staircase, stepping from edge to edge as necessary. I learn to glide across the kitchen floor with scarcely a sound. I congratulate myself on my stealth and consider using my skills for breaking into other people's homes rather than out of my own. But a life of crime hasn't been kind to me so far and it isn't something I give over-long consideration to.

Owen and I talk. My tongue tied self from our first visit evaporates. The new me discovers she can talk to Owen about nearly everything. I tell him about my life and my parents and my siblings. I tell him about my dreams, including the one about living in Boston and being a fine lady and visiting shops and plays and galleries. He doesn't laugh but adds his own ideas of what we could do in Boston. He talks about us as a couple-a couple with a future. He tells me about his family-all of them in Wales-and how he'll take me there, one day, to visit his ma. He even sings me little Welsh songs and helps me wrap my tongue around the words.

I find myself saving up things to tell Owen-a precious trove of thoughts and ideas I want to share. I carry them with me through the day, savoring them and polishing them and imagining his response. If he can't come I fall asleep vaguely depressed, as if I've missed some great event that will never occur again. But of course when he does come we have even more to talk about. Our visits involve sitting around the corner of the house, out of sight of neighbors or anyone looking out a window. On windy or wet nights we sit on the steps in the shelter of the porch, which feels oh so much more dangerous. We clasp hands and Owen leans over to kiss me occasionally. Owen's kisses have become hungrier with time but he's always the gentleman and pulls away when he feels he has gone too far. I've told him about Wells and about some of the things that happened there. But, of course, I haven't told him about Wyre and the terrible things he did to me. Many times I wish he would not pull away but I'm grateful that he's not Wyre and isn't interested only in being physical. My world is very small but Owen has become it's very center.

The weeks move on and the weather warms. When Owen and I are out together we take to walking arm in arm rather than huddling by the house. I hope that anyone seeing us will take us for any young couple out for a stroll. Clothing is a complication. I can't go to bed in my clothing without the girls asking questions. Nor can I stroll about the neighborhood in my nightgown. Instead I carry my dress downstairs with me and pull it on over my nightgown. Owen helps me with the buttons, and we laugh about him dressing me like a child.

I know we're doing a dangerous thing, but I'm like a frog in a pot of water, slowly coming to a boil. Things happen gradually and I'm only slightly bothered by each new dangerous step we take. I don't jump out of the pot because the present danger doesn't seem so bad and the water feels so delightful. But of course, one evening, it all comes to a boil.

CHAPTER NINETEEN

It's a beautiful warm evening in April. Owen and I have been sneaking out together the entire winter, stealing moments of time once, sometimes twice a week. I'm tired all the time, lying awake listening for his whistle or turning a recent conversation over in my sleepless mind. Owen has repeatedly asked me for permission to speak to my parents, to ask if he can court me properly. I've refused. I know it has to happen. We simply can't continue this way forever, but I'm afraid. Maman appears to have forgotten about Owen. I think that's why she hasn't been more vigilant and why we've been able to get by so far. I know in my heart, once she knows we still have feelings for each other, she'll forbid me (again) from seeing him and do what she can to keep us apart.

Owen has suggested running away together. I've run that idea around in my mind like a toy train on an endless track. How wonderful it would be just to hop on that train with Owen and leave my old life behind. The problem is I'm not sure how I can leave the little girls with Maman. I would even miss Henry Jr. and Martin, though they're older and mostly off these days running around town getting into trouble, teasing girls and doing odd jobs at the quarry to help pay for their tobacco. They might not even notice if I go missing.

If I won't run away, then maybe I can live with Owen in the boarding house. I'd still be close to the girls and could keep an eye on them. But I know Maman will disown me and will never let me see the little ones. Then there are all the other considerations. Owen's landlady, Mrs. Gambol, runs a tight ship by all accounts. It's not likely she'll let us live in sin under her roof. And who would hire me if they knew my living situation? The solution, says Owen, is simple. We'll get married. He believes my parents will eventually forgive us and we'll be a respectable married couple. I can only shrug. I'm so confused.

So we continue, one day leading into the next. Owen is becoming frustrated with me but insists it's my decision to make. I love him for that but, honestly, I sometimes wish he was a cave man who'd just knock me on the head and drag me away in the night so I won't have to think about it anymore.

To make it up to Owen I agree, one night, to go with him to his boarding house. It's a long walk there and before we're even there I'm fretting about the time. Owen holds a finger to his lips as he swings the door open, and we tiptoe as quietly as we can up the stairs to his second floor room. Once inside he takes my coat and we sit together on the bed. He takes me in his arms and kisses me and for the first time touches my breast and runs his hands over my back and my belly. I have been so hungry for him but I can't relax. I'm going to be so late getting back. I've never been gone this long. Eventually I pull away and ask Owen to take me home. It's been an awkward and wholly unsatisfying evening for both of us.

The second time I agree to go to Owen's I'm more relaxed. It's May. The trees are greening, the night fragrant and love is in the air. This night we hurry to Owen's boarding house, anticipation electrifying every look, every touch. Once inside we're on the bed in a flurry of skirts and heated kisses. I wrap my legs around him and he presses against me. I behave in a way that startles me. I allow him to touch me in secret places under my clothing and that touch makes me writhe with wanting him. We are almost overcome by the months of pent up passion. But still, I'm not so far gone as to not recognize the consequences of the act we're moving towards. I pull back, having almost to shove Owen off me. He's panting and looks pained. But when I tell him we must stop, that I must go home, he nods sadly in agreement and I love how his hair falls over his sad, beautiful face.

Owen walks me home and leaves me a block away to return to his boarding house. As I round the corner toward my house I stop dead. There's a light in the front room window. I'm uncertain what to do. Do they know I'm even gone? Should I wait until whoever is up goes back to bed? Against all reason I think maybe Papa or one of the boys just got up to get a drink. But I know they wouldn't light a lamp. Lighting a lamp in the middle of the night is serious business.

Then I spot Viola through the window. Even from this distance I can see her stricken face lit by the coal oil lamp and I can tell she's crying. I also see my mother's dark shadow cross the room-repeatedly. She's pacing. I'm tempted to leave, to run back and catch up to Owen. I nearly do it too, and maybe I should have. But all I can think of is that I can't leave without Owen's notes and my few possessions. I have no grand thoughts of courage or standing my ground or leaving on my own terms. I only want my things.

And so I enter the porch and climb the three steps to the front door. It seems my legs are carrying me in spite of themselves. I'm no longer in control of anything. My hand reaches out and turns the knob; the door swings open. Even I'm surprised at the speed at which Maman is on me.

"You whore!" She screams into my face. Her hand cracks me across the cheek, quickly followed by a backhand that takes me to the floor.

"Maman," I whisper, the metallic taste of blood flooding my mouth. Behind Maman, in the front room, I see Viola, her eyes wide with horror. Papa has half risen from his chair but stands there frozen, afraid.

"You left these little girls alone!" She screams. "What kind of a sister are you?" Maman is screaming, her face red and splotched with anger. "Viola woke up and didn't know where you were." I try to tell her the girls weren't alone, that they were in a house with their parents and two older brothers. But I see that reason isn't going to work on the hideous woman that my mother has become.

"Get out of our house," Maman screams. "Get your clothes and get out. You can sleep in the street for all we care."

I hear Viola gasp "No, Maman, no." Papa takes a step forward, uncertain what to do.

But I, I know just what to do. I regain my feet and run for the stairs. In my room I pull Owen's letters from their hiding spot and stuff them in the pocket of my dress. I grab a few articles of clothing and some personal things and throw them into my bruised old valise. Then I run down the stairs and out the door without a word to anyone. I can hear Maman screaming at me as I leave, but her words have no more meaning.

Once outside, the enormity of what has happened hits me hard. I'm on my own, in the middle of the night, with no money. I have only one option and that's Owen. I run hard, anxious to make space between myself and Maman, but eventually I must slow to a walk. I'm sobbing in great heaving gasps, surely waking up people in nearby houses. No matter. I can't be any more humbled than I am right now.

I retrace my steps to Owen, a route I followed just a few minutes ago, full of love and hope. Owen has never asked his landlady whether she would countenance an unwed couple in her house but it doesn't matter right now. I have nowhere else to go. Owen promised to take care of me and he's the only person I want to see right now.

I think I might catch up with Owen before he gets home but I don't. I let myself into his boarding house, thankful that no one in Pittsford locks their doors, including Mrs. Gambol. I tiptoe up the stairs to his room and tap lightly on his door. I can hear the bed squeak as he gets up to come to the door. He's in his undershirt with his suspenders down around his hips, one boot in his hand. Not yet in bed then. Of course not. He's hardly had time to do anything but get back to his room. In the space of time it has taken him to get home and remove his shirt, my whole world has fallen apart.

Owen takes one look at me and folds me into his arms. I sob into his chest while he, like a strange dance partner, gently shuffles me inside and shuts the door. Eventually he helps me to the bed and we lay together and I tell him what happened. Later he gets up and dampens a wash rag in the basin to clean my face, moving the cloth gently over the area where my teeth have cut the inside of my mouth. Owen assures me it's getting "proper ripe" and for the first time I smile. It hurts.

We make love for the first time that night. Owen is a gentle and patient lover. He almost makes me forget those awful times with Wyre. Later we fall asleep in each other's arms and for that moment, before sleep comes, the world seems good and kind.

I'm not feeling so hopeful the next morning when Owen says we have to go and lay ourselves on the mercy of Mrs. Gambol, his landlady. I offer to hide in his room, suggesting maybe he can smuggle food up to me. I have no answer for the obvious questions like what will happen when Mrs. Gambol comes up to clean the room. No, there's no help for it. We file sheepishly down the stairs to catch Mrs. Gambol alone before the other boarders come down for breakfast.

We find Mrs.Gambol in her kitchen, whisking eggs. She's an ample woman in a crisp apron over a flowered house dress, gray hair pin-curled and covered in a hair net. She stops short when she sees trespassers in her kitchen, takes our measure, then immediately resumes whisking with a vengeance. Her huge upper arms sway dangerously over the bowl of eggs. Her voice booms. "Wingham Owen Jones. You know perfectly well guests are not allowed, and particularly ones of the opposite sex. I run a clean and wholesome establishment. This is not a flop house where you can bring your floozies. And don't be thinking I'm going to feed her either. Out! Out! Both of you out!" Mrs. Gambol now has the whisk raised menacingly. I find myself fascinated by a yellow string of egg that's meandering its way down to the counter top. I start to back away but Owen holds his ground, both hands raised as if showing her he has no weapons.

"Hold up, Mrs. Gambol. My friend Erminie here, she's got herself in a bit of a situation and she needs a place to stay. It's not what you think. We're going to be married, but just now she has nowhere to go. We want that she should stay here, with me. We'll pay double rent on the room. You won't miss out on any income. It'll be two rents for one room, see?"

I watch with some relief as the whisk is lowered, the yellow string of yolk reunited with it's kin in the mixing bowl. Mrs. Gambol's face is still a hard mask though. She isn't happy with us and it's plain. She waves a plump hand at the chairs around the kitchen table and moves to slide the pocket door closed, separating us from anyone who may come into the dining room. She moves a few things around on the stove to put breakfast on hold for the moment, then organizes her ample self onto one of the kitchen chairs. Owen and I have already settled but I'm perched about as close to the edge of the chair as gravity will allow.

"Relax, Pet. I'll not be serving you for breakfast." A trace of a smile creases the folds of her cheeks. "Now Owen, tell me what's going on here and be quick. The others will be down for breakfast right quick and they don't pay me to palaver with strange girls in my kitchen."

And so Owen, words tumbling over each other in his haste to get them out, explains my fight with Maman and her hitting me and sending me away in the middle of the night. Mrs. Gambol listens gravely to his story, swaying her head like she doesn't know what to make of it all.

In the end she lets me stay, but not with Owen. And only until the end of the month. She has a vacant room on the third floor that she keeps for short-stay workers. I can have that, she says, as long as she gets paid for it, same as all her other rooms. At the end of the month she wants us both gone. We both nod and I feel like I might cry from gratitude. After she lays out her terms real stern-like she softens quite a bit and leans in close to me. "Pet, I'm saying you can stay for a bit but you really need to go home and have a talk with your folks. See if you can work things out with them. It won't be easy for an unmarried couple to find a place in this town and it won't be easy for you to find a job neither. Now I don't know your folks but you seem nice and it would be sad if people got the wrong idea about you." She lays a large meaty hand over mine. "Talk to them," she says.

Then she's back on her feet, moving in complete defiance of her size, shooshing us out of her kitchen. I offer to help but she tells me there is only room for her in her kitchen.

And so, that morning, I join the other tenants for breakfast for the first time, conscious of curious looks from the six other residents who eventually assemble around the enormous dining table. Mrs. Gambol takes a moment to introduce me as Erminie, the new girl who has taken the room on the third floor. Then she's off bustling back and forth with their breakfast fixings. There's plenty of painfully polite "pass the eggs please ma'am" and "would you be wanting the toast, miss?" In spite of the awkwardness, though, they're kind to me and I'm grateful that they ask no questions about my sudden arrival. I'm pleasantly surprised when an older man, who Owen introduces as Harry from the quarry, approaches us after breakfast and welcomes me to the house, saying Owen has talked a lot about me. This surprises and pleases me. I've not been able to tell anyone about Owen and I wonder what it will be like to talk openly about him.

After Owen leaves to catch the train that takes the men to Hollister Quarry, Mrs. Gambol consents to let me help her clear the breakfast things. She doesn't say much but moves with amazing speed and efficiency. When things are tidied away to her satisfaction she takes me to Owen's room to collect my things, telling me firmly that it is the last time I will be in that room. I nod obediently. I don't think anyone argues with Mrs. Gambol. Then she takes me up a floor to my new room. It's a tiny, sparely furnished room with a steeply sloped gable roof and a tiny window at one end. There's a single bed with a chipped white iron bedstead and a frayed blue coverlet. A small dresser, a wooden chair and a wash stand with a flowered basin and pitcher are the only other furnishings.

"It's not much," says Mrs. Gambol gruffly. "I keep this room for some of the quarry workers who come into town for short stays and they aren't too picky about their accommodations."

In truth I'm delighted. The room is clean and it's all mine. I've not had a room to myself since Ethel was born.

"Now just like I don't want you in young Owen's room, I won't tolerate him coming to yours. If you want to ogle your young man you're going to have to do it over the breakfast table or in the common room. Anything unseemly goes on and you'll both find yourselves on the street right quick." She turns to huff out of the room but swings back. "One more thing, pet. You'll be telling your folks where you are. I don't want no police officer showing up thinking we're holding you against your will. You go see them and tell them what's what. You hear me? And you try to work something out with them so's they'll take you back."

I nod numbly, though I can't imagine how I will ever get the strength to return to that house, let alone confront my mother again.

I spend the day in my new room. I really have nothing to do but I'm afraid to go out because I feel awkward about bumping into Mrs. Gambol, or one of the other boarders, though I can't say why. I move the few sticks of furniture around then put them back as they were. I pace the small space. I take a nap. I look out the window maybe a hundred times, hoping to see Owen coming down the street. Finally, in late afternoon, I see him with several other quarry men, coming down the street. They are talking and laughing and jostling. One slaps another on his back over some joke and quarry dust rises up around them in a dirty white cloud. I tiptoe down to the landing to greet Owen before he goes into his room. After a quick glance over his shoulder he gives me a kiss and a hug. But it's his smile, radiating out of that dust-caked face, that makes my day of waiting worthwhile. Then he disappears into his room with a warning to brush the dust off my clothes before supper.

Owen and I sit together in the common room after supper is all done and put away. I tell him what Mrs. Gambol said about talking to my folks and wonder out loud if maybe we can just pretend we talked to them. Then I could tell Mrs. Gambol that everything is all right but that I'm not going back to live there.

"Mrs. Gambol is right, though," Owen says, irritating me with his common sense. "Your folks will be worried. They have a right to know where you are. They'll be worried, even your ma 'cept she probably won't admit it. We'll go together. They can rant and rave all they want but what's done is done and we're together and we're going to stay together." Scanning the room quickly to make sure no one else is about, he leans over and gives me a peck on the cheek.

"Tomorrow we'll go-after work."

I nod in reluctant agreement, but I get not a lick of sleep that night.

CHAPTER TWENTY

The next day I see Owen off to work and put on my best dress. Well, really, I only own two threadbare dresses, but this is the better of them. I head out to search for work. In my pocket is a piece of paper where Mrs. Gambol has written the addresses of two families of her acquaintance who might be looking for a hired girl. She has included a note of recommendation. I'm surprised by the kind words she's written, given the strain of our initial meeting just two days ago. But I don't even get to show anyone the letter. The first woman turns me away flat out, saying they've just hired someone. At the second address no one answers the door.

I contemplate going to Loveland's Mercantile as kind of a joke, but as I think it through I realize the real entertainment would be for those passers-by when Harry's father tossed me out on my backside. Instead, I decide to try some of the other merchants along Main Street. I visit Drake's Grocery, Chatterton's Hardware and the Otter Creek Hotel, all with no luck. I almost pass by the office of Drs. Swift and Pinkney. What, after all, could I do in a medical clinic? Still, I think perhaps they might need some office help so I poke my head in the door. A stylish young woman at the desk pauses and smiles. "Come in. Don't be shy. Do you have an appointment?"

"No," I stammer, realizing she thinks I'm a patient. "I just wondered if you might be needing some help. Office work, or cleaning or…?"

The young woman is already shaking her head. "No, I'm so sorry. There's just me here-and the two doctors of course. We already have a lady who comes in after closing to clean. I'm sorry I can't be more help."

"That's fine. Thank you for your time," I say, backing out the door that I haven't even gotten completely through.

"Wait," she says suddenly, startling me. "There's Mary."

I pause. "Mary?"

"Mary Armstrong. She's a nurse at the hospital. She's looking for a girl to care for her two children while she works. Is that something you might be interested in? No promises of course!" She adds hastily. "Here, I'll write down her address for you. She'll be at the hospital just now but she might be home this evening." I've moved inside to stand in front of her desk and she slides the paper to me. "You go and see her after seven o'clock and tell her that Eileen sent you."

I debate telling the nice young woman-Eileen-that I have something else to do this evening, but decide it won't help my job prospects, nor is it of interest to Eileen who has already gone back to wrestling files into an oak filing cabinet behind her desk. Instead, I call out a thank you, assure her I will call on Mary Armstrong and tuck the piece of paper, along with Mrs. Gambol's, in the pocket of my dress.

"You're welcome!" the girl calls cheerily from the depths of the file drawer.

I try a few more businesses in the area with no luck. So, even with Mary Armstrong's name tucked in my pocket, I head home tired and discouraged. After dinner Owen and I talk and decide we should stop at Mary Armstrong's house on the way to Maman and Papa's. We reason that, if we can tell them I already have a job and a place to stay, things might go more smoothly. And so, just before seven, we set off to the home of Mary Armstrong on Granite Street. As agreed, Owen stays back. I don't want to present myself as someone with a man lurking behind me, though I take a great deal of pleasure in knowing that he's waiting there, just around the corner.

Mary answers the door herself. She's a brassy young woman. I can easily picture her at work in the hospital, efficiently caring for patients and taking no nonsense from them. Two children peek out timidly from behind her skirts. I introduce myself and tell her about Eileen's kind referral. She tells me that she's been informed I might stop by and would I be so kind as to come to her sitting room. Once we're settled in her cozy front room she introduces the two scrubbed children who have trailed us. Two-year-old William has already wriggled his way up onto her lap and four-year-old Sarah is perched on the arm of Mary's chair eyeing me with frank curiosity.

Mary has the expected questions. Do I have experience caring for children? I tell her about how I care for my younger siblings. Can I cook and clean? Yes, I have skills in both those areas. Am I able to work unusual hours? Yes, I can be very flexible as to time. Do I have references? I present her with Mrs. Gambol's letter. No, sadly I have no other references, having recently moved from Rutland and never having been employed outside my parents' home. Have I had any trouble with the law? I've prepared for this one in my head before-hand so the lie comes out smoothly. No ma'am. Never. Mary Armstrong does not need to know about Wells Industrial School.

After what is obviously the formal part of the interview, Mary seems to relax and becomes less intimidating. I'm pleased. She's not hurrying me out the door and I feel I've passed inspection. Even the children seem to sense that some important event is over and they move off to play nearby, though I see them peeking at me curiously from time to time as I chat with their mother.

I learn that she's a widow, her husband having been killed in an accident at the quarry eighteen months earlier. Her parents in Georgia have been helping her out financially, but she's recently decided to return to her nursing work. She's tried a variety of child care situations, none of which have ended well. She tells me I'm her last hope. If she can't make things work she'll be forced to pack up and move back to Georgia. She doesn't outright say it, but I can tell this isn't something she wants to do-be dependent on her family. My heart goes out to her and right then and there I vow to be the best housekeeper that Mary Armstrong, or Pittsford, has ever seen.

We discuss money and duties. Mary will pay me $20.00 every two weeks. I've never had money of my own so it seems like a fortune but Mary is apologetic at the sum. She becomes firm and business-like again. I must come by early tomorrow to tour the house and review my duties. I'm expected to care for the children and keep them clean and well fed. I'm to keep the house clean and have an evening meal ready when Mary returns from the hospital each evening. If Mary is called to go to the hospital at night I must be available to come on short notice. The boy next door will come for me. She asks me where I'm living and I give her the address of the boarding house. It will do until I have a more permanent address to give her.

She shows me out and, to my surprise, Sarah follows me to the door and gives me a hug. I'm pleased and Mary seems surprised. I'm sure it's a good omen and tell Owen so when he materializes out of the growing twilight to meet me. I'm going to be paid for doing what I have done for free since I could walk. I'm so over the moon about the job I almost forget that our next stop is my parents' house. As we get closer though, dread replaces my excitement and Owen has to coax me along to keep me from bolting. I calm myself somewhat by considering how difficult this will be for Owen, yet he's marching at my side as if we're invincible. Together, maybe we are.

Hand-in-hand we enter the porch and climb the three steps to the door. I feel Owen's grip tighten. I tap lightly on the door and hear a rustle of activity inside. I hear one of the little girls asking excitedly who it is and Maman hushing her. It's Papa who comes.

"Erminie," he says, with a nervous glance over his shoulder. "Come in." I feel a moment of overwhelming love for my Papa, but it's tempered by a flicker of anger that he's so uncomfortable to see me. I step into the kitchen with Owen following behind. Maman has come to the doorway that separates the kitchen from the front room. She stands there silently, glacial.

I know she's told my siblings to stay in the front room. She is a human barricade to keep them from running to see me.

"Why are you here?" she demands. "Have you forgotten something?"

"No, Maman. I have everything I need. I just want to let you know that I have a room at Mrs. Gambol's boarding house on Garden Street. Mrs. Gambol asked me to tell you so you wouldn't worry," I add hastily.

"How kind of you to let us know," Maman says coldly. "Are you exchanging sexual favors for your room and board?" Papa puts up a hand, silently beseeching Maman to stop. I sense Owen tensing at my side.

"No, Maman. I have a job caring for two children. I will pay my own board." This is a tiny lie. Owen will be helping me with my rent until we can get a place together, but I'm damned if I'm willing to give Maman the upper hand.

"Well then, since you have delivered your message and you don't need anything I think you had better leave. I must get the children to bed." With that Maman turns and disappears into the front room where I can hear the young ones peppering her with questions about what's going on. Owen and I turn to leave the house. Papa, who has remained standing by the door during this short conversation squeezes my shoulder gently as I turn to leave. At that moment I'm angry. I have no words for him.

"I'm sorry Min. I should have told you."

"Told me?"

"I knew you were seeing Owen-going out at night. I should have stepped in but I wanted you to have some time." His voice is low; a whisper. "Things haven't been good for you. I wanted," he pauses, struggling, "something nice for you. Now this." He waves his hand toward the front room as if all the evil in my life lies in that direction. At that instant Maman's voice crisply demands that Papa help her get the children to bed. He looks sad and apologetic as he ducks his head and hurries away.

Once outside I'm so angry and frustrated that my legs move like pistons. Even Owen struggles to keep up with me. I know he's looking for some words to calm me. I'm angry at Maman's hurtful words and Papa's pathetic lack of courage. I'm even angry at Owen for not stepping in and defending my honor. As I run the conversation over in my mind, though, I know things happened too fast and Owen, always careful with his words, probably didn't even have a chance to react. By the time we arrive back at Mrs. Gambol's my anger has been replaced by despair. We sit in the common room, Owen chastely holding my hand while I cry quietly. None of the other boarders are around but Mrs. Gambol materializes without a word, carrying a tray of tea and cookies. She sets the tray down, urges us not to stay up too late, smiles sympathetically and leaves. Eventually I cry myself out, Owen and I share the tea and biscuits and talk about the future. He says I mustn't be undone by my mother and I know he's right. I'm in love and that will make everything alright. Eventually we climb the stairs to our respective rooms where I fall into bed and dream of Leona being kidnapped and screaming for me to save her. In my dream I can hear her crying but my way is blocked by a series of walls and obstacles. I run and run but can get no closer to that little voice.

Owen taps on my door the next morning so I won't be late for my first day of work. But I'm already awake and dressed and fussing about what to do with my swollen face and puffy eyes. I've always admired those girls who can cry and still look good. I'm not one of those. Breakfast is a quiet affair. I've already learned that a certain telepathy exists among the other boarders. Even though Mrs. Gambol actively and vocally discourages gossip, they all know something is going on. I'm sure my face only confirms it. Though the details may be hazy the other residents know I'm going through a rough patch and they're kind and solicitous and pretend not to notice.

After breakfast I get my coat and walk part of the way with Owen to where he catches his train. When we part he hugs me and kisses me and wishes me luck. I feel blessed to have at least one person who cares.

Mary Armstrong is an efficient woman with very firm ideas on how her home is to be run. In that she reminds me of Miss Bette and I like her immediately. I like having a very clear idea of my duties and have every intention of doing a good job. Besides, overlaying her crisp efficiency, Mary has a kind heart. I can see it in the way she interacts with her children and the patient way she explains things to me. Though I feel that no one with eyes could overlook the fact that I've spent the night crying, Mary doesn't mention it. I feel like I'll get along with Mary Armstrong just fine.

We spend two hours that morning going over my duties, where things are kept and interacting with the children before Mary heads off to her work at the hospital. Once she's gone I get down to work, doing up the breakfast dishes, sweeping the floor and dusting Mary's simple, utilitarian furniture. The children hover nearby, curious and a little apprehensive. They pretend to play but I feel them watching me. Finally I put down my dust cloth and invite them to sit with me for a story. A few minutes later I find myself on the sofa with a child pressed close on either side as I read a well-worn copy of *Queen Zixi of Ix*. Sarah gazes at the illustrations in blue-eyed awe while William pops his thumb in his mouth and settles in with a tattered blanket across his knee. The warmth of the childrens' bodies stirs a longing for Ethel and Viola and Leona and little Donny-even for the wild boys. I'm hurt and angry that Maman kept me from seeing them last night. She's always understood how to make a deep cut. While I'm happy to put distance between myself and Maman I'm desperately going to miss the little ones. And what will Maman tell them about me? I shudder to think what a villain I'll become in their eyes. But for now, Mary's two delightful children are mine to enjoy and I feel that maybe life may finally have given me a break.

At supper I'm over the moon about my job. I chat with the other boarders and sit with Owen after dinner to tell him about the children and what a beautiful and strong creature Mary is. He smiles and tells me he's happy that I'm happy.

CHAPTER TWENTY-ONE

I love working for Mary. I keep the house scrubbed and clean and plan and prepare the evening meal before I leave for the day. Mary has only to do the final assembly. I take pride in doing a good job and Mary seems delighted with my work. My favorite part is caring for her children. Sarah and William are bright little buttons who love stories and games and making things. I make up stories for them, invent games and build forts under the kitchen chairs. What feels strange to me is that I can leave at the end of the work day and be free. I can go shopping or stroll by the creek. I no longer feel like a prisoner. I've not felt so much a grown-up since Wells. Best of all, at the end of the day, I go home to Owen and my new family at the boarding house. Owen and I don't go to church any more. I really don't want to see my parents there and I know the congregation will be wallowing in the news that Jenny Menard's daughter is shacked up with that young Welsh lad from the quarry, and didn't they all see that coming? In spite of this I'm happier than I can ever remember.

Life isn't all a bed of roses. Owen and I still have to find a place to live before the end of the month, now just a week away. Mrs. Gambol remains adamant that we can't share a room while unmarried, and she has a quarry worker needing my room for the start of the month. Our problem is temporarily solved by Maggie Turnbull, one of the other residents of the boarding house. Maggie suggests the name of a woman of her acquaintance who's planning a trip to Boston for a few weeks to visit her daughter and new grandson. Maggie thinks the woman might be pleased to have someone stay in her house while she's away. Though not a permanent solution, it will buy us some time, and Maggie is willing to provide a reference for us.

So it happens that we find ourselves visiting the very posh home of Adeline Carruthers, a throaty, poker-thin, thoroughly irreverent widow who already seems to know all about our unmarried status and doesn't give a fig. In her words, if her friend Maggie says we're reliable, it means more than a priest muttering a few words, waving some incense around and calling us married. She offers us a whiskey neat (which Owen accepts and I decline, having never tasted hard liquor). She puffs on a cigarette, making her the first woman I've seen smoking, up close, since Boxer. Adeline is planning on going the following Tuesday to Boston to visit her daughter who's just had a new baby. Her plan is to stay in Boston for six weeks "If my daughter doesn't throw me out sooner," she cackles. All she requires of Owen and I is a clean house when she comes home and a few dollars rent to cover any of her food and electricity we might use. And here is the real joy in the deal- Adeline Carruthers is one of the few people in Pittsford to have electric lights and a telephone in her home. She offers to call us when she's ready to catch the train home, but I beg her to send a letter instead. I've never talked on a telephone and have no idea how to work the thing.

"Pish posh," scoffs Adeline. "Time to learn." She proceeds to teach us how to use the contraption, calling through to one of her friends to demonstrate how to call central and make a connection. Owen and I each then muddle through a call to the same friend who must think we are all addled. "I need to know that you can make a call if there is an emergency and you need to get hold of me."

"We will," promises Owen who's only slightly less intimidated by the thing than me, but less willing to admit it.

We say our goodbyes to the other tenants at supper on Monday evening. There's much hand shaking and hugging and well-wishing and promises to stay in touch. I thank Mrs. Gambol profusely for taking me in, given such unusual circumstances. Before we leave, Mrs. Gambol takes me aside and tells me that Maman was by earlier in the day. The purpose of her visit was to advise Mrs. Gambol to evict me since my presence would be certain to soil the good name of her boarding house. An indignant Mrs. Gambol reports she told Maman, in no uncertain terms, of her skill in judging the quality of her tenants and that she most certainly would not put me out on the street before the agreed upon day. She did not, to my relief, tell Maman we were moving to a new location.

Owen and I move our few possessions into Adeline's home that evening, the day before her departure. There's excitement in the move, certainly, but I'm preoccupied with thoughts about the lengths my mother will go to hurt me. I wonder what drives the actions of this woman who was once my mother.

Living in Adeline's feels like playing house. We shop together for food and sleep in the same bed and get to know each other in a way that wasn't possible in the common room of Mrs. Gambol's boarding house. Aside from some nagging problems with my stomach I've never felt happier. Each morning I go to Mary Armstrong's to tend the house and look after the children. Each evening I return home to cook our dinner and wait for

Owen to come home from the quarry. On rare occasions Mary sends for me at odd hours by way of her neighbor's boy. On these occasions my only job is to get to Mary's as quickly as I can and stay with the children until she returns. When this happens it usually means there's been an accident or an injury or a critical illness that requires her nursing skills at the hospital. Often she returns looking drawn and pale and I know the outcome hasn't been good. Once I could tell she'd been crying. But she never says much about what's gone on and I sense it's best not to ask.

Over the weeks I become quite close with Mary. She's my employer first and foremost, but I also begin to consider her a friend. One day she asks me about my living arrangement. I've already told her I'm staying at Adeline Carruthers, so I know she's asking something more. I feel like I can trust her so I plunge into my story of how my parents threw me out for seeing Owen and that we're staying together at Adeline's until we can be properly married. Her expression makes me think I'm confirming something she's already suspected. She doesn't scold me but she does have a strange response. She sits me down and begins to ask me some very embarrassing questions. Are Owen and I having intercourse? Do I know about contraception? Has Maman ever talked to me about sex?

I'm stunned. I've never heard sex discussed so matter-of-factly. Even the tough girls at Wells, who loved to talk of their sexual exploits, never used words like intercourse and contraception. In fact, I feel like I had a pretty thorough orientation to sex at Wells, between Wyre's pestering and listening to the other girls talk about their experiences. But when Mary patiently schools me on the entire process of intercourse and conception, using the illustrations in one of her nursing books, I realize there's an awful lot I don't know.

"Your mother should have told you this, Erminie."

I'm silent, ashamed at my ignorance, but mostly trying to picture Maman talking about such things. I can't even imagine such a thing happening. Maybe, if I could only see my younger sisters for a short time, I could tell them some of this.

Mary moves on to discussing contraception. She produces a box of condoms she says Owen should wear when we make love. She goes on to talk about stages in a woman's cycle and when she's most likely to conceive a baby, and how to tell if she's pregnant. I mention that I haven't had a period in a couple of months and wonder how that might affect my chances of becoming pregnant. Mary stops talking, her mouth hanging open in an expression that would have been comical if she hadn't looked so pained.

"You haven't had a menstrual cycle?"

"Not for a couple of months," I repeat, beginning to feel a little defensive. What on earth is wrong?

"When was the first time you had intercourse with Owen?"

"In May. But only that once at the boarding house. Mrs. Gambol wouldn't allow it after that." I feel the need to add that last bit, but Mary interrupts me.

"How are you feeling? Any sickness, upset stomach?"

"Sometimes. Not every day."

Mary grabs me by the shoulders and gives me a not-so-gentle shake. "Erminie, feeling sick to your stomach is one sign of pregnancy. And not having your monthly cycle is one of the most sure signs. It could be because you've been under a lot of stress lately, but I'm going to ask Dr. Swift to take a look at you."

I'm horrified. "I can't afford a doctor!"

"Relax. He'll see you for free if I ask him. He's a kind man. You'll like him. Don't be afraid Erminie. We don't know anything yet. This is just a precaution."

I nod, suddenly feeling dull. A headache is taking over the front of my skull and I want nothing more than to be home at Adeline's, curled up on the bed with Owen. Owen! What will I tell him? I decide that, for now, Owen doesn't need to know, at least not until I hear what this Dr. Swift has to say.

Two days later Mary hands me a piece of paper. On it is written the day and time I'm to present myself at Dr. Swift's clinic, the one where I was first connected with Mary. Mary has another girl come to stay with the children for the afternoon so I can get away. I have no idea what to expect but I'm nervous just the same. All sorts of thoughts crowd my head. Is it possible there's a baby growing inside me? Owen's baby? Then of course there are all the things I find to worry about. What will the examination be like? Should I be walking this quickly, or might it harm the baby? I slow down a bit, just in case. But I don't want to be late.

I arrive at the clinic and push the heavy door open. A tiny voice wonders if the effort in pushing the door might harm the baby. Chipper Eileen is at her desk, though she shows no sign of recognizing me. She has me fill out a form and tells me to have a seat. The only others in the waiting area are a heavy-set woman with a boy of about four years draped lethargically across her knee. The child's cheeks are ruddy and his head rests against his mother's sturdy shoulder. Am I going to have one of those? A child of my own? Will I know how to care for a sick child like this boy? How can I afford to bring it here to the doctor if it gets sick? I have a lot of experience dealing with children-but a baby? I was young when the girls were babies and don't remember when the boys were born so Maman must have handled the feeding and bathing. Oh God! What is Owen going to say? What is Maman going to say? My mind is so busy that I almost miss the doctor who has come to the waiting room and is calling my name. I wonder how many times he's actually called me already. He looks amused.

Dr. Swift is a fatherly man with wire-rimmed spectacles and a fringe of unruly gray hair exploding around a gleaming bald head. In spite of his kindness, or perhaps because of it, the examination is the most humiliating thing I've had to endure with the exception of my times with Wyre. He asks questions about my monthly cycle, when Owen and I last had relations and whether we used any contraception. Then he has me remove my dress and underwear leaving me only in my shift. He has me lay down on his examination table while he pokes and prods my stomach and my breasts. Then he has me put my feet into a contraption that brings my heels up near my bottom and forces my knees apart. I will myself to die. This cannot be happening. He takes a cold shiny instrument and inserts it into my most private area, murmuring what I suppose are meant to be comforting words. "Be still now dear. This won't hurt, hon." But it does hurt and I feel sweaty, exhausted and humiliated by the time he tells me to get dressed and meet him next door in his office.

Once alone I put my dress back on, try to smooth my hair and take some deep breaths to slow my heart. Then I go next door and take a seat across from Dr. Swift, now sitting at his cluttered desk.

"My dear," he begins, kindly. "I understand you are an unmarried woman and so I'm sure this is not news you want to hear, but you are most decidedly going to have a child. In my estimation you're due to give birth in early February."

I sit in stunned silence. For all my fretting and worrying I mostly didn't believe pregnancy was a real possibility. "What now?" I wonder, but say nothing.

"Do your parents live nearby?" Dr. Swift asks.

I nod, feeling the first tears beginning to burn at the back of my eyes in spite of my resolve to act like I receive this sort of news every day.

"Would you like me to talk to them for you?"

"No. No! That won't be necessary." I begin to babble. "Thank you for your time, Dr. Swift. I have a bit of money. I can't pay your full fee but I can give you part of it now and more later."

"My dear, please don't fret about the money. I did this as a favor to Mary Armstrong. She's the best nurse I've had and she thinks a lot of you. Your fee is taken care of. It's more important to talk about your plans for this baby. Have you thought about that? I can recommend a couple of adoption options," he offers kindly.

"I-I'll have to go home and talk to my-to Owen-the baby's father," I stammer. Adoption? I hadn't even considered that. This is my baby. Mine and Owen's.

"You talk to your Owen and if you need to discuss the various options please do come back to see me with your young man. Promise?" I nod. "You are a fine, healthy young woman and there's no reason to suspect you won't have a fine healthy strapping baby. But babies require a great deal of commitment from both parents. You need to be able to provide a stable home."

I nod, but my dry throat has sealed up and no words will come. Dr. Swift walks me to the door of his office, hand on my back, talking about some things I should and shouldn't do to keep the baby healthy. I hardly hear, let alone comprehend, what he's saying. I feel like I am viewing myself from a very great distance.

At the door I mechanically thank Dr. Swift for his time. I leave the clinic and walk home in a fog, one foot in front of the other with no awareness of people or carriages passing by. It's still two hours before Owen is due home from the quarry. I use the time to practice how I will tell him about the baby. In my favorite scenario I'm a calm confident version of myself. I deliver the news of the baby to Owen in a straightforward, factual way. When Owen actually comes through the door all that is forgotten. I run to him, blubbering like a child. He wraps his arms around me and murmurs comforting sounds while maneuvering me around to sit beside him on Adeline's gaudy, orange brocade divan.

"What is it Min? Are you sick?"

"I'm going to have a baby," I wail, around a new flood of tears. There it is. No art. Rehearsals forgotten. Nothing to cushion the blow. "You're going to be a father," I add hopefully, thinking maybe I should include him in the equation. There's a long silence during which I keep my face buried in his dusty work shirt that smells of sweat and stone dust. I am convinced, in equal measure, that he will ruin Adeline's divan with his dirty work clothes and push me away and storm out of the house.

"A baby? We're going to have a baby? A boy or a girl?"

I nod my head, face still buried in his shirt. I ignore the boy/girl question, sure he's probably already realizing it was a silly thing to ask. "Do you want to have a baby?" It's a hopeful question mumbled against his chest.

"I haven't given it any thought. It's a surprise," he adds needlessly.

"Yeah. For me too. Do you want to keep it?" I ask. I know there are ways of disposing of unwanted pregnancies, though I don't know what they are. Perhaps that's one of the "options" Dr. Swift mentioned. "I could ask about-you know-ending it?" Even as I say this I know I'll probably rot in hell for even thinking such a thing.

"Oh Min, no! It's too dangerous. I've heard of women dying, bleeding to death."

"Women die having babies too," I retort, and immediately wish I hadn't planted that particular seed in my own brain. If I'm destined to rot in hell, I don't want it to happen quite so soon.

We sit in silence for a bit, each rolling ideas and thoughts privately around in our heads. I'm the one to finally break the silence once it grows from merely uncomfortable to painful. "I'll talk to Mary tomorrow. She'll know what to do."

I spend the whole of my walk to Mary's the next morning wondering how to broach the subject of my pregnancy to my employer. She meets me at the door. "Well?" She demands, arching an eyebrow. "What did Dr. Swift say?"

"I'm going to have a baby. In February. Oh Mary! I don't know what to do. We have no real home, no money, we're not even married."

"Calm down Erminie," she says firmly. "Sit. You're not the first girl to find herself in this situation and you sure as hell won't be the last."

I sit and Mary settles beside me on the sofa, a comforting arm around my shoulders. In all my life I've never been able to abide people being nice to me. It brings the tears right up.

"Listen Erminie, you have three choices here. One is to keep the baby and raise it. If you and Owen get married it will be easier. Raising a baby by yourself is very difficult, even for me and I'm older and I had a husband for the first while. Your second choice is to have the baby and give it up for adoption. Your baby would go to an orphanage until it can be adopted out to a couple who can't have children of their own. I can help you work through all of that."

"Your third option, though I don't consider it a real option, is to have an abortion-end the pregnancy. You would need to find a doctor willing to do it and it will cost a lot of money. And Erminie, I have to tell you, it's very dangerous even if it's done by a qualified doctor. There are backroom quacks who will do it cheaper but they're no better than butchers. You could end up bleeding to death, or getting an infection. Even if you come through it you might not ever be able to have children again. Erminie, if you decide to abort this baby I will do what I can to help you find someone to do it, but my name must never be mentioned. You don't have to decide what you are going to do right away, but if you decide to abort this baby you need to do it very soon, alright?"

I nod, my head swimming.

"What does Owen say? Does he want the baby?"

"He didn't really say much. He just looked kind of shocked. Mary, I love children. I want to keep this baby. I just don't know how I can."

"Well, you and Owen will have to talk this through and decide together. I have to go to work now love, but we'll talk more and if you have any questions about any of this, you know you can always talk to me, right?"

"I know, Mary. And I can't thank you enough for all this."

"Oh Erminie, I just want you to be happy and this baby to be cared for. If not by you, than by someone who will love it to bits." Mary gathers her coat and bag and hurries off to the hospital.

I keep myself busy but the day passes slowly. Knowing now that there's a baby growing inside me, I wonder how I could not have known. It seems so real. So obvious. My queasiness, the changes in appetite. It all makes sense. I have a baby growing inside me. Swimming, sleeping, doing whatever tiny babies do in there, a passenger in my body.

When Mary returns from work she gives me a huge warm hug and releases me from my day's duties. I return home and wait for Owen. After our supper we curl up in bed under the covers where everything feels safe and we talk long into the night.

We both agree the idea of aborting the child is far too frightening, even excluding the possibility of eternal damnation, which we have probably signed on for any way. Could we raise a child? I'm really good at looking after other people's children so it stands to reason I might have some skills. Mary hasn't mentioned terminating me so she might let me work there for a bit yet, maybe even until the baby comes. We could rent a small house. Owen says he'll write to his family in Wales but he doesn't seem optimistic. Owen's been promised a position doing accounting for the quarry. If that happens the extra income would certainly help. I consider writing Grand-mère , but I haven't heard from her since we visited Rutland at Christmas and I know she's not been well. Even though she's shown a softer side recently I don't know if I can ask for charity from my fierce old grandmother.

Three evenings later Owen proposes to me. We've tiptoed around the issue recently, both seemingly afraid to speak the words. But, though we're young, we're both practical people. Raising a baby will be so very much easier if we're married. Our baby will be socially accepted and it will help me as well. Life isn't easy for single women with babies, unless, like Mary, they have the good grace to be widowed. People will still talk, of course. They always do. It's a preoccupation of the human race. That can't be helped. The practical points aside, though, I love Owen to the moon and I know he loves me. I know he'll find a way to take care of me and the baby we've made.

After all our talk about babies and marriage and being together you'd think a proposal wouldn't come as any big surprise. But, when Owen arrives home from the quarry that Friday evening, he's acting oddly. He's restless, jittery. He sits a while, then jumps up to do some silly task, then sits again, fidgeting and smoking non-stop. He was late getting home so I wonder if he stopped for a drink before coming home, though there's no smell of alcohol. It even occurs to me that maybe he's seeing someone else, or maybe he's going to tell me he isn't ready to be a father and is fixing to leave. That last worry burrows itself into my brain and makes me so scared that I feel even sicker in my stomach than usual. I visualize how, with good grace, I will accept his bad news, right before I kill him.

Just when I can't stand his strangeness any more Owen wanders into Adeline Carruthers posh sitting room, sits down beside me on the sofa, takes my hand and says, "Erminie Menard, will you do me the honor of being my wife?"

I've been preparing my breaking up speech in my head so I suddenly find my head empty of words. I can't find a single intelligent thing to say. Owen takes my hesitation as a sign of doubt and jumps right in with both guns blazing.

"This isn't just about the baby. I love you and I want to be your husband and I want us to be a family. I talked to your father today after work and asked his permission to ask for your hand."

That shakes me out of it all right. "You asked my father? Did you tell him? About the baby?"

"No I didn't tell him about that because I want to marry you anyway. They don't need to know about the baby until we're married."

"Maman will know. I swear she will know somehow! And she will never approve of us getting married."

Owen looks at me strangely. "What more can they do? They've already thrown you out of the house and they haven't come to see us since. It doesn't matter Erminie. Your father gave his blessing and if you agree we'll get married with or without your mother."

"Well of course I'll marry you," I spout. Owen's right. Maman can't object if Papa has already approved. And even if she tries to interfere we'll find a way. I hug Owen tight and he scoops me up and carries me, giggling and squirming, upstairs to Adeline's startlingly large four poster bed.

The next few weeks are marked by a flurry of activity. I suggest that we get married in a simple civil ceremony but Owen insists on a real church wedding. He says he doesn't want me having regrets down the road and blaming him for being too poor to provide the real thing. I tell him there's no way that will happen but he's so insistent and so excited that I agree to a church wedding with a white dress and a few close friends.

All of our wedding plans are overlaid by our need to find new accommodations. Adeline will be home from Boston soon. She sent a pretty postcard of Boston Common full of spring blossoms. On the back was a short note saying her daughter was driving her mad and her new grandson kept the whole house up at night with his squalling. She felt she must soon come home to get a good night's sleep. I chuckle at Adeline's crustiness. She isn't outwardly a very maternal woman but I would trade her for my own crazy mother any day. I prop the postcard up by the kitchen sink so that I can see the photo while I cook and clean. I picture myself pushing our own son (for surely it will be a boy!) in an elegant buggy along the Common. Passersby will stop and coo and admire our lovely baby. Our baby, of course, will never "squall" or fuss like Adeline's grandson. Our baby will be beautiful and delightful and so very, very loved.

We're able to locate a house for rent not far from my parents. The distance between the two houses is not a positive attribute, but the quarry is expanding and there's been a small influx of workers that has put some pressure on housing. The house is small and run-down but one of the few that's within our means. The best part of the deal is that it comes with a few sticks of furniture. With a good cleaning and some repairs it will make a passable home for our little family until we can get away to Boston. Besides, my mother rarely leaves the house except for church. I don't expect her to be dropping in.

We move our few possessions on a lovely sunny day at the end of what is otherwise a winter so unseasonably cold there are news reports of Niagara Falls freezing over. This sunny, spring-like day feels like a good omen. I know I have a bounce in my step as we walk back and forth to Adeline's carrying as much as we can on each trip.

Adeline has returned from Boston with a trunk of purchases. Learning of our upcoming wedding she pulls out a lovely quilt in a design she calls *flying geese*. "Consider this an early wedding present my dears." She wraps the quilt around my shoulders and gives me and the quilt a hearty hug. "I'll get you something nice for the baby a little later."

My jaw drops. How does she know? I haven't told her about the baby and I know Owen hasn't either.

Seeing my reaction Adeline waves a careless hand my way. "Pish posh. I've been around a while. I know a pregnant woman when I see one." I lay a hand on my still flat belly. "Your face dear. It's in your face."

Now I'm spreading Adeline's beautiful quilt over our newly-made bed, one of the relics left from a previous tenant. I smooth the covering and try not to think of the stained and questionable mattress underneath. We can replace that soon. For now, we finally have a home so we can settle for a time and begin our family.

One day, while we are still 'nesting' and settling into our little home, Owen brings home a note from Papa. In it he tells me that Grand-mère has passed and that he and the boys drove to Rutland for the funeral. Maman, of course, refused to go. No one asked me if I wanted to attend and the letter gives no reason. Perhaps Maman forbade it, or perhaps Papa thought I wouldn't want to go. Whatever the reason I'm heartbroken and angry. Grand-mère was very old and lived a good life but I regret not having a chance to say goodbye. That night I pray for the first time in a very long time. I pray for the soul of my tough old Grand-mère and ask her to watch over my little family.

CHAPTER TWENTY-TWO

Plans for our wedding are progressing nicely. We have a date in late April, just three weeks away. Everything in our lives, it seems, needs to be done in a rush. I want no sign of a baby when I walk down the aisle. Once we're married, people can count on their fingers and speculate about dates, but I want to make it hard for them. Amidst the turmoil we get some great news. Owen finally gets confirmation that the bookkeeping job at the quarry is his. Old Mr. McLean is retiring and has agreed to work with Owen for a time to help him pick up on the job. He'll start the week before the wedding. The pay isn't as much as we hoped but it's more money than he makes now and it's clean, safe, indoor work with a future. We're over the moon with plans for our little family.

Mary has the day off which means I have the day off. I've just returned from Mrs. Chamberlain's shop. I'm sewing my wedding dress but Mrs. Chamberlain has kindly agreed to help me with some design ideas and has given me a lovely lace remnant to use for a veil. Mary has offered up her treadle sewing machine, encouraging me to do the sewing in the afternoons while the children are napping.

I hurry up to the door of my new little home. It's been raining off and on all day and the most recent shower has me drenched to my underthings. My mind is taken up with wedding plans and I'm clutching the bag with the precious lace inside. I'm planning how, with a little care, I might be able to salvage an extra piece of the snowy lace to attach to the bodice of my dress. I'm so distracted that, at first, I don't notice the fresh footprints in the mud leading up to, but not leaving, the door. Owen isn't due home for hours and these are large tracks made by a man's heavy boot. I hesitate, wondering if someone is inside waiting for me with some evil intent. But, as I hesitate there on the door step, the door opens and Papa steps out.

"Papa!" I cry. I haven't seen him in weeks and certainly wasn't expecting him to stop by for a visit. But I'm oh so glad to see him. Something in his face stops me cold though. "Papa?"

"Come in Min. It's raining." He takes me by the elbow and guides me inside the house. I feel panic clutching at my belly. He drags a chair over from beside the kitchen table and sits it down beside the door, forcefully sitting me down on it, coat, boots, bag, lace and all. "Erminie, it's Owen. Honey, I'm so sorry. He's been injured at the quarry. He's in the hospital. Mary is with him and she sent me to get you. She told me where you live."

I feel a momentary stab of guilt. I haven't told my father where we're living. Then Papa's words come around to form something solid in my brain. "Owen? He's hurt? How bad is it?"

"It's very bad Min. We have to go to him right now."

We half walk, half run the several blocks to Pittsford's hospital. On the way Papa tells me that Owen was helping attach the rope harness by which the huge slabs of marble are lifted to the surface. One side of the contraption gave way and a two-ton marble slab swung sideways. It caught Owen in the head and shoulder. "He's very badly hurt," Papa adds, pausing mid-stride to glance at me.

"Then let's get there," I scream at him and quicken my step. I have to get to Owen. He'll be fine if I can just get to him.

I've never been inside the small cottage hospital that caters to the health needs of Pittsford and the surrounding area. Most can't afford hospital care but quarry injuries are treated, with costs being picked up by the various companies for whom the men work. Papa leads me past a desk where a stern looking matron is keeping watch. She makes no move to stop us. We hurry down a long antiseptic-drenched hallway with rooms opening up on either side. Each room holds four beds, one in each corner, some occupied, many not. About halfway down the hallway Papa guides me into one such room and points to a bed in the corner. Mary, minus her crisp nursing uniform, sits beside a nondescript heap of white blankets that must be Owen. I remember she isn't supposed to be working. She jumps up as I come in the room and intercepts me near the door. Papa melts into the background, obviously relieved to turn me over to someone with more experience in dealing with illness and fear.

"Erminie, Owen is very seriously injured."

"I know, Papa told me." I like Mary but I swear to God I will hit her if that's what it takes to get to Owen's bedside. "Let me see him." I push forward, trying to get past Mary's solidly efficient body.

"You can see him, Erminie. But you need to be prepared. He's unconscious. He won't be able to speak to you. He might know you're here, or he might not have that level of awareness. We don't know. He looks bad. There was a lot of damage to his head and his upper body. There are lots of bruises and bandages." I move impatiently to get past her, but she grabs me fiercely by the shoulders. "Erminie, Owen isn't going to wake up. He has bleeding inside his brain. He might last the night but not much more. You need to say goodbye. The priest from the company just left. He's been given his last rites."

A chill slides down my spine. I dart past Mary and rush to the side of the bed. Mary's words mean nothing. Of course Owen will wake up. But I gasp at what I see under those blankets. Owen is horribly pale, even against the starched hospital sheet. The left side of his head is bandaged but bruises bloom out from under the bandage, stark against his pale skin. The visible parts of his face are swollen, the unwrapped eye puffy and closed. Someone has cleaned blood from his face but his hairline is crusted with dark blood. A small bit of his left shoulder is exposed and I see more bandages and more bruising and more crusted blood.

I know Papa and Mary are prepared for hysteria but what I feel is numb. I watch myself, from somewhere above my body, reach under the blankets and find Owen's right hand. I see myself examine it for injuries. It's dirty and the skin is dry and cracked but it is whole and very much Owen, right down to the tobacco-stained fingers. There's no movement though, and it's cold to the touch.

I watch myself sink into the chair vacated by Mary. "Owen, it's Min. I've come to see you." My voice seems to come from a long way off. "Please open your eyes." There's no flutter of the swollen eye, nothing to indicate he hears. As I watch that other Erminie, she begins to talk. She talks about the baby, the house, the lace for the dress, his new job, how much she wants to see Boston in the fall. I think I should tell her Owen can't hear but I know she won't listen. The words flow in a quiet stream. I'm aware that Mary and Papa have left the room. The other beds are empty. We're alone and that other Erminie talks.

Sometime in the small hours a nurse comes to check on Owen as she has several times through the night. She checks his pulse and lifts his exposed eyelid. Then she quietly pulls the sheet over Owen's face.

"He's gone sweetie. Your friend is gone."

"He's not. That's not possible. We've been talking this whole time. He must have just fallen asleep. Please uncover his face. He can't breathe."

"He's gone dear," the nurse repeats patiently. "He's in God's hands now."

Suddenly Papa is at my side. His strong arm is around my shoulder. "Say goodbye to Owen, Minnie, and I'll take you home." The nurse turns down the sheet again, exposing Owen's poor broken face. I touch his cold cheek and gingerly run a finger into his blood-crusted hair. "Owen?" I ask hopefully.

"He's gone Min. He's gone to be with God and you must let him go in peace. Father Roger came to see him when they first brought him in. He's at rest. Let him go now."

I lay my head down on Owen's chest. I'm no longer watching from across the room. I'm back inside my body and the pain is too much. I've not shed a tear all night but now they come in a rush with great gasping sobs that shake my body and even the bed on which Owen, my precious Owen, lies. In that moment it seems that every bad thing that has ever happened to me has come together in one mighty surge of grief. Through my tears I curse God, my mother and even Owen. He's left me and the baby and there's no one to take care of us.

Eventually Papa and Mary (when did Mary come?) take me to an empty room and put me to bed. A doctor I've not seen before comes by and asks a nurse to prepare a sleeping powder for me. I drink the bitter concoction, without comment or resistance, and lay my head on the pillow. I wish I could sleep forever.

I wake with no idea of the time. Sunlight pours through the window so I know I've slept a while. Papa is there, his long frame hunched onto a hospital chair. He smiles at me sadly. "Hello Minnie." He reaches for my hand. "I'm going to take you home now." I nod absently and swing my legs over the side of the bed, still feeling groggy from whatever they gave me to help me sleep. Just as I'm testing my legs, Mary arrives, now in her uniform and obviously on duty.

"You're not going anywhere until you eat something."

I mumble that I'm not hungry but I don't know if Mary even hears me. She's darted out of the room and I hear her barking orders in the hallway. I sit on the side of my bed feeling that terrible pain fill my chest again. Surely I can't survive this.

Mary comes back and sends my father off to rent a buggy. She forbids me to walk home and I can't even argue. She sits with me and talks about God and peace and things that have no meaning. The sleeping medicine has left me without substance. Mary holds my hand and, more than anything, her touch seems to be the only thing keeping me from drifting away.

When Papa comes, Mary gives me a hug and walks me to the hospital door. Papa helps settle me into the buggy. We stop at my house so I can gather a few things. I want to stay there but Papa won't hear of it. He's uncharacteristically firm. I must go home with him, to be with my family. The idea of going back there fills my stomach with knots but I don't have the energy to protest. I'm like a blade of grass in the wind, pulled whichever way the breeze blows. I hold my valise on my lap as we bounce along the last bit of the way to Maman and Papa's house, feeling like I've lost not only Owen but a piece of my soul.

Papa helps me out of the buggy. We're greeted by Maman who's the very picture of concern. She fusses over me and helps me with my coat and my boots like I'm a small child. "We're so glad you came home Minnie. This is where you belong, where we can all take care of you." I hate her for her hypocrisy but I'm too numb to fight.

My sisters and brothers are all there with expressions ranging from curiosity on the younger faces to caution and open grief on the older ones. They've been told to give me space, I guess, because they hang back looking awkward and uncertain. Finally I squat and open my arms and little Leona flies at me. All hell breaks loose for a few moments until Maman gets everyone under control again and takes me up to my room. Henry Jr. follows carrying my valise.

I pull back the quilted bed cover and crawl gratefully underneath. My whole body feels chilled. Here I am, back again, in the house I've worked so hard to get out of. There's a difference though. This time I have a child growing in me and, aside from Dr. Swift and Mary and Adeline, I'm the only one who knows. I lay my hand over my belly and let sleep take me away.

OWEN

Stupid. Stupid. The number one rule is to keep your eyes open. Stay alert. Daydreaming can get you killed.

Now, here I am. I don't remember much of what happened but I know it isn't good. Min's friend is here with me, moving around the room like a ghost, fixing blankets and blinds. She's really just a shadow, an image. My eyes are slits-one is covered I think-but I can neither open nor close them. I don't feel any pain. In fact I don't feel anything except a terrible need to see Erminie. I need to tell Mary to get her but nothing works. My lips don't move. My voice won't come. They must have given me something.

Another woman, a nurse, comes and lays a hand on my brow, forces an eye open, takes my pulse. Her touch is gentle but it feels too personal. I don't like her touching me. I want to tell her to leave me alone. I'm fine. Except I'm not. Because if I was fine I'd be able to tell her to get her paws off me.

Then she's there, in the doorway. I can make out a silhouette and I can hear her. She sounds angry. Not with me. With her friend. Someone else is there, her father maybe. Then he's gone and Erminie is beside me. I smile at her with my mind but I don't think my lips are moving. She looks so scared. I want to tell her it'll be ok. Her hand moves my blankets, then comes to my head, but strangely I feel none of it. It's like I've checked out of my body. But I can still hear and almost see and I know her touch is different than the nurse's. It soothes.

She's talking to me and I have to concentrate so hard to hear her. I don't want to miss anything. She's telling me she loves me and then about the baby we've made. Her voice is a soft crooning in my ear. So soft. I wish she would speak louder. Her voice is just a rhythm now, rising and falling.

I recall that first time in church, seeing a beautiful girl with chestnut ringlets sitting between her parents. I knew I had to talk to her. I set my mind to it. She seemed so shy and she blushed so prettily when she caught me looking at her. Then came the visits at night, the long walks, the kisses, the first time we made love, I see it all again like I'm right there. She became my everything. Beautiful, calm, patient, practical and so full of love. And we made a baby. What a miracle! Poor baby to have me as a father, but oh how he'll be loved. Or maybe it will be a girl and will have slate-blue eyes like her mother.

Min's still talking. The sound is like waves rising and falling. I'm very tired but I mustn't sleep while Erminie is here. But as hard as I try, I feel like I'm being pulled out to sea, away from her.

Someone-the nurse-comes again. I know she touches me but she seems so far away. Then it's dark. I can't help it. I'm drifting away. I understand now. I'm dying. I'm dead.

ERMINIE

CHAPTER TWENTY-THREE

I put off telling my parents I'm expecting their grandchild. I tell myself it's because I'm not ready for any sort of confrontation. But really I know it's because I have a need to keep this little piece of Owen my secret as long as I can.

The company pays for a coffin and a graveside service for Owen. He has no family in America so I think it will only be me and some of the men he worked with. I'm delighted when Mary and Adeline come. Adeline, bless her, pushes her way to stand at my side by the grave, leaving my mother scowling. Adeline doesn't notice, but wraps her hand over mine and gives my hand a squeeze. Maman has to shuffle around to the other side. Almost everyone from Mrs. Gambol's boarding house is there and many people from the church. I'm not even sure how some of the church folks know Owen since he never seemed to talk to anyone there. It seems everyone loved him though, and it makes me proud that I was his girl and that I'm carrying his child-although of course most don't know that. When the service is over everyone files by to offer condolences. They all tell me how much they'll miss Owen. I feel like he was loved by everyone.

Maman will not endure having me lie around idle. She loses no time in giving me chores around the house. Her theory is the sooner I return to a normal routine the sooner I'll feel better and able to move on with my life. I know what she really means is she wants me to forget about Owen and get back to being her servant. That will never happen. But I'm glad to be busy so I move around the old house like a wraith, dusting and tidying and helping the younger children. On the surface it seems that nothing has changed. But in my heart nothing is the same.

One afternoon, a few days after Owen's funeral, Mary comes to visit on one of her days off. We go for a walk together and Maman is plainly annoyed. But even Maman is no match for Mary, who tosses me my coat from the hook and tells me to hurry along; that fresh air will do me good.

As we walk, Mary tells me she's made some inquiries. If a couple are married, the surviving spouse is eligible for a pension from Northwest Marble. But because Owen and I did not marry there's no such support for me or for my baby. Mary assures me I can come back to work for her once I'm able, and stay as long as I want. She's currently employing her neighbor's daughter, but the girl is young and shiftless and Sarah and William miss me. That makes me smile for the first time since Owen's death.

"I'll start back next week, Mary. Thank you for giving me this time. I haven't felt up for much of anything. I've been thinking a lot about things though. I'll have to give up the house, of course. The rent is paid until the end of the month but I won't be able to carry the rent on my own. Maman and Papa have said I can stay as long as I want but I don't know what will happen when I tell them about the baby."

"You haven't told them?" Mary stops dead in her tracks and swings around to face me such that she startles me. "Why ever not?"

"I will," I stammer. "I just haven't found the right time or the right words and honestly, I haven't felt up to facing Maman. She'll throw a fit."

Mary turns and continues walking. "You never know. Sometimes finding out you're going to be a grandparent softens people. Give them a chance."

"I'm not worried about Papa. I think he'll be over the moon. But he doesn't stand up to Maman and seems to make sure he's somewhere else most of the time."

"Well you can't put off telling them much longer. You'll be showing soon."

When we get back to the house Maman is lying down. Ethel says she has one of her headaches and I know she's pouting because I left the house with Mary.

I spend the next few days thinking about what Mary said. Yes, I have to tell my parents about the baby, and soon. But how best to do it? I just feel like I don't have the strength to tell my mother. Mostly I want to curl up and sleep and let my problems drift away. I even consider ending my life. I imagine meeting Owen in heaven and spending eternity in a place where I no longer need to worry. Except suicide is a mortal sin and I won't go to heaven. I would also be taking our unborn child's life and that is a sin even the most forgiving god couldn't overlook. Besides, I have no idea how people kill themselves. No matter how I imagine it I can't see having the courage for that final jump or shot or swallow of poison.

The whole problem of telling Maman is taken out of my hands by Maman herself. She comes to me one evening just after supper. I'm sitting on the floor playing with Donny. Papa has gone out, Martin and Henry Jr. are at a friend's and the little girls are playing fort upstairs. Maman's expression is serious. She knows, I think. She knows I'm going to have a baby. I'm not really surprised. Adeline guessed long ago and Maman is determined to control my life. Even the workings of my body can't stay secret from her for long.

She takes me into the front room and we sit together on the worn sofa. My heart leaps up into my throat when Maman takes my hand. I really want to pull it back but I don't. I suck in a big breath of air and focus with all my might on a water stain on the ceiling as Maman begins to speak. "Erminie, I'm expecting another baby," she says quietly. I hear the words just fine but my mind can't quite make sense of them.

"*You're* having another baby?"

Maman nods. "Yes, it came as quite a surprise. I thought I was done with all of that after Donald. But it's true."

I sit motionless, staring at the stain, part of my mind thinking how its shape resembles the outline of a sheep. The other part of my brain is frantically trying to process what Maman has just told me. I'm not even sure how this could happen. Papa is hardly around. "You're having a baby?" I repeat, aware that I must sound feeble-minded.

"Yes, in January. But there's more, Minnie. We're moving to Montreal. You're father's work here is not good. We've decided there'll be more opportunities for him in Montreal. And, of course, I have family there."

I stare at her. To my knowledge, Maman hasn't seen or corresponded with anyone in her Canadian family for years. Where has this all come from? Maman continues to talk. She talks about the opportunities in Montreal, how they speak French there, how it will feel like home, how we'll finally be in a place we belong. I think, but do not say, that no one in our family really remembers how to speak proper French; our family has been in Vermont for three generations. Vermont is home. Maman herself has driven us all crazy by expecting us to embrace our French culture with one breath, then demanding we be American with the next. She insisted I go to French school, then pulled me out of school all together. She insists we all call her Maman but has paddled us in the past for speaking French. Like so much in Maman's life, her relationship with the French language has puzzled our family. Now, though, she is reaching out for it like a life raft.

"I'll need you to come with us to help with the baby, of course. Having a baby at any time is difficult, of course, but at my age…." She sighs and shrugs her shoulders helplessly.

I really look at her for the first time since we sat down. I've always considered Maman to be well kept in an austere sort of way. Now, though, I notice new lines on her face and her eyes look tired. Seeing these things I think maybe Maman may be more approachable at this moment.

"Maman, this is a very strange situation, but I'm going to have a baby too…in February."

Maman gazes at me, her expression unreadable. "Is it Owen's?" she asks finally.

"Of course it's Owen's, Maman! Who else would the father be?" I splutter. Even at her kindest Maman knows how to make words sting.

She just shrugs like she thinks the baby could belong to anyone. I try very hard not to react.

"Maman, I don't want to go to Montreal with you. I want to stay here in Pittsford and raise my baby until I can save enough to move to Boston. It's what I've always wanted. I have a job with Mary...."

Maman cuts me off. "And where will you live? You can't afford to rent anything on your own with what that woman pays you." She manages to make "that woman" a sneer. "No one will have anything to do with an unmarried woman with a baby. You'll have no prospects. This town feels nothing but revulsion for us. We are all shamed." Maman rises unsteadily and, without another word goes into the bedroom she and Papa share. The door slams. I know I'll not see her again until sometime tomorrow. I'm left wondering what just happened.

What on earth does she mean we're all shamed? Nobody knows I'm pregnant, we've been very careful to keep the theft and my stay in Wells quiet. True, I lived in sin with Owen briefly before his death but, after all, it is 1911.

In spite of Maman's nasty reaction to the news about my baby, having the telling over and done is a load off my shoulders. Now, how best to deal with Maman's news? Maman is right about one thing. I can't afford a place of my own on my salary, let alone look after a baby. I could, perhaps, move to Rutland and stay with family there, but I'd be starting over there as well, with no job and a baby to care for. I wrap my arms protectively over my stomach and ponder my options. There are not many to ponder.

Surprisingly, Maman appears from her room an hour later. It's clear she's been crying. Her eyes are puffy, her skin blotched. I've never known her to cry and I'm shocked that she's even capable of it. She gets right to the point.

"You'll be showing soon. There are places where you can go. I'll see what I can find out. You'll have the baby, put it up for adoption then join us in Montreal." It's clear I was not the only one considering options.

"No, Maman. I'm keeping this baby. It's all I have left of Owen."

"This isn't up to you Erminie. You are a child. Your father and I must make the difficult decisions for you. You can't possibly raise a child alone and I will not have your bastard baby under my roof."

And there it is. My options as laid out by Maman, clear as day. There's nothing soft in Jenny Menard, grandmother or no. I don't even try to reason with her. I stand and leave the room. I know I'm not giving up my baby and if I have to prostitute myself to support us then that's how it will be. In the meantime I desperately need a plan.

The next day I return to work at Mary's, her tidy little house a refuge from life with Maman. With Mary I can speak freely and not be judged. Mary has to hurry away to work in the morning but when she returns late that evening I lay out my dilemma.

"Christ Erminie! That mother of yours is as cold as a witch's tit." She quickly checks over her shoulder to make sure her children haven't overheard her language. She lowers her voice. "I thought sure she'd thaw when she found out she was having a grand baby."

I smile bitterly. I don't want to say "I told you so" but no one knows the depth of Maman's orneriness quite like me.

"First, you are not a child. You are 18 and perfectly capable of making your own decisions. What I think you both need most right now is some breathing space. There's a place in Burlington. They take in women who have no place else to go. Most of them are girls and women like you who've gotten pregnant. It's run by a charitable group so you can stay there for free until you have the baby. That is, if they have room; and I think I can pull some strings to get you in. That will put some space between you and your mother and she can't refuse since it's what she suggested in the first place. Then you have some time to rest and think about what you want to do."

I've never been to Burlington but I need a place where I can escape everything that's happened - Owen's death, my pregnancy, news of Maman's pregnancy, my family's upcoming move to Montreal- it sounds like a gift. "I would like it very much, Mary, if you could check on this place for me. I don't think I can stay with Maman any more knowing how she feels about my baby."

"Do you want to stay here with us for a while until we can make other arrangements?" Mary asks.

I consider the offer, but Mary's house is tiny and it would involve rearranging Sarah and Matthew's sleeping arrangements. "Thank you Mary. That's a kind offer but I can manage for a while yet. I'll just try not to get drawn into a fight with her. It leaves me feeling sick inside. It's probably bad for the baby and I never ever win."

Mary writes to the Home for Friendless Women in Burlington on my behalf. As their name implies, they are a last chance home for women who have no place left to go. Normally the fact that I'm still living at home would disqualify me but Mary tells one or two white lies in her letter. Three weeks later she receives a reply from them in the post. They will take me at their next available opening. They have arrangements with a doctor who will oversee the birth of my baby. The decision will be mine as to whether I keep the baby or turn it over to nearby St. Joseph's Orphanage. Mary reads the letter to me and we do a silly little dance around her kitchen. I realize it's the first time I've felt any sort of positive emotion since Owen's passing.

I think even my baby is smiling.

I don't share the news about Burlington with my family. My relationship with Maman is brittle. I think she's upset because my pregnancy is taking something away from her pregnancy. Neither of us even mentions our developing babies. Maman has told Papa but I only know this because one day he catches me alone and tells me he knows I will be a great mother. It doesn't escape me that he's assuming I'll keep the baby.

One day, a few weeks after the initial letter from Burlington, a second letter arrives. They expect to have an opening for me at month's end in December. Mary says she'll write them back to tell them I'll be there.

I go home that evening, help with supper, wait until the dishes have been cleared and Papa has retired to the front room. "Maman, there's a place in Burlington that has accepted me for the end of December. I can stay there until I have the baby."

Maman nods. "I'm told it's a good place. I was going to suggest it myself. I think we can delay going to Montreal until you are settled there, and, of course you are welcome to join us in Montreal once you've delivered the child."

"Maman, I'm planning on keeping the baby. I could not bear to part with this child. It's all I have left of Owen. I owe it to him to raise his baby."

"Well, Erminie, you know my position. I'll not stop you from keeping the baby if that's really what you want, but if you do you'll be dead to this family. That's all I have to say on the matter." Maman rises from the table and busies herself rearranging some items on the sideboard. The discussion is clearly at an end. It's not the response I want, but it is the response I expected.

The latter half of August and then September roll onward. I marvel at the changes in my body. The earlier queasiness has passed leaving me feeling better than I have in weeks. My belly is swelling and I have to let my dress out to accommodate my growing child. At the same time I watch my mother's belly swell at an even faster rate. This is her ninth pregnancy and she's approaching forty. She wears pregnancies like a worn sweater. I admit to being a bit embarrassed by her. Who would have guessed a women of her age still made love, let alone could become pregnant? But I know my embarrassment of her is more than matched by hers of me. The pot can hardly call the kettle black. Maman and Papa have stopped going to church because of the shame of my pregnancy. On the rare instances when Maman ventures out, she always returns with stories of what "they" are saying about me. Since I rarely go out, I'm unclear how "they" even know me to be pregnant. It makes no difference that Owen and I were about to be married, I'm a fallen woman. So we co-exist in an uneasy truce while the male members of the family tiptoe around afraid to say or do something that will unleash the ire of either of us. Donny is too young to understand any of this and the little girls are mostly oblivious. They know they are moving to Montreal, but it seems Maman has not yet told them about the imminent arrival of a new baby brother or sister. Nor have I told them about my baby. I know the questions would be endless and I can't face that right now.

We make it through a sullen, uncomfortable Christmas. As December draws to a close I pack up my few possessions while my parents and siblings pack up the household for their move to Montreal. Papa suggests they delay their move until after the baby is born but Maman is adamant that they are leaving the moment I am out the door. The atmosphere in the house is awkward. Maman is holding firm. I must put the baby up for adoption and join them in Montreal or I make my own way with the baby. I'm equally adamant I will keep the baby. In spite of his earlier support Papa has become aloof and says little.

Of the boys, Henry Jr. and I have always been the closest. He's caught up in the adventure of moving to the wilds of Canada and insists I need to join them. "I know you can't put up with Maman, Min. I have trouble putting up with her too. But maybe you could keep the baby and still come to Montreal. You could get your own place there. Maybe we could get a place together. Besides what's the difference. Boston? Montreal? They're both big cities. I bet when Maman and Papa see the baby they'll want to be around it. They'll forget about being so mad about everything."

"I need my own life, Henry. Maman would either keep ignoring me or try to control every bit of my life again. I feel like she smothers me. I want to raise Owen's baby in my own way-the way Owen and I would have raised him. I want to be a better mother than she's been to us," I add, feeling some powerful emotion bubbling to the surface along with the words.

Henry Jr. nods sadly. "They haven't been the same, Maman and Papa. All the rows since we moved here to Pittsford. I hear them after they go to bed-well anyway, I hear Maman. Papa doesn't say much. Maman is a hard woman. Once I'm old enough to get out on my own I'm going to head west and get some land and never look back. Maybe you and the baby can come with me," he adds hopefully.

I laugh. "Henry, I've spent my whole life trying to get myself out of small town Vermont and now you want me to move to the wilds of the Canadian West?"

"It's going to be an adventure. Come along and you'll see."

I laugh again at my brother's earnest face. As much as the idea of parting company with Maman appeals to me, I'm going to miss my brothers and sisters and Papa. Will I ever see them again? Well, anything is possible. In the meantime we all make promises to write. Henry Jr. vows to write me at the womens' home to give me their address in Montreal. Even little Leona promises to write though she's been slow to learn her letters.

"Maybe you can draw Min some pictures and put them in with my letter," Henry Jr. suggests helpfully. But Leona insists she will write her own letter and I feel like my heart is going to burst for love of all of them.

On the appointed day I say my final goodbyes and go with Mary to the train station. Maman insists they are all too busy packing to go with me. Papa's face is unreadable and the boys are angry, though not with me. The little girls cry and cling to me and beg me not to leave them again. It's a very messy parting.

Mary and the children walk me to the train station to catch the 9:15 to Burlington. Carefully folded in my bag I carry a letter of introduction from Mary to the staff at the Home for Friendless Women. It's possibly the last time I'll see Pittsford, which has seen some of the best and the worst times of my life. After the baby is born I'll head to Boston and make a new start where no one knows me. It will be hard but I'm young and strong and willing to work hard. I'll find a way. If I ever return to Pittsford it will be to visit Mary and the children as a successful mother and working woman. The thought makes me walk just a little taller beside my friend.

Saying goodbye to Mary and the children finally brings the tears. Mary has been nothing but kind, one of my few real friends in Pittsford. We hug each other among the other travelers crowding the platform. Through my tears I thank Mary for all her help and promise to write. I give Sarah and Matthew each a final hug and Matthew says "Yuk" and wipes the wet from my tears off his cheek with a sleeve, making everyone laugh. The conductor is shouting at everyone to get aboard. I grab my valise and climb the steps, stopping once to turn and wave. Then I find myself a seat, perch my bag on my lap, dig out a handkerchief to dry my eyes and settle in for the trip to Burlington.

JENNY

The world is an unkind place. The Lord judges and people gossip. It's so important to always tread the right path and not give anyone reason to doubt your morals. I've tried to teach my children this, to prepare them for the world. But Erminie, especially Erminie, has always wanted to go her own way. And where has it gotten her? Reform school? An unwanted pregnancy? All my hopes for my eldest have been plucked from me one by one.

And Henry. Ah yes. Henry. I loved him once. He was funny and charming and had big plans for us. He promised me the world in those days. He would be an artist one day, creating beauty from stone and commanding top prices for his work. We'd live in a beautiful home and be the envy of our neighbors. But Henry was never satisfied, never good enough, never happy. Truthfully he wasn't talented enough either. When he felt the truth was getting too close he would pack us all up and move. Getting a fresh start was his calling card. We had so many fresh starts I've lost count. His family, especially his uppity mother, blamed it all on me. Somehow his wanderlust was my fault. It was up to me to hold our family together and make the money stretch to cover the needs of our growing family. Children are a gift from God and he blessed us again and again. And yes I felt blessed, but also so very very tired. And always the headaches.

This final move to Montreal? This time it's my idea. I'll claim full credit for it. The situation in Pittsford has become unbearable for all of us. We could have smoothed over Erminie's foibles, but Henry's are quite another matter.

CHAPTER TWENTY-FOUR

I arrive in Burlington in mid-afternoon. I have the address for the Women's Home on Shelburne Road in my bag. I've never been in Burlington before but I'm reluctant to ask for directions in case people realize where I am going. Still, I can't stand around in the cold indefinitely. Eventually I gather my courage and ask the ticket master where I might find Shelburne Road. He draws me a small map on the back of an envelope, complete with cross streets. He never asks specifically where I am heading, for which I'm grateful. I head off in the direction he's indicated, eventually arriving at Shelburne Road. I make an arbitrary decision to turn right, walking several blocks before I realize I'm heading the wrong way. I trudge back the way I came, past the original intersection where I turned, and onward for another two blocks. Finally I see it. The Burlington Home for Friendless Women is a large brick house tucked among residential homes but set well back from the street. I have to double check the address to make sure it's the right place. I realize, in my mind, I've created a place more resembling the sprawl of Wells than this discreet, pretty home.

The place resembles Wells only in that there's a large metal gate that closes behind me with an ominous clank. Hearing it, I wonder how it is that I come to be alone in a strange city on a freezing day in December, preparing to enter a building that calls itself a home for friendless women. Well, I know the answer to that and there's nothing to be done but get on with it. I climb the steps leading to a heavy, ornately carved door. There's a rusted metal knocker and I tap it lightly three times. Then, considering the size of the building and the weight of the door, I tap it again, harder this time.

Almost immediately I hear heels tapping briskly on a wooden floor. The door is opened by a tiny birdlike woman, bundled in what appears to be many layers of clothing topped off with a heavy knit sweater.

"Erminie?" she asks, her voice a chirp totally in keeping with her appearance.

ERMINIE

"Yes, I'm Erminie. Mary Armstrong sent me," I add, though the woman seems to need no additional information.

"Come in. Come in. We've been expecting you," the tiny woman tuts, stepping aside and pulling the door wide. Hurry, please, we don't want to heat up Vermont, do we?" she chuckles at her joke. "You can leave your boots here for now." She indicates a rag rug where three other pairs of outer footwear rest. "Keep your coat with you." I slip my boots off and set them carefully beside the others on the mat.

"Is this all you have dear?" she asks, gesturing at my single bag.

"Yes, this is all."

"Good. Come then. Come. Come." She trots off toward a stairwell then abruptly turns in her tracks, nearly causing me to run into her. "Oh dear me! How rude. I forgot to introduce myself. I am Charlotte Manning, Lottie to my friends. And I do hope we will be friends, Erminie. My, that is an unusual name, isn't it?"

I respond that it is, but Lottie has already turned and is clicking up the stairs, gesturing for me to follow. Apparently no real response is required. She leads me up to the third floor, chatting the whole way about the cold and how I must be freezing. Indeed I am freezing after my long walk from the station and I don't feel much warmth in this old house. I'm glad I didn't have to surrender my tatty brown coat at the door. Lottie ushers me into a small bedroom. There's just one bed-no room-mate then. Having a room to myself is something I've only experienced briefly at the boarding house. The room is simply furnished, but comfortable. A colorful quilt lies across the bed and another rag rug covers a substantial portion of the scuffed wooden floor. A wooden stand holds a pitcher and basin for washing. Plain yellow cotton curtains make the room feel bright and welcoming and a painting of the White Mountains hangs over the bed.

"This will be your room during your stay with us. There's a lavatory down on the second floor that you'll share with the other girls. There are eight girls staying here at the moment. We serve supper in the dining room downstairs promptly at six o'clock. Breakfast is at eight o'clock and you are responsible for fixing your own noon-day meal in the kitchen. Everything else you can learn as we go along. For now I'm going to leave you to rest. I'm sure you're exhausted after your trip." With that, Lottie flits out of the room, closing the door quietly and leaving me alone.

I am indeed tired. My growing belly has made walking more difficult, especially on the ice and snow where I feel off balance and in constant danger of falling. My hips feel as if I've waddled all the way from the train station. After the noise of the train and Lottie's chatter the quiet of this plain, sunny room is delicious. I run a hand over the hand-made quilt. It's beautifully made and makes me think of the flying goose quilt Adeline brought from Boston for Owen and I. I left it with Mary for safe keeping, it being too bulky to carry with me on the train. I test the bedsprings gingerly with my hand and finally lay down, still wearing my coat. I allow myself to melt into the over-soft mattress and feel I might easily slip off to sleep, but my need to visit the lavatory exceeds even my need for rest. Still wearing my coat against the chill I find my way downstairs to the lavatory, which currently, thankfully, is unoccupied. There are two cubicles, each with an elderly chain pull water closet. A long counter runs the length of the opposite wall with two sinks that look to provide both hot and cold water. Shelves along both sides of the counter hold towels. A small room off the main one holds an old-fashioned tub, rusty in some places, but a wonder of luxury for me.

Mary told me a bit about this place; I know the home is run through a charitable organization headed by a wealthy Burlington woman. Her family donated the house when they built a newer, larger house on property just out of the city. That explains the aging grandeur of the house. According to Mary, the woman dedicated herself to raising funds to provide a home for women preparing to give birth who had no other place to go. She wanted them to have a safe place to give birth and so reduce the number of women turning to illegal and sometimes fatal abortions. None of the women are required to pay anything for their time here, but those that can, or their families, are encouraged to make donations. Such donations, along with various fund-raising events provide food and other necessities for the women during their time in the home. A local doctor donates his time to ensure the women are well cared for during their pregnancy, and delivers their babies when the time comes. It's a lovely place and I'm grateful that Mary has secured me a space. Someday I'll make it up to the home and the people that run it.

I use the lavatory and clean the travel grime from my face and still have time to rest before joining the other girls for supper. I'm quite surprised by my first glimpse of the other women staying here. They represent nearly every female stereotype I could have imagined. There's Delores, undoubtedly pregnant, but one would not have been able to differentiate baby from the great rolling mounds of flesh that cover her body. She rolls into the dining room, holding chair backs to move to her place at the table. I'm unsure whether this is to support her enormous weight or because she can't see the floor around her. Regardless, I relax some when she gets herself down onto the chair safely. Already seated at the table when I arrive is Eloise. She is a scrawny young thing, all bony arms and legs protruding from a huge swollen belly. Next to Eloise, and already in her seat when I arrive is a woman named Martha. Martha looks closer to Maman's age than mine. She's well-advanced in her pregnancy. She says little, keeping her head bent forward, intently moving the food around on her plate. I wonder what twist of fate brought her to a home for friendless women. The cast of characters is rounded out by Marcelline, a pretty blond French girl who welcomes me warmly and chatters through dinner in lightly accented English that reminds me of Grand-mère.

Three girls are missing. I'm told two are visiting family for a few days. The third, someone named Bessie, has gone into labor. Marcelline tells me that the doctor decided she might be better in the hospital and they've taken her away after several hours of labor.

"You should have heard the screaming," pipes Eloise helpfully past a mouthful of mashed potatoes. This prompts uncomfortable looks around the table and a bit of a scowl from Lottie, though she doesn't say anything. Anyway, the long and the short of it is that no one has heard anything of Bessie since they took her away.

As dinner wears on I learn other tidbits of information. Lottie is a staff person who lives permanently in the home. She prepares the meals and keeps the place tidy with help from the girls. I hear other names, notably Dr. Fennimore, who tends to the girls and delivers their babies. There's also a lot of chatter about someone named Helmer. Helmer is the subject of much blushing and tittering around the table (except for Martha who keeps her eyes firmly on her plate and doesn't join in the conversation). After Helmer's name comes up for the third time I have to ask about him. It turns out he's the maintenance man-a young Dane, though his country of origin is in some dispute-who comes to shovel the walks and repair what needs repairing. The girls say that they hardly understand a word he says but that he's fine to look at.

The food is plain but it's good and plentiful. Martha has eaten almost nothing but the same isn't true for the other girls. I guess that most of these girls, myself included, are not used to such plenty. I worry that tiny Eloise might explode if she shovels any more food into her mouth.

I settle easily into life at the home. In spite of the unfortunate choice of name, the Home for Friendless Women is the nicest place I've ever lived except for the brief time Owen and I stayed at Adeline's. I have privacy and quiet and a chance to grieve Owen in a way I haven't been able to until now. Most of the time I enjoy the company of the other girls. We're a sisterhood of girls in trouble. No one has to hide the fact they're expecting. We talk freely about our situations and the men who put us where we are. Saddest of all is pretty Marcelline's story. She was raped over and over by an uncle over several months until she became pregnant. Now her family has sent her here to avoid the scandal. She's heard nothing from any of her family since she got here three weeks ago but is certain the uncle in question is carrying on happily now that all traces of his indiscretion have been removed to Burlington. Still, Marcelline doesn't let the situation get her down and, because of my experience with Wyre, I feel a particular soft spot for her. We become fast friends. It's to her I tell the story of Owen, how he courted me, how we lived together and the terrible day of his death. We cry together, sitting on the edge of my bed holding hands and weeping for all we've lost.

It's from the other girls I eventually learn Martha's story. She's married to a drunk who beats her. When he found out she was pregnant with their fifth child he was incensed and beat her nearly to death. She woke up in hospital, taken there by neighbors who, finally unable to listen to any more, had come to the house. The neighbor's husband took Martha's husband by the scruff of the neck and shoved him against the wall while his wife tended to Martha, lying unconscious on the floor. Together they got her to a hospital and, by some miracle she kept the baby. She's never gone back to him, nor does she know the whereabouts of her other four children. The girls say she's mourning for these children as well as for her husband who she says she still loves. The girls whisper that Martha isn't right in the head—that the beatings have addled her brain in some way. Still everyone here has experienced some sort of tragedy and they more or less accept her.

Charitable donations are used to purchase food and basic necessities for the home, but there's never enough money to run the place. So we cut back where we can. The house is always cold and, while there are electric lights and hot running water, we're discouraged from using them. Instead each room has a coal oil lamp and a wash basin. The food continues to be plentiful, though, because local merchants donate older produce and bread and cash donations buy the rest. Dr. Fennimore preaches that eating well is essential to easy pregnancies and healthy babies.

I'm happy to help Lottie out with the cooking and cleaning. It seems the least I can do to help pay for my stay. Besides, I'm not one to sit idle. Too much free time leaves me missing Owen.

I'm helping set the table one evening when a stabbing pain tears through my lower belly. I quickly sit down on one of the kitchen chairs, then double over my knees in pain.

Lottie lays a bony concerned hand on my back. "What is it love? Is it the baby?"

"No, it can't be. I'm a month before my time."

Lottie chuckles. "Well you wouldn't be the first girl ever to have your baby early, you know. Let's get you upstairs, shall we?"

Lottie recruits Eloise to help me upstairs. They're both so scrawny I wonder how much they can really help if I collapse. But then, I have no intention of collapsing and they're both eager to help. We reach the second floor and I realize that having one of the two rooms on the main floor would be a benefit. Too late though. We keep moving. Midway up the second flight of stairs another pain tears through me. Now I really wish I had someone more burly to support me than tiny Lottie and the brittle and very pregnant Eloise. In spite of my concerns, though, they successfully herd me up to my room once the contraction subsides. For it is a contraction and no amount of denial will serve. I'm going into labor.

Lottie rolls back the quilt, helps me change to my nightgown then guides me down to the bed, all with efficient practiced hands. "Now dear. This is likely to go on a while with a first baby. Eloise will sit with you a bit if you want, but you should try to get some rest. I'll send word to Dr. Fennimore that you're in labor so he knows he'll be needed soon. Sometimes the pains stop when you're early like this but it seems like they might be here to stay." With that she hurries out of the room and I hear her quick heels on the stair.

Eloise looks at me questioningly, one hand on the back of the only chair. "Should I stay?"

I start to tell her she should go and have her supper when another pain wraps around me, stealing my breath. I feel I'm being squeezed and ripped open all at the same time. How are such contradictory feelings even possible? Eloise pulls the chair over and sits down without comment. She takes my hand. I worry I might crush it as I ride out the contraction.

Once the pain has passed I assess my situation. I'm in labor! But so early. How can my baby survive being born so early? What if the baby dies? What if I die?

The pains go on and on. Between them I doze. At some point I wake to find Eloise has been replaced by Marjory, one of the girls who was away when I first arrived. Still later it's Marcelline who sits beside the bed humming and stitching a pillow case. I'm never left alone and I'm grateful.

Eventually, Dr. Fennimore arrives. He's a long, lean streak of a man with graying hair and a tanned outdoorsman's face. I can imagine him out fly fishing on a hot summer day. He apologizes for taking so long, saying he had other patients to attend to. I don't know the time but I know that it's night, probably late. Maybe he was delivering other babies. Marcelline is still sitting with me and he asks her to step out. When she's gone he does a lot of poking and prodding that is painful and humiliating, all the while murmuring in such a way that I am not sure whether he's talking to me or to himself. He smells of spearmint which I find comforting even given the humiliation of the whole procedure.

Eventually the doctor pulls my nightgown down and the quilt back up to my chin. "Well, young lady. You are most certainly in labor. A bit early, but everything seems to be in order. This might take a while. I'm going home to get some sleep. In the morning I'll stop by the hospital to check on my patients there, then I'll come by again. In the meantime, Lottie and the other girls will take care of you until I can get back. I must know though, what your intentions are? Do you intend to send the baby over to St. Joseph's? That's the usual thing here."

I feel myself stiffen at mention of the orphanage. "No sir. I'm keeping my baby, sir."

Dr. Fennimore looks at me and I think his face looks sad. "Think carefully about this dear. Do you have a place to go? Do you have the means to raise a child?"

In truth, I thought I'd have more time to think things through. Before laying down in this bed with my insides being pulled out through my private parts, raising a baby seemed like an easy enough thing. Suddenly I feel overwhelmed. Where will I go? How will I look for work with a baby in my arms? Who will look after my baby while I work and how can I pay them? My mind goes to the one person that I think I can count on. "I have a friend in Pittsford. I'll go there. She'll help me, sir. Her name is Mary."

"Ah yes. She's the one who sent us the letter about you, is she not?" I nod. "She implied some health issues, none of which I've noted. She must be a good friend indeed." He gives me a tiny wink and I relax just a bit.

Yes, Mary will help me. I'm confident of that. She said she would.

As Dr. Fennimore gathers up his equipment, he tells me I should give the matter of the placement of my baby more thought over the next few hours. As he turns to leave I stop him with one last question. "Dr. it's too early for this baby to be born. Are you sure everything is going to be alright?"

The doctor has already put his gloves on but he takes my hand and looks at me kindly. "My dear, I make no promises on God's behalf. But so far everything looks normal and you are young and strong. I see no reason why your baby shouldn't survive. It is very small though, and will require close attention for a while." With that he gives my hand a tiny squeeze and is gone with a promise to return in the morning.

I labor through the night. The girls take turns sitting with me as I grind through contraction after contraction. In between I sleep, only to be awakened by the next. The doctor arrives as promised in the morning, declares it will be some time yet, gives my shoulder an encouraging squeeze and is gone again.

I'm devastated. I can't go on. Yet what choice do I have? My body is now running the show and I'm just along for the ride. Another contraction is upon me before I can even feel properly sorry for myself. My hair is wet and matted and my nightgown clings to my damp belly. Funny how my stomach looked so huge before but now seems much too small. The girls help me up to use the chamber pot when necessary and encourage me to walk, hoping it will advance my labor. But as time wears on I'm too exhausted to keep my legs underneath my body.

It's about eight in the evening. I've been laboring for over twenty-four hours. Suddenly I feel a rush of fluid that soaks my nightgown and spreads over the waterproof sheeting Lottie has put on my bed. I believe it to be blood and I shriek loudly enough that Lottie and Eloise come running into the room and Marjory, who is sitting with me flops her arms around in a panic that would have been funny in other circumstances.

Eloise waddles off, at the request of Lottie, to get some towels. Lottie delicately lifts the bedding away from me and an encouraging smile warms her face.

"It won't be long now, love. I'm going to send one of the girls to get Dr. Fennimore."

"What is it? Am I bleeding?"

"No, no. It's just the fluid that surrounds the baby. Your baby is getting ready to come," she adds encouragingly, leaving me to wonder just what the last twenty-five hours were all about if the baby is just now getting ready to come.

Still, Lottie's words and her air of perky optimism cheer me and I experience a new resolve to stay alive long enough to get the job done. Lottie helps me up and onto a chair so she can put fresh bedding on the bed and position a thick towel in the center. Marcelline has appeared and helps me change into a fresh nightgown. Then the two of them help me back into the bed and position my derriere, minus my underwear, on the towel. Marjory has been running back and forth fetching things for Lottie, and I suspect it's more to keep her busy and calm than for real need. But now she appears with a cup of broth. Lottie encourages me to drink it and, unlike my earlier attempts at eating, the soup is actually quite welcome.

Dr. Fennimore arrives after most of the girls have gone to bed, beaming with pride at his patient's progress as though he's somehow responsible. I hate him. How dare he flit in and out and leave me to simmer in sweat and body fluids. I want to tell him to leave-that I can manage with Lottie and my friends, but manners prevail and I bite my tongue. He examines me and coos and proclaims that the baby will arrive within the hour. Good news indeed! All of us are exhausted. Dr. Fennimore barks some orders to Lottie which she obviously finds annoying, since she seems to know exactly what to do without his instruction. They shift me up onto a pile of pillows so that my upper body is elevated. They remove the blankets, open my legs and make me bend my knees. I have never felt so exposed and vulnerable but I'm in no position to argue. I'm a soggy rag doll they can bend and twist at will, pausing only when another contraction takes over. Dr. Fennimore protects my ragged dignity somewhat by draping a sheet over my knees, creating a little tent through which my baby will make his or her appearance. It's that thought that crystallizes, as nothing before has, the thought that I'm going to have a baby. A real baby. Owen's baby. I settle in to do battle for Owen and our child.

And a battle it is. The one hour promised by Dr. Fennimore turns into two hours, then three. I am in a fog of pain and exhaustion. Dr. Fennimore stays with me this time though, as does Lottie. The other girls have been asked to leave the room but take turns huddling outside the bedroom door and relaying news to the others.

Finally, in the early hours of the morning, my baby is born. Dr. Fennimore catches the baby and I catch a glimpse of a tiny purplish body streaked with blood before he hands it over to Lottie. He cuts the cord that connects me to the child. The baby makes no sound and I'm sure it must be dead. How could something so small have survived that ordeal? Now both Dr. Fennimore and Lottie are huddled over the baby who lies on a towel on the washstand. Dr. Fennimore has laid out a number of pieces of equipment next to a pile of clean cloths and towels. The two of them lean together over the baby's tiny body for what seems like hours. They've clearly forgotten about me! Suddenly I see Dr. Fennimore turn my baby upside down, hold it by the ankles and swat its tiny bum. A second swat. There is a splutter and a tiny mewling sound.

"You have a baby girl Erminie," Lottie proudly announces. "We had to clear some mucous from her mouth and nose, but she's breathing well now." Lottie has wrapped the bundle in one of the towels and hands her to me. I have held many babies and children over the years but I feel a moment of panic. I'm uncertain even if I should take her. New contractions are wracking my body and I'm afraid I might damage my tiny baby during one of these.

"Is there another baby?" I ask Lottie, unable to understand why the contractions haven't stopped.

"No dear. You're soon going to pass the afterbirth. Those contractions are normal. Don't worry. There's just one baby."

Lottie chuckles as she lays the baby on my stomach in spite of my apprehension. She's an alarming little creature. She's a heavily mottled purple and pink. Her little face is contorted and swollen and her head seems unnaturally pointed. Lottie has wiped her down but there is some blood crusted along her dark hairline. I have a momentary flash of Owen dying in his hospital bed and the power of the memory takes my breath away. It's all I can do to force my mind back to my beautiful daughter. Because she is beautiful. She looks just like Owen.

We stay like that for a few minutes. I take extra care during these last few contractions not to squash the baby until, finally, I pass the afterbirth. At that point Dr. Fennimore takes the baby while Lottie cleans up, explaining that the doctor wants to do an examination before he leaves, to make sure the baby is healthy. Meanwhile Lottie expertly turns me to remove the soiled linen. Once I'm settled again she offers to make me some tea and toast. No meal from a fancy restaurant could have sounded as good as that offer of tea and toast.

Eventually, Dr. Fennimore returns the baby, now squalling angrily. He has re-wrapped her snuggly in a soft blanket. "She is small, of course, but she appears to be in relatively good health. We'll know better in a few days but, for now, everything looks as good as can be expected when they arrive as early as this little one." He sits on the edge of the bed. "Are you still planning on keeping this baby, Erminie?"

"I am," I respond without hesitation. "I'm going to call her Dorothy." I'm about to tell him that Dorothy is Owen's mother's name but he isn't interested. He interrupts me.

"Well, you have some time to change your mind. It won't be easy for you. The world isn't kind to children born out of wedlock, or to their mothers."

"I know that doctor. But she's my baby, my responsibility-no one else's."

Dr.Fennimore nods and rises to collect his hat and overcoat. "Then I'll be on my way. Lottie will be back to help you and the baby get settled for the night, what's left of it. She'll show you how to feed the baby as well." With that he jams his hat on his head and is gone.

I enjoy my tea and toast while Lottie holds baby Dorothy, cooing and rocking her gently. Once I have a little something in my stomach, Lottie shows me how to get Dorothy to fasten on to my breast. She does this with only a tiny amount of fussing and I'm greatly relieved. I can tell Lottie is too. Dorothy nurses enthusiastically for a minute or two, then pulls away and begins to fuss. In spite of Lottie's best efforts and my desperate offerings the fussing builds up to a full-on wail. I burp her and encourage her and rock her but she's inconsolable.

I'm very aware the other girls will be awake by now but Lottie assures me it's what one has to expect, living in a house with pregnant women and new babies. Dorothy's high piercing cry continues for what seems like hours. It ends only when the poor wee thing throws up the little bit of what she's managed to consume. She falls into an exhausted sleep and I feel my shoulders slump in relief.

Lottie, who has only had snatches of sleep over the last two days, suggests we all get some rest. She sees my worried, tired face, and quickly assures me it isn't uncommon for newborns to have an upset tummy, that perhaps she's colicky. In spite of the parade of thoughts going through my mind, I do sleep. I awake just a bit later to Dorothy's piercing cry. It's a cry already so familiar to me I believe I could pick it out from a whole room full of crying babies. I take her up and try to feed her with no more luck than before. She screams again until she throws up a bit of yellow fluid, then sleeps fitfully. This happens almost every hour. When Lottie checks back in she looks far from rested. She assures me that learning to nurse takes time for both mother and baby. Still, she sounds much less assured than she did earlier and I read concern on her doll-like face. This tiny new life needs nourishment and so far she's not been able to keep anything in her stomach.

Dr. Fennimore checks in with me the next afternoon. Dorothy has still not eaten any appreciable amount and I feel on the edge of physical and mental exhaustion. Lottie isn't in much better shape. The other girls in the house, while sympathetic, are looking bleary eyed and irritable. Dr. Fennimore examines my nether regions and proclaims me battered but well. Then he unwraps a wailing Dorothy, pressing on her distended belly, listening to her heart and lungs and running a finger up her tiny bottom. I watch my baby girl, face red and contorted, as she screams in pain and indignation. My heart aches for my helpless little bundle. But I also detect a slight change in Dorothy's cries. They seem less angry somehow, less vigorous. After he completes his examination, Dr. Fennimore breaks the news to me.

"I'm going to take the baby to the hospital. You, and the rest of these ladies, need some rest and I need to run some additional tests on this young one."

"What's wrong," I ask. I can hear a thickness in my voice.

"I don't know just yet. It may be she has some sort of blockage in her intestine. We'll take care of her at the hospital until you can get some rest and get back on your feet. Now say goodbye to your young miss." He hands a re-bundled Dorothy to me. I search her face, seeing a hint of Owen's nose and my own blue eyes, but I also see pain and discomfort and I have no help for it. My first hours as a mother have been a miserable failure. I don't realize I'm crying until a tear falls on Dorothy's blanket, then another.

Dr. Fennimore puts a kind hand on my shoulder. "This isn't your fault Erminie. Let's not get the cart before the horse. Let me do some tests and we will see what can be done to make her more comfortable."

I nod. I have no words. I hug the bundle and reluctantly hand her over to Dr. Fennimore.

"We'll take good care of her," he assures me as he leaves my room.

Everything about the moment seems wrong. To watch my newborn baby disappear in the arms of a near stranger makes my gut clench in fear. If anything happens to that baby, how will I ever make it up to Owen? But I'm powerless. I'm weak and exhausted and I don't know how to stand up to Dr. Fennimore's brisk efficiency. I'm crying into my pillow when Lottie and Marcelline come to comfort me. "Everything will be fine," Lottie coos to my heaving back. "They'll take real good care of her at the hospital and once you're both well you can take her back to Pittsford. You'll see. It will all work out."

I sit up and put my arms around her thin shoulders, blubbering my thanks for her help and her kindness amidst gulps and sobs. I'm sure I'm getting tears and probably snot on her soft cotton dress. But it turns out that isn't her first concern. She gently takes my shoulders and pushes me away from her. I follow her gaze.

"That is something else we're going to have to take care of," she chuckles. I see that the front of my dressing gown is wet and I've transferred some of the wet to her chest. I'm mortified, but Lottie is matter-of-fact. She brings me a jar and shows me how to squeeze enough milk out to give me some relief for, until now, with everything that has gone on, I haven't realized how much pain I'm in. Once that's done, Lottie has me lay down. She tucks me in like a child and rubs my back and croons comforting words to me until I fall into an exhausted sleep.

The next morning I gingerly climb out of bed for the first time. I squeeze some of the milk from my breasts again. Never in my life have I imagined myself doing such a thing. I dispose of the milk in the chamber pot, then gather up a pen and some paper and pull the chair up to the small bedside table.

After a few false starts, crumpled pages and pen-gnawing I write:

Dearest Mary,

I have a new baby girl. She was born early yesterday morning. She is such a beauty. I can hardly wait for you to meet her. She has some difficulties with her stomach and the doctor has taken her to the hospital for some tests. He has assured me that she will soon be back with me. When we are both ready to travel I hope you will be kind enough to allow me to stay at your home until I am able to get a job and find a place of my own. I promise this will not be for too long, as I know your house is small. I will repay my expenses once I am employed. It is just that I seem to have few options at the moment.

Your good friend,
Erminie

I seal up the letter and give it to Lottie when she comes to check on me. She clucks like a mother hen, agrees to post my letter, and hurries me back into bed.

CHAPTER TWENTY-FIVE

There's no word from Dr. Fennimore all the rest of that day and into the next. I question the girls when they come to visit and they swear there's been no word. Eventually I get out of bed, get myself dressed and make my way downstairs. I have it in my head to go to the hospital but Lottie is predictably horrified by the idea.

"I can't lay there any more Lottie! I need to know what's going on." I think I see a look of discomfort cross Lottie's face briefly, but she agrees to see if she can get some news about Dorothy if I will see fit to go back to my bed. Reluctantly I agree to give her some time to find out what's going on. She shepherds me back up the stairs and tucks me back into bed, clothes and all. This bed, and this room, have become my prison. My mind seeks out all sorts of horrible, unthinkable possibilities.

That evening Lottie ushers Dr. Fennimore into my room. Lottie nudges the door closed behind them. Both of their faces are long and grave. This isn't good. Dr. Fennimore has lost most of his brisk manner. He pulls the single chair over to the bed, sits heavily on it and takes one of my hands in both of his. They're cold. Lottie hovers behind him, her arms folded over her skinny chest, her face a picture of misery. It's clear no good news is going to come from these two.

I try to speak but can find no sound. Thankfully Dr. Fennimore isn't given to dramatic suspense.

"Your daughter is very ill, Erminie. Initially, we thought she had a blockage or a twisting in her gut that we might be able to correct with surgery. But I'm afraid it's more complicated than that. She seems unable to digest her milk–probably a metabolic problem. Right now we are feeding her goat's milk with a tube directly to her stomach until we can come up with a better solution. She seems to have better luck with the goat's milk."

"Can I see her?" I interrupt, impatiently.

"Erminie, we'll take you to see Dorothy but we need to talk first. Dorothy is very ill. If she is to survive she's going to need some very special care, perhaps for the rest of her life-special food, special equipment. It's very likely there will be some level of mental retardation because of her inability to absorb proteins. We just don't know it all yet. Erminie, you are going to have to leave her with us. My recommendation is that you turn her over to the hospital and to St. Joseph's. The hospital can give her the medical care she needs and St. Joseph's can look for an adoptive family with the resources to give her the sort of care she'll need."

He gets no further. I'm overcome with a blanketing red fury. I know my fists are flying and I know I'm screaming but I see it all as an observer. I'm shocked, I confess, by my own behavior.

"No! You will not take my baby. Has my mother put you up to this? No one will raise my baby but me. No one! Take me to her. You've kept her from me because you don't want me to have her. You're all in this together. I want to see her now." I am out of the bed, pummeling Dr. Fennimore around his head and chest. He has raised his arms to deflect my blows.

Lottie has moved closer and reaches for me but thinks better of it and raises her hands in a gesture of surrender. "Erminie, for God's sake, calm yourself. You must be reasonable. You have no money, no husband, no job, not even a home to take this baby too. How can you take care of her? How will you take care of her? You will kill that baby. As much as you love her, you'll be killing her."

"Take me to see her now!" I lurch around the room spastically, collecting my coat and gloves, aware that Dr. Fennimore and Lottie are watching me helplessly.

Dr. Fennimore finally comes around to speaking. "Alright, Erminie. I'll take you to the hospital to see Dorothy. Visiting hours are long over but I'll take you. You must promise to calm down though and act like a lady or I'll bring you straight back here."

I care nothing about whether Dr. Fennimore thinks I'm a lady or not and he can rot in hell for all I care. I'm going to see Dorothy if I have to find my own way to the hospital. I should have been there hours and hours ago. I fling the bedroom door open to discover all the girls hovering on the landing, eyes like saucers. I brush past them, pulling my coat closed over my nightgown. I run down the stairs to the front door and fling it open. Only then do I realize two important facts. My feet are bare and I don't actually know where the hospital is. It's the last straw. I collapse in the open doorway and cry. I cry from anger and embarrassment and fatigue and fear. Dr.Fennimore catches up and helps me up from the frosted step.

"Now, he says reasonably, how about we get you properly dressed and get you over to see your daughter?"

Dr. Fennimore waits for me outside in his cutter while Lottie helps me dress. We say almost nothing. I'm fuming because she's a part of this, even though a rational part of me knows she meant no harm. Still, I'm angry and

I won't be distracted from that anger. If I am, I know I'll shatter into a million tiny pieces.

Once dressed, I run down the stairs again, suddenly feeling the tenderness of my breasts and places still sore from childbirth. Strange, I never noticed that on my first tear down these stairs. Anger must serve as an anesthetic of sorts but now it's running out.

Dr. Fennimore is waiting outside. He jumps down and helps me into the sleigh, then tucks a fur robe solicitously around my knees.

"Let's just go," I mutter angrily. I'm determined that no kindness go unpunished.

He sniffs, settles himself in his seat and takes up the reins without comment. Since arriving in Burlington I haven't seen much of the town. None of us liked the idea of being stared at as we waddled around the streets, so we all stayed pretty close to home. In another set of circumstances I might have enjoyed the ride as Dr. Fennimore urges the sorrel mare along the frozen deserted streets. The stars are brilliant and the harness jingles merrily. But my thoughts are full of my baby and Owen and how I might somehow make this horrible situation right. I'm so lost in my thoughts that I'm startled to realize that Dr. Fennimore is not talking to the horse, but to me.

"She has a feeding tube right now that takes food directly to her belly. It seems to be helping to get the food where it needs to go. Don't be alarmed when you see her. Inserting it is quite a trauma for her, so we leave the tube in." He looks at me, requiring some sort of acknowledgment, so I nod.

It's late by the time we reach the hospital. One lone nurse is in the hallway as Dr. Fennimore ushers me inside. He nods curtly at her and she pretends to go on with what she's doing. I feel her eyes on me though, and I know she's probably sizing me up right now; no husband, sick baby. I want to turn and smash her face but I focus on the middle of Dr. Fennimore's back and keep moving. We don't have far to go. He stops at the first door on the right. It's plainly a children's ward. The room is dim but bright paint lights the walls and toys are piled in a box in one corner. Several tall iron cribs line the walls but I can see only one other child in the room, a toddler I guess, based on what I can see through the gloom.

Dr. Fennimore hushes me, telling me not to wake little Emily or she'll wake the whole hospital. "Quite a voice, that one."

I'm already heading to the only other occupied crib. My little Dorothy looks tiny and lost in this giant crib. I can't even reach her until Fennimore helps me lower the heavy side rail. She's silent but not asleep. In this light her eyes are dark orbs fixed on my face. The feeding tube disappears into her left nostril. I lift her from the crib, blanket and all and bring her to my chest, murmuring something, I don't know what, into her soft hair.

"I'll show you to a private room where you can visit." Fennimore takes my arm and steers me to the door and into the hallway. Next door is a room outfitted with a comfortable chair and even a rocker. Someone has lit a lamp and it casts a soft glow over the room. "I'll leave you here. If you need anything there are two nurses on duty. One of them can help you if you or Dorothy have any problems. I'll be back in a few hours to take you back to the home. If you need to sleep, tell the nurses I said they should find you an empty bed." With that he crushes his hat onto his head and is gone.

I become aware of movement within the blanket. I settle on the upholstered chair and lay Dorothy along my thighs. Two huge eyes stare up at me. To me they seem full of pleading, of longing. Below the eyes, in the nose that so reminds me of Owen, is the feeding tube. I have a better look at it. I somehow imagined it would go into her mouth and am now amazed and appalled at the process that would thread that tube into a tiny baby's nostril. Her little face contorts momentarily in a look of discomfort. A gas bubble? Something more?

"Look at you lovey," I coo. "Mommy is here now. It will be alright. And Daddy is here too," I add, suddenly sure that Owen must be watching, puffed with pride at his beautiful daughter. I lift her to my shoulder and pat and rub the tiny back and sing bits of a French lullaby I remember Maman singing to the younger girls. How strange that memory seems. Breathing in Dorothy's baby smells and feeling her warmth soothes my jangled nerves. I lean back in the chair, cradling her close to my body and marveling that I have produced this perfect little person. Shortly Dorothy begins to squirm and root at my chest making clear she's looking to be fed. I'm at a loss. I'm a bit afraid of the feeding tube and Dr. Fennimore's warning about my milk not agreeing with her. Still, she's getting out of sorts and the urge to feed her and calm her is strong. Finally I offer her my breast and wince as she latches on with surprising enthusiasm. I close my eyes. A while later I hear a nurse come in to check on us but I pretend to sleep and she leaves without speaking. Eventually I really do doze off with Dorothy snuggled into my chest.

I come fully awake to the sound of Dorothy mewling weakly. I realize it's really the first sound she's made since I arrived at the hospital. I feel her diaper. It feels fine but I decide to change her just in case. A pile of fresh nappies are stacked on a table nearby. The process of changing her is really the first good look I've had since her birth. I've seen babies before and I know they come in all shapes and sizes, short and round, long and lean. But Dorothy looks skinny in a way I've never seen in an infant. I hurriedly finish changing her because she's becoming visibly angry and kicking in a half-hearted kind of way. I offer her my other breast and she attaches without hesitation. But after a few frustrated tugs she pulls away and begins to cry. I use every trick I know to comfort her but she's inconsolable, drawing her legs into her body, her face red and angry. Suddenly she goes rigid. The crying stops. In fact, my baby is making no sound at all. I worry she's stopped breathing. I shake her gently, then more vigorously. In a panic I bundle her to my chest and bolt for the door. A nurse is coming down the hallway, no doubt alerted by Dorothy's earlier cries. I run to her and hold Dorothy out to her like an offering. "She isn't breathing. Help her. Please."

The nurse takes Dorothy with infuriating calmness and cradles her. "She's having one of her seizures. She has had several before. Did Dr. Fennimore not tell you?" I shake my head mutely. "All we can do is keep her comfortable and safe until it passes." I watch as the nurse moves the blanket aside and gently strokes Dorothy's tiny limbs until they begin to relax. Eventually she gasps, begins to cry weakly and throws up some milk. Her movements seem weak, lethargic. "She'll perk up," the nurse assures me, sensing my concern, "but these spells seem to take a lot out of her. I hope the doctor can find a way to help her. It's so sad to see her going through all this at such a young age. She's such a dear baby. Look at all that lovely hair." The nurse re-wraps Dorothy snugly in her blanket and hands her back to me. "If she has another seizure, just hold her and talk to her. Be calm and don't let her sense that you're afraid."

"I fed her-from my-I mean". I touch my breast. "I wasn't sure because of the tube, but she seemed hungry. Did I hurt her?"

"Don't fret dear. I don't think it can really hurt anything. She's having trouble in her tummy. She seems to be in greater pain when she sucks than when we feed her through the tube, but neither seems to be particularly to her liking. Dr. Fennimore hasn't yet decided on the best way to feed her, or even really what to feed her. She doesn't seem to do well with cow's milk or goat's milk. Every time she has even a little bit to eat she seems to be in terrible pain. Then, of course there are the seizures. It's a lot for such a little one."

The nurse has, by now, walked me and the baby back to the visitors' room. She turns to leave us there. Then, abruptly, she turns back. "It's not my place to ask this, but are you thinking of keeping this baby? I only ask because usually, when they are going to be adopted, the mother doesn't spend any time with them. It just makes it harder on everyone. I know you don't have a husband or much support…" she trails off.

"I'm going to take her home with me. She's my baby. She's all I have left of her daddy. He was killed in a quarry," I add lamely, realizing that I sound angry and defensive and the nurse has done nothing to deserve it.

She gently takes my arm and guides me into the room, urging me to have a seat. She pulls the rocking chair over and sits nearby. "I could get into a lot of trouble for interfering in this, but I'm sure I'm not telling you anything Dr. Fennimore isn't going to. You just can't raise this baby on your own. She's very sick and she's going to need constant care. On top of that she's going to need special equipment, medicine and maybe even special food. How are you going to give her that? If you turn her over to the state it will be hard but at least she'll be cared for. St. Joseph's will try to find a family willing to take care of her. It will be hard now, but it will be much harder if you find you can't take care of her and have to give her up in a few weeks or months."

I sit in silence. I know I probably look angry but I'm holding back tears because, for the first time, I'm beginning to think this woman, and Dr. Fennimore too, are right. How can I give my baby what she needs?

The nurse gets up and moves the rocking chair back to its place in the corner. "Well, I think I've said enough. Please think about it though. I know you love her. Any fool can see that. But sometimes love isn't enough." With that she's gone. I hug Dorothy close to my chest and a hot tear squeezes through my tightly closed eyes.

By the time Dr. Fennimore arrives to take me back to the home, Dorothy has had another seizure and several episodes of listless crying. Even with my inexperience, I can tell her movements are weak and lethargic. A baby with simple gas pains would have been screaming and kicking the covers off with rage. But my little Dorothy seems not to have that kind of energy. I kiss her goodbye, hand her over to the nurse and follow Dr. Fennimore out to his cutter. We travel in silence. He doesn't press me about my night but I feel him glancing at me from time to time. When he drops me off I thank him for the ride and go straight inside. Some of the other girls are just sitting down to breakfast but I decline their invitation to join them and go straight up to my room. I climb under the covers fully clothed and bury my head under my pillow. There's a minute or two of calm. Then I rage. I kick. I pound the pillow. I pound my own thighs until they're bruised. I rage until I'm exhausted. Then I cry. I cry for Dorothy, I cry for Owen and I cry for the unfairness of life. Outside my door I'm aware that some of the girls have gathered, wondering if they should come in or stay away. I can hear their muffled voices. Finally Marcelline opens the door and pokes her head in. I give her a feeble smile. She visibly relaxes and tiptoes over to sit on the bed.

"I don't really know what to say, Erminie. I feel so bad for you. We all do." I shrug and we hug each other wordlessly. Then we lay down with our arms around each other and she stays with me until I fall asleep.

When I wake up the next morning Marcelline is gone. My eyes are swollen nearly shut and my thighs are black and blue where I pounded them with my fists. But my mind is clear. I know what I have to do. I dress and go down to the kitchen where I find Lottie making breakfast.

"Can I talk to you?" I ask.

Without answering she pulls a saucepan off the stove and sets it aside, then pours us each a cup of coffee from the white enamel pot that perpetually simmers on the back of the stove. She hands me the coffee, pushes the sugar bowl in my direction, then sits down across from me. "My poor dear. How can I help you?"

"I know you have other girls waiting for a room and I am so grateful you've let me stay and work through," I pause feeling a little lump of emotion trying to work its way into my throat, "all of this" I finish lamely. "I stayed with Dorothy last night and I know now I can't take care of her. She's so ill and I don't have any way to care for her. I don't even have a home." Lottie reaches over and takes my hand. She looks so sad. "I just pray that someone adopts her who can love her and take care of her. She's so tiny, Lottie. She's so helpless. It will kill me to leave her but I just don't see any other way."

"It's likely the hardest thing you will ever have to do. It's not been easy for any of my girls. But for what it's worth I think you're doing the right thing. I just don't know how you could manage with her. Do you know what you're going to do-when you leave here, I mean?"

"I'm going back to Pittsford for a bit to visit Mary, I think and, you know, get myself settled a bit. Then I might join my family in Montreal. I've always wanted to live in a big city." I smile wryly, knowing Lottie doesn't know enough about my family to understand all the ironies involved in this. "Montreal is big. I think I can get lost there-start over where no one knows me. My father's family lives in Rutland but I don't think they would be interested in taking me in. The only one who used to care for me was my grandmother and she's gone now. Besides, I wouldn't be in town a week before everyone would know everything about me. I've not had the kind of life they can boast about to their church group."

Lottie nods. "A lot of the girls feel the need for a fresh start once they leave here. As long as you never forget us," she adds with a teasing smile.

"I will never forget you Lottie. I don't know what I would have done without you and the other girls and having this place to come to. I hardly even notice the cold anymore!" We both laugh and it feels almost normal.

"Will you ask Dr. Fennimore to make whatever arrangements are necessary, you know, for the adoption?" Lottie nods, then rises and gives me a hug. Just then a sleepy-eyed Marcelline comes into the kitchen looking for her coffee. I tell her about my decision and she sits there rubbing her huge belly. She doesn't say much but I know she understands how hard this is.

Lottie sends word to Dr. Fennimore who stops by later that day with a sheaf of papers. He goes through them with me. One of the papers is Dorothy's birth registration which he asks me to check over. In bold letters up the side margin someone has written *ILLEGITIMATE* and where it asks for the father's name, the same someone has written *unknown*. I stab my finger at the paper. "There. Her father's name is Owen Jones-Wingham Owen Jones." Dr. Fennimore, looking a little sheepish, makes the correction and hands me the next paper. This is an adoption paper. I read it over and sign it without comment, though my stomach churns. It's done. I'm no longer a mother in the eyes of the world and the state of Vermont. I'm overwhelmed with sorrow. There are no tears left, nothing more to say. I'm just expected to pick up and move on with my life as if Owen and Dorothy never existed. I've failed at this like I've failed at everything in my life. I've disappointed everyone I love. Even Owen would be disappointed with me now. But he's gone and I had to do the best for our baby. God help me. I hope I did the right thing. I wish I could have talked to Mary.

CHAPTER TWENTY-SIX

I pack up my few things and take leave of my friends at the home. Marcelline has taken to her bed because of swelling in her ankles, so I say goodbye to her in her room. The others gather in the foyer to see me off. They each give me a hug. Lottie takes my hands in hers, makes me look her in the eyes and tells me I've done the right thing. The kind words bring tears to my eyes but I wipe them away. I am done crying. It serves for nothing. Instead I give Lottie a final hug, marveling, even now, at how such a tiny frail body can house such strength and compassion.

It's only mid-morning but the winter sun is surprisingly warm. I trudge through the slush to the train station, gripping my trusty valise, my companion now through so much. On the train I sit beside an elderly woman. She clearly wants to chat but I turn away and pretend to sleep. I know I'm being rude but don't care. I have no energy to talk about the unseasonal weather or the woman's family or anything else that people talk about on trains.

Lottie has been kind enough to telegraph Mary to let her know I'm coming. She and the children are waiting on the platform at the Pittsford station. I hug them all, happy to see Sarah and William, but also saddened at the reminder of what I've just given up. Mary asks no questions on the walk to her house. She chats instead about the children and the shortcomings of the woman now in charge of their care-then reprimands Sarah who is a little too quick to agree with her mother. It's only when we're back in Mary's cozy living room with a mug of tea that the words tumble out. The children have been given a treat and sent out to play. Mary listens without interrupting while I tell her about Dorothy's birth, her illness and my decision to give her up. I recite all of this dry-eyed. Mary listens with pain in her eyes. When it's all out we embrace. Mary tells me how badly she feels and assures me I did all I could. Everyone has told me this but I wonder if I will, some day, believe it.

I stay with Mary and the children for a few weeks. I don't feel judged when I'm with Mary and I love her children dearly. It's a healing time for me. I take some time to visit Mrs. Gambol at the boarding house and pay a quick visit to Adeline, currently chafing under doctor's orders to stay in bed. She tells me, in a voice oozing sarcasm, that she's recovering from a "ladies' ailment." She entertains me with colorful stories about how she imagines her doctor's demise whenever he pokes and prods at her. We laugh together and it feels good. These are people who love me and I'll never forget their many kindnesses. But I know I can't stay in Pittsford. Every building, every blade of grass, every face reminds me of Owen.

I have no money but Mary loans me enough for a ticket on the Grand Trunk and packs me food for the trip. And so I'm on the move again, this time to Montreal to join my parents and siblings. The idea of going back into the family fold is painful. But at least I know they'll let me stay until I can get a job, and I promise myself I won't let myself be imprisoned by my mother and her problems. I'm an adult now and so much stronger than I ever knew I could be. Besides, I'm over the moon about seeing my sisters and brothers again. There is even a tiny secret part of me that hopes my mother will hold me and offer me some comfort.

CHAPTER TWENTY-SEVEN

My arrival in Montreal is terrifying and exhilarating. It is, in many ways, the city of my dreams. I step out of the train station to a sea of tall buildings and hordes of people. Beautifully dressed women hang on dapper men. Streetcars, bicycles, automobiles and various horse-drawn conveyances plough through spring puddles and vie for space on the crowded streets. Everywhere I hear French along with a stew of other languages. I can't believe a train ride of a few hours has brought me to this exotic place. It feels worlds away from Pittsford, Vermont. Maman insisted I attend French school briefly when we were in Rutland to "keep up my language," but I've never considered French my language. Besides, that school and those lessons seem like a million years in my past. Still my dream has always been to make it to a big city so I'm not about to turn tail and run now.

I pull out the address that Papa gave me and approach a stout, kind-looking woman with a young boy in tow. "Pardon madam," I begin shyly, holding out the crumpled bit of paper. "Ou est…"

The woman interrupts me, not unkindly. "I speak English," she says, and I cringe. My French is that bad then. "Is this the place you are looking for? Rue Henri Julien?" Her voice is richly accented but her English is impeccable. I nod. "It's a long walk. Best you take the streetcar. There's a stopping place for them on the other side of the station. You can ask one of the drivers. He'll help you get the right one."

I thank her and hurry in the direction indicated. I have no problem finding the correct streetcar but I'm embarrassed to realize I have no Canadian coins for the fare. The driver, at first, looks at me with a hint of consternation, then smiles and waves me on. It turns out the ride is short. In spite of the advice from the nice woman I think, in hindsight, I could easily have walked. But the weather is warm and it's nice to sit with time to plan what I'll say to my parents. I sent a postcard from Mary's telling them I'm coming, but there was no time for a response to have arrived before I left. I have no idea if they even received it. There's a chance they've moved, since the apartment they had was located through the generosity of some distant relative of Maman's.

The driver lets me off on Rue Henri Julien and I ask another passer-by which way I need to go. It isn't far and soon I find myself in front of 4117 Rue Henri Julien. The houses are set close to the busy street. Carriages clatter past and people flow around me as I stand in front of the house, gathering up my courage to knock. When I do knock, no one comes. After the third attempt a stooped elderly woman opens the door and peers out at me suspiciously.

"I'm looking for Monsieur et Madam Menard." The woman mutters something in a language I don't recognize, but steps aside and opens the door marginally wider for me to squeeze through. Third floor, she mutters in a heavy accent, then shuffles off to what appears to be her main floor apartment. I catch a glimpse of an equally elderly man sitting in a worn chair in an undershirt surrounded by a haze of tobacco smoke. I thank the woman, but the door bumps closed before my words are finished. I shrug and climb the stairs. The walls are grubby with hand prints. Old cooking smells ooze from the pores of the building. I wonder about Maman. She must, by now, have had her baby. How did she manage all these stairs?

At the top is a single door, a relief since I feared I'd have to make even more inquiries when I got to the top. Through the door I hear young girls voices and my heart skips a beat. How I've missed my sisters, and Henry Jr. and Martin and little Donnie. They've been my only true friends for so much of my life. I tap on the door and immediately hear shouts and running feet on the other side. The door is thrown open and Viola is upon me.

"Minnie, we were hoping it was you," she shrieks. "We've been waiting and waiting." The other little ones have gathered around the door, all bouncing in anticipation of a hug.

"We have a new baby brother. His name is Freddy." This from Leona.

"You might let her in the door. And girls, lower your voices." The voice trails from inside the apartment; my mother.

"Oh Erminie, I'm so sorry. Do come in. Here give me your bag, You must be thirsty. I'll get you some water." I smile at Ethel's take charge attitude. She's the big girl of the house now and is taking her role seriously.

"I would love some water," I tell her as I wiggle in the door around all the little bodies pressing in on me.

Maman is standing in the middle of the room. Her tousled hair and rumpled look tell me she's been lying down. She pushes her hair away from her face. "I was resting," she says, simply. "Come and sit down. Did you walk from the station?"

I ignore her request to sit down, instead walking over to embrace her. Maman seems surprised but responds with a kiss on each of my cheeks.

"No, I took the streetcar. I didn't have the right money but the driver let me ride anyway. I could have walked, though. It didn't seem far." Maman and I settle on a worn settee. Ethel quickly arrives with a glass of tepid water for each of us while we exchange small talk about the weather.

"Your father is away just now. He has a job helping with street repairs. Henry Jr. is working with him. They should be back by supper. Martin is away too." She stops and appears confused. She doesn't know where Martin is, or has forgotten. She seems still half asleep. She shakes her head slowly and goes on. "I've been getting terrible headaches. I'm afraid they make me quite dozy."

"How are you feeling Maman-with the baby I mean?" I've been struggling with this on the train ride and more recently on the streetcar. The subject of babies is difficult but I feel a need to get all the awkward topics out of the way. "Is your baby well?"

Leona answers on Maman's behalf. "He's the most beautiful baby in the world, Min. Wait until you meet him! He's asleep now, though."

"It's so hard this time. I'm very tired," Maman goes on as if Leona hasn't spoken. "Things are not good." She waves her hand vaguely around the apartment. "Frederick has been colicky and seems to cry non-stop." Suddenly Maman focuses on me as though she's only just realized who I am. "Girls. All of you go down to the grocery. We need a round of cheese."

Dutifully, reluctantly, Ethel rounds up her younger siblings. Normally they'd be pleased to go to the grocer but right now it's clear they'd prefer to stay here. "Be careful on the street. Hold Donny's hand, oui?"

"Oui, Maman." Ethel takes some coins from a cracked teapot on the window sill and herds her younger siblings out the door. I hear them clatter down the stairs and hope the other tenants are as deaf as the two on the main floor.

Once the children have gone Maman settles herself more comfortably on the sofa, tucking a strand of hair behind her ear. "Now, Erminie. Tell me about the baby. We must not speak of it after this time. You changed your mind about keeping it? That was wise."

I feel a familiar prickle of anger but I swallow it. "The baby was a girl. I named her Dorothy- after Owen's mother," I add. I can hear the acid in my voice, but Maman just nods. "She-the baby-Dorothy, was not well. She couldn't digest my milk. The doctor told me it would be better for her if I gave her over for adoption so she can be placed with a family who can afford to take care of her. She'll need special food and care. I can't give that to her, not alone. Not without Owen." Again Maman nods, her face a mask. How I wish she would wrap me in her arms and hold me and tell me she loves me and how sorry she is that all this has happened to me. Instead she sits ramrod straight on the settee.

"You did the right thing, of course. It was God's will. Raising a child when you're not married is impossible. I'm sure the whole thing was difficult but you'll get over it. It would have been better if they had not let you see the child. It's easier that way. But there will be other children. And now that you've come to your senses and joined us here, you have your brothers and sisters to care for. Mind you, we are in tight quarters here so I think it would be wise if you start looking for your own place as soon as you can."

And that's it. We're done discussing my unfortunate accident. I know Dorothy will not be discussed again unless it serves Maman to bring it up in some future argument, possibly to illustrate my lack of moral character.

Maman goes on. "I don't mean to rush you but Ethel is able to take care of things here for me and, as you can see, there isn't much room for all of us. It will be nice to have you close by though, to help out with things."

I smile inwardly. So I've been replaced by poor little Ethel. Does she understand that caring for Maman will be a prison sentence until she can find a way to break free? Still, it's good news. I've been fearful Maman will try to keep me under her thumb and I have no intention of being under anyone's thumb, not now that I have this exciting city to explore.

Baby Freddy wakes up from his nap, the children return from their errand and Papa and the boys arrive home for dinner, all in rapid succession. Papa gives me a warm hug and has tears in his eyes. The boys seem glad to see me in their own awkward way. We share a meager supper of potatoes and a rubbery piece of beef, but there's happiness in the room and that's something I've not enjoyed with my family for a very long time. Henry Jr. and Martin are eager to share stories about their adventures in this new city and the girls have stories about school and the nuns who run it. Leona is quiet but I see her studying me, no doubt trying to reconcile me as the older sister who has been away for so long. I know I've made the right decision in coming to Montreal. Back at Mary's I questioned myself, wondering if I should make a clean break and go my own way. But, my heart aches for my family even if they can be impossible to live with.

I move, temporarily, into the girls' room. It's already crowded and I don't want to cause any more disruption than necessary. I make a bed of blankets on the floor. Viola brings me two books, one that has traveled with them from Vermont, the other I haven't seen before. She asks me to read them because "Leona would so enjoy it." I grin. I know Viola is the bookworm and will enjoy it most of all. I take the books and the three girls curl around me on my little nest on the floor. By the time I've read both books, Ethel is the only one still awake. She kisses me goodnight and climbs up into the bed. The little ones stay where they are and sleep with me through the night.

The next day I walk the streets near my parents' apartment. I stop in at shops asking if they need help, and watch for signs in windows. I feel the urgency to find work, but I'm also enjoying the vibrancy of the neighborhood. I love the elegant women and the handsome men. Of course, not everyone is elegant. There's poverty too, at a level I've not experienced in Pittsford or Rutland. Dirty children play in the streets and sometimes beg for money as I pass. I've nothing to give them but my sympathy. Everyone seems in a hurry to get somewhere and the air is full of unfamiliar sounds and smells. I feel like I'm finally where I belong. A place where I can get lost and start fresh and be someone new. How I would love to push Dorothy along this street in a buggy and have other mothers stop to coo over her. But, of course, that will never happen. I pass a school, quiet now since children are in class, and feel another twist in my gut. Where will Dorothy go to school? Perhaps she's already been adopted by a very rich family and will go to an exclusive school. Perhaps she'll be brought up to mock working people like me and my family. I'd hate that. There's nothing to be gained by dreaming about what might or might not happen. I've made my decision and deep down I know it was the right one. I just wish I had someone to talk to. Someone to tell about the silky smoothness of Dorothy's hair or the clean baby smell of her; even about the feeding tube and how scary it looked in her tiny nose. But Maman has closed that chapter of my life on my behalf. I'll write to Mary, I decide. With Mary I can be honest about how much I miss my baby and how I think about her all the time.

I'm so deep in my thoughts I almost miss a hand drawn sign in a dressmaker's shop window. It's tucked in amongst a display of Easter finery. Clean, reliable seamstress required. Apply within. I don't especially enjoy sewing but I'm competent and patient and it will do no harm to inquire. I think of kindly Mrs. Chamberlain back in Pittford, who gave me the lace for my wedding dress. At the time I thought it would be fun to work in her busy shop where women chattered over colorful bolts of cloth and exclaimed admiringly over delicate lace and pretty buttons. I push open the door to the store. A bell over the door jangles jarringly. The inside of the store actually resembles Mrs. Chamberlain's shop, though perhaps larger and less cluttered. A lone customer is browsing the bolts of material. The sound of the bell has attracted the attention of a plump woman in a wildly floral dress pretending busyness at the back of the shop. I feel her evaluating my shabby dress and worn boots and suddenly feel like running. Still, her words are kind enough as she calls, in French, that she will be right with me.

"Merci," I respond, and turn to feign interest in a bolt of garish green fabric. Eventually the woman finishes what she is pretending to do and winds through the store toward me. Again she asks if she might help me. I reply, in French, that I have seen her sign. She immediately switches to heavily accented English.

"Where are you from, child?"

"Vermont. Pittsford, Vermont, madame. I arrived in Montreal yesterday. I'm sorry but my French isn't so good yet, but I wondered about the sewing job I saw posted in your window." Again, the woman appraises me with uncomfortable frankness.

"Come into my office and we'll talk. She stops and speaks to the other woman in the store in rapid fire French that I can't understand. The woman waves her off with a gloved hand and she guides me into a tiny curtained room at the back of the shop. "My shop girl is off today but my customer says she will call me if she requires me." As she talks she moves bolts of fabric and stacks of papers onto a cabinet along one wall. Once she has cleared off a chair and a space on her desk, we sit. "Now then. My name is Mathilde Berneau. This is my shop. Have you sewn before?"

"Not for hire," I answer, wanting to be honest. "But my mother taught me to sew and I was taught pattern making and needlework in school. I sew my own clothes. I was sewing my wedding dress but my fiance was killed in an accident." Now why on earth did I say that? I mumble an apology.

Madame Berneau is quiet. "Did you sew that dress you're wearing," she asks.

"I did, but I've been traveling and it's very old." Even to my own ears I sound like a silly school girl.

"It is good work. Are you fast?"

"Pardon, madame?"

"Can you sew quickly? Have you used a machine?"

"I have used a machine," I reply, grateful that Mary let me use her treadle machine when I was working on my wedding dress. I decide confidence is the way to go so I add, "I can be fast if necessary, but I would rather be good."

Madame Berneau lifts a delicate eyebrow and smiles slightly. "Indeed?"

I nod, vigorously.

"Where else have you worked…in Vermont, was it?"

"I was a housekeeper and a mother's helper. Before that I was in school." I feel it prudent not to mention the exact nature of the school. Surely I can leave Wells behind in this new city, this new country.

Madam Berneau has several other questions, some about my character and my honesty and some about my family and living arrangements. I keep my head up and tell the woman that she can count on my trustworthiness. Finally she nods. "I think you might do. When can you start?"

"I can start tomorrow madame."

"All right. Come by promptly at 8:30. I'll show you your work station and introduce you to the other girls. I expect nothing but your best work, mind."

"I won't disappoint you, Madame Berneau. Thank you for this

opportunity."

I hurry out of the store, nearly skipping so elated am I about finding work so quickly. I feel it in my bones. This new country is going to bring a new and better life for me. Maybe, finally, I can leave all the bad that's happened behind me.

I hurry back to the apartment, eager to share news of my job. Since Maman tried to sabotage my jobs in Pittsford, I hope by sharing my excitement I might prevent the same thing from happening here. I've nothing to fear though. Maman knows Madame Berneau's shop and, predictably I suppose, believes the woman's work inferior. But about the job itself, she is ecstatic. Ecstatic and quick to point out the rent I will pay will be very helpful to the family. I'm happy to pay rent if it means I can work outside the home and become a productive member of this new community. It is, after all, what I've always wanted. Everyone else in the family is happy for me too, though I wonder about Martin. He's not yet been able to find work. Having his sister arrive and get work on her first day leaves him sullen, though he tries to hide it.

The next morning I hurry to Madame Berneau's shop to arrive promptly at the appointed time. The store is not yet open to customers but she's waiting for me. She unlocks the door, lets me in and locks it again behind me. "In future there is a entrance up the back stairs you can use. That door is open by 8:00. Today, I'll take you through this way."

We take stairs up to the second floor of the building and enter a cavernous space that must take most of the second floor. Large cutting tables run down the center of the room and a treadle sewing machine sits in front of each of two large windows, positioned to take advantage of the natural light. One girl is getting her machine set up for the day. Another is spreading some fabric over one of the cutting tables. They are the only ones in the room, though a third girl hurries breathlessly up the back stairs, excuses herself in French as she sees us and hurries over to the other machine. Madame Berneau looks annoyed but says nothing to the girl, instead turning to tell me how very important it is that I arrive on time. "You can make decent money here but you must be prepared to work long hours and that means starting on time."

"I have only two machines so you'll have to work out with Rosie and Madeleine here, when you are most in need of one. I expect you to work this out peacefully among the three of you, mind you. The other girls don't use the machines. When no machine is available there's always a lot of handwork to be done. I'll be giving you pieces once I see what you can do."

Madame Berneau goes on to explain how much and when I'll be paid. She assigns me a dress that's been cut but needs to be assembled, as well as two dresses and a nightgown that need finishing work. These are laid out neatly on one of the cutting tables, along with scissors, pins, a measuring tape and a small metal box filled with thimbles and the small detritus of a seamstress. Instructions done, Madame Berneau returns to the shop below, leaving me with the other girls who, to this point, have been industriously cutting and paddling away on the machines.

"You speak English." It's a statement not a question. It's the girl who was in the room when I first arrived. "My name is Rosie. Welcome to Madame Berneau's. I hope we'll be friends."

"I hope so too." The girl is about my age, startlingly tall and lean with long dark plaited hair hanging down past her waist. Her face is plain enough, but that hair! I can't take my eyes off it. The braid that contains it is as thick as my forearm. "My name is Erminie. I'm new in Montreal. I've only recently moved here from Vermont. I speak French but not well, I'm afraid."

"Ah well," she shrugs. "Madeleine over there speaks no English, so perhaps I can help you both." At mention of her name Madeline waggles her fingers at us in a shy wave then quickly returns to winding some white thread onto a bobbin. And over there is Cecilia, Rosie points to the girl who came in late.

"Bonjour," Cecilia calls out from around a mouthful of pins.

"Bonjour," I call back.

"This is a decent place to work. There are worse, I can tell you that. Madame Berneau is strict about being on time and not bringing friends up here, but as long as you get your work done she's pretty reasonable. The last girl stole some fabric though, awful stuff it was too, some horrid orange cotton. But it was enough to get the police up here. Not sure where she is now but I can tell you she doesn't work here any more!" Rosie laughs with a most unladylike snort. "I'm working on a wedding dress, so I'll be at that for a while. I need machine one for a couple of hours but after that you can use it for this." She sweeps a hand carelessly over the cut pattern pieces stacked on the table.

I like Rosie fine but I'm anxious to get to work. I want to make a good impression on my first day, but Rosie seems determined to chat. "Where are you staying?" she asks now.

"I'm with my parents on Rue Henri Julien-just a few blocks away. You?"

Rosie shrugs. "I share a room with a girlfriend. My parents live out west. I came here to study fashion but until I can get a break…get in with the right people, you know?" She trails off, looking around the shabby work room.

I nod. "I'm sure you'll be a great designer some day."

Rosie smiles, a little sadly, it seems to me. "Everyone tells me it's not a job for a woman. But really, shouldn't a woman design clothes for women? What do you want to do?"

I haven't really thought much about it. I wanted to get out of Pittsford, that's for sure. Now that I'm here I'm not really sure what I want to do. "Get married and have children, I guess," I answer lamely.

Rosie smiles. "Well I don't expect you'll have no trouble there. You're beautiful."

I feel color creeping up my neck. No one, except Owen, has ever told me I'm beautiful. I wonder if Rosie needs spectacles or just likes to flatter. In any case I decide I like Rosie who is as cheerful as her name and beautiful in an odd, eye-catching way.

Rosie's singular flaw is that she likes to talk. As I spend more time working with her I learn it's perfectly all right to continue my own work and listen with the part of my mind not focused on the sewing. Rosie takes no offense. To do otherwise would mean never getting any sewing done. Rosie has an opinion on everything from Madame Berneau's wardrobe ("truly, you would think a woman who sews dresses for a living would have a better sense of style") to the political situation in Europe (about which I know nothing and care less). From time to time Rosie turns her attention to Madeleine and Cecilia, speaking in French that sounds as fluent to me as her English, though assuredly I am not the one to judge. There are other women who come at various times. Some have arrangements to work only one or two hours at a time. Others come and collect hand sewing to take home. These mostly are women with children trying to earn a little extra grocery money.

Of the three full-timers, Madeleine is the most content to sit by herself and mind her sewing. Rosie assures me she's pining for a young man, which only makes Madeleine blush and turn away. She does understand some English then.

Having secured a job, I now set about to find accommodations of my own. I feel it's important to do this quickly before Maman becomes too attached to my rent money. While she seems much more anxious to have me move out than she did in Pittsford, Maman still insists I move to a respectable place where she can visit with the children without fear of being accosted on the street. I note that my reputation is no longer a topic of conversation as it was in Pittsford. Maman undoubtedly has decided that ship has sailed. When I mention to Rosie that I need a place to stay she makes it her personal mission to find me a suitable place. In the end though, it's Madame Berneau who provides the solution. On one of her frequent trips to the second floor to check on our progress or to pick up a finished piece, she asks if any of us are in need of a room. Genevieve, the shop girl, currently stays in a room on the third floor, the rest of that floor being occupied my Madame Berneau herself. Genevieve is engaged to be married and she and her beau are moving to a house. I expect that Madame Berneau particularly wants Madeleine to take the room as, perhaps, it would cure her chronic tardiness. However, Madeleine shakes her head, saying she's happy in her current situation. Rosie gives me a little shove. "I would consider the room Madame." And so it is that I move my few possessions to the third floor of the shop on Rue Lamirande. My mother is plainly perturbed that I've not asked her advice on the room. She finds all manner of things wrong with it, from bedbugs to nesting bats to villainous thugs. She grouses that the room is on the third floor and wonders how she will manage the stairs with little Freddy. All this and she has not yet set eyes on the room. She lets the matter drop relatively quickly though, and I know she's glad I'll soon be out of her way, yet still close enough to come on command. I also know she has no intention of visiting me.

Happily, Madame Berneau turns out to be much less demanding a landlady than an employer. Long widowed, Madame has a beau named Frank who she speaks of in glowing terms. Most of the time, when the shop is closed, she's with Frank and is seldom in her rooms. In fact, she's away so much I feel it wise not to comment on the fact to Maman lest she come to believe that Madame Berneau is inadequate as a chaperon. It comes down to me being alone most nights, a situation totally foreign to me. I don't allow myself loneliness though. I'm finally beginning to live my own life as an independent working girl in a bustling city. All the horrors of Wells, the death of Owen and the loss of Dorothy are behind me and I'm determined to make the most of my life.

Rosie, though, isn't content for me to sit home and read by lamplight. She begins to organize outings for us. These are thinly disguised matchmaking opportunities. Rosie has a particular group of friends she travels with and I begin stepping out with them from time to time, sometimes to the cinema or a play. Sometimes we go dancing.

I haven't lived long above the shop when Maman, Papa and their brood move. Papa has a new job as a stonecutter and has located a house for them on Degenais. I think he will be happy but Papa rarely seems happy any more. I know the move to Montreal has been hard on him, though they have moved so often in the past I think he must be used to it. Still the house is good news and when I help them move in I find it bright and spacious and certainly a step up from the rooms on Henri Julien. It's a considerable distance from the shop and my apartment but I see that as a plus, not a minus.

Maman is out of sorts, even for Maman. During the move she directs traffic and barks orders until one of her headaches drives her to lie down, causing everyone to breathe a sigh of relief. Meanwhile, Ethel has charge of wee Freddy. The lad is a constant reminder to me of my own pregnancy and of Dorothy. I wonder where Dorothy is and pray daily that she's been adopted out to someone who will love her in spite of her medical problems. I wonder too about my friends in the home, cheerful Marcelline and brooding Martha. They'll both have had their babies by now. Both planned on giving them up. Have they changed their minds? I hope so. Their babies would be competition for my lovely little Dorothy in the orphanage.

All these thoughts aside, I'm settling into life in Montreal. Madame Berneau keeps me busy during the day and Rosie finds an endless array of fairs and dances and plays to keep me busy in the evenings. I sometimes find the language dichotomy unsettling. There's a mistrust of Francophone for Anglophone and vice Versa. As an English-speaking French Canadian born and raised in Vermont, I don't even really know in whose camp I belong. My French is improving quickly and shopkeepers no longer switch to English out of pity, but still I sense I'll never quite belong to either side. Come to that, I never really belonged in Vermont either where my name and my French words and going to a Catholic church all earned teasing at school. Maybe God just created me a misfit. Still I'm happy. I feel like I've found a place where, if I don't fit in perfectly, at least I can make my own future. Even being near my family, though a double-edged sword to be sure, is a positive thing. The entire family, including Papa is united in their exhaustion with Maman and her moods and that brings a strange sort of closeness. The boys sometimes find their way to come out with Rosie and I to the cinema and I become closer to them than I've been in years. Though, in truth, Henry Jr. seems more interested in getting to know Rosie, four years his senior, than he is in connecting with me.

I often join the family for mass at St.Zotique on Sundays, then stay at the house on Dagenais to entertain my sisters while Maman rests. It's a lovely life and I'm glad I've come to Montreal. For a single girl, family is important. As for Maman, she's uniformly unkind to everyone so, for once, I don't feel singled out. Nor is there any reference to my pregnancy or my "loose moral character", as I had feared.

CHAPTER TWENTY-EIGHT

Rosie is intent on finding the "right man" for me. A continuous parade of eligible young men come and go from the fringes of our social group. Most hold no interest for me. I'm still healing from so many hurts that I have no energy for courting. I know I'm getting a reputation as a cold fish because I show no interest in these aspiring suitors. But men have caused me a lot of heartache in my nineteen years, intentionally or not. No one can replace Owen in my heart. I'm civil to these young men, but try never to give them hope.

The only one I'm remotely interested in is Gus, a dark-haired bear of a man with a background similar to mine. Born in a village outside of Montreal, he tells me his family shipped him off as a boy to live with an uncle in upstate New York when his mother died. His uncle was a drinker and a mean drunk, but he worked as a driver and taught Gus how to drive and maintain a vehicle. When he was seventeen Gus fathered a child and his uncle, fearing reprisal from the girl's family, threw him out of the house with nothing but the clothes on his back. He managed to work his way back to Montreal. Now he works at odd jobs and saves to buy his own motor car. So far he's saved only enough to buy a stiff brimmed chauffeur's cap that he wears whenever he's had too much to drink. I enjoy Gus' company and the more I learn about him the more I find him a kindred spirit. Like me he's soiled, not quite acceptable in polite society, not quite belonging in either the French or the English world.

Gus tells me these things about his past in bits and pieces as we get to know each other better. I feel his confidences require something in return, so I tell Gus about Owen and our relationship, though I leave out the parts about the pregnancy and baby Dorothy. We talk a lot about family, Gus wanting nothing to do with his, and me wishing mine could just be normal. We begin to step out together without the rest of the group, something that sends Rosie into a flutter about the success of her matchmaking. Gus and I go for walks or to a movie if we have enough money for the admission. In the flickering light of the theater, Gus takes my hand in his huge warm paw and it feels good. I've never been courted in the conventional sense before. Best of all, Gus never takes it any further than hand holding. I don't know if it's respect for me or fear of fathering another child. He doesn't say and I don't ask. It's simply more comfortable that way. Our friendship is easy and undemanding. Eventually I introduce Gus to Henry Jr. and Martin, who, it turns out, already know him peripherally through the gang that we all hang out with. I'm in no hurry to introduce him to my parents. I already know Maman will not approve of Gus's history, or of his dreams of being a driver. Maman would consider that a frivolous goal.

Maman is always asking if I'm seeing anyone. Even though she was eager to get me out of their crowded house, it irks her that I'm no longer under her thumb. She wants to know what I do during my evenings and my days off from the shop. She wants to know who I chum with and if Rosie is a respectable sort of girl. She finds out that Henry Jr. and Martin travel in the same circles as some of my friends and begins to pump them for information. They stymie her though, as they always have, with grunts and shrugs and incomplete sentences that give nothing away. Papa, meanwhile has become more and more withdrawn. He simply hugs me and tells me he hopes I'm happy and that he's pleased the move to Montreal has been good for me.

I must admit things are going well for me, Maman and her meddling aside. I have freedom, independence and friends. I've never had these things before and I finally feel life is moving in the right direction. I even take time to sit down and write a letter to St. Joseph's Orphanage in Burlington to see if they have any word on Dorothy. It occurs to me that perhaps now I could manage a baby, though there are aspects of that I still can't reconcile in my head. It doesn't matter anyway because when, after a long while, I get a response from the orphanage it is short and blunt.

"State law prohibits us from releasing any information about children given to our care. This is for the protection of both the child and the adoptive parents. Thank you for your correspondence."

The letter is signed by a Sister Ursula. On the day I receive the letter I tuck it away in a little jewel box that Gus gave me. I shed some tears and feel down in the mouth the rest of the afternoon. When Rosie stops by after dinner to see if I want to go for a walk with the gang I finally tell her about Dorothy and the letter. It's the first time I've told anyone here in Montreal about my baby. Rosie holds me and we cry together and I swear her to secrecy. She wants to know all about Dorothy. How big was she? What color was her hair? Was she beautiful? I cannot believe how good it feels to talk about my daughter and her beautiful turned up nose and her thatch of dark hair. I tell Rosie about my decision not to keep Dorothy and the medical problems that decided the matter for me. Rosie doesn't seem to think less of me. She just nods sadly as she listens, and shakes her head in frustration when I show her the letter from the orphanage.

"Does Gus know all this?" Rosie asks.

"No, and you have to swear to never tell him-not ever!"

"Min, he'll understand. He got a girl in the family way in the States. He knows this kind of thing happens for heaven's sake!"

"Don't you ever tell him. Or anyone else. Swear to it."

Rosie raises both hands in surrender, then crosses her heart. We go for a walk, just the two of us and I feel better for having a real friend to share my story with.

CHAPTER TWENTY-NINE

Everything begins to unravel during the last few months of the year. Maman, even after bearing eight other children of varying temperaments is clearly at a loss as to what to do with young Freddy. She's carried and delivered nine children in twenty years and she has nothing left for this one. Papa is becoming even more withdrawn. The younger girls do what they can but Ethel is only twelve and it's too much to ask of the two younger girls who are in school and have studies to attend to.

Maman clearly cannot cope. I find myself spending nearly every moment, when I'm not at work, at my parents, helping out where I can. Mostly it means carrying and rocking the baby so Maman can sleep. Often I take him for walks in an old carriage that a neighbor gave to Maman. These walks are the only time little Freddy settles and I sometimes allow myself to pretend that the baby in the carriage is Dorothy. In my mind I'll return, after our walk, to the beautiful little apartment I share with Owen. But, of course, I'm always jolted back to reality sooner or later.

It becomes increasingly clear that I'm being pulled back into my mother's orbit for all my intentions to not let that happen. The woman who, even at her worst, presented herself to the outside world as straight-backed, regal and prim seems incapable now of caring for herself, let alone her family. Papa is worse than useless, and the boys always have someplace they have to be.

In late November, Ethel shows up at the dress shop. She's never been there before, so Madame Berneau quickly shows her up to the work area. The child is sobbing so hard it takes me some time to understand what she's saying. Papa is gone, it seems. He left a packet of money on Maman's dressing table along with a note to Maman. Ethel doesn't seem to know what the note says but she is distraught. Madame Berneau excuses me from work and Ethel and I rush to Maman's. Maman is sprawled on the bed, her face swollen from crying and her knuckles raw and bleeding. Later the girls tell me how she flew into a rage when she read the note, pounding her fists against walls and any other solid object that got in her way. Finally, exhausted, she collapsed crying onto the bed and has been there ever since. The girls are frightened and Freddy is wailing in his crib, hungry, wet and angry. I hardly know who to tend to first.

I set the girls about making tea while I change Freddy and warm some milk for him. Freddy somewhat calmed, I pass him off to Ethel and tell her to feed him then take the little girls and Freddy out for a walk. I pour some tea for Maman and me, adding a shot of Papa's whiskey to Maman's cup hoping it will calm her. It's the very least Papa can do for us at this moment. As an afterthought, I put some in my cup too. I feel like I'm going to need some fortification. Aside from Maman's now subdued weeping, relative calm has settled over the apartment. I take a deep draft of my spiked tea, murmur a few encouraging words to Maman and pick up Papa's note. It's crumpled and laying in a corner where Maman has probably thrown it. It's been staring at me since I entered the apartment. It's brief:

Jenny,

I write this with deep sadness, but I cannot continue in this marriage. Please tell the children I love them. I never wanted to come here. I am leaving all the money I have saved and will send more when I can.

Henri.

And that is that. Papa is gone, leaving Maman with a sickly baby and six other children still at home. In some ways I can't blame my father-life with Maman is never easy-but I'm deeply angry. And if I'm honest with myself I'm angry at what he's done to me. To leave his family in a new city is selfish and cowardly. And now it will fall on me to look after them. I peek in the envelope and count two hundred dollars. Hardly enough to last to the end of the year. Christmas will be a bleak affair.

In the evening the boys come home from work. Maman is asleep and I'm dozing in a chair beside the bed, fuzzy from three cups of tea. Warily they seek us out in the bedroom. It must be obvious even to two teen-aged boys that something is amiss. I dread telling the boys that Papa is gone but Maman doesn't open her eyes when they come in the room. I usher them out of the bedroom quietly and sit them down in the front room. I tell them what's happened, showing them the note and the envelope of money. They are predictably sad but don't really seem surprised except by the money from Papa which seems to them a windfall. I wonder if they suspected Papa was leaving, but when I suggest it, all I get are the same grunts and shrugs they have been using to deflect Maman for years. In any case, it changes nothing. Papa is gone and we need a plan to move forward.

Maman has no job and has never held a job. The girls are still in school and can't be expected to bring in much more than pocket change. Henry Jr. and Martin both have jobs and that will help, but it's clear I'm going to have to contribute some of my income from sewing in order to get the family through.

Over the next few days I pray for two things. I pray that Papa will have a change of heart and return and I pray that the money in the envelope will somehow multiply like the fishes and loaves of biblical times. Neither of those things happen and I finally must face the fact that I will have to give up my apartment and move back in with my family. The rent I'm paying can be better used to support the children. I'm out of options and silently cursing my father for his weakness.

When I give a sympathetic Madame Berneau my notice on the apartment, I ask her if I might be given additional hours. To her credit, she asks no questions, though I suspect she's already asked Rosie what's going on. If so, they've both kept mum about it. Whatever the reason, she's very understanding and offers me some hours doing sales in the shop, a job that pays two cents more per hour than sewing.

The next few weeks are a whirlwind. I get the three girls off to school in the morning making sure everyone is washed and fed and has a lunch. I make sure the boys have breakfast and Donny and the baby are fed and clean. I work long days at the shop, come home to make dinner for the family then supervise homework and bedtimes. Saturdays I work on the sales floor at the dress shop for four hours in the morning and Sundays I get everyone ready to go to church. I have little time for myself and none for Gus. I soon hear via Rosie that he's seeing a girl who works winding film onto reels at the cinema and who likes to tell people she works in "entertainment". I hardly have time to mourn my relationship with Gus and I certainly don't blame him. I do miss him though. I miss him a lot.

Maman sinks into a deep well of sadness and is hardly able to climb out of bed most days. I'm desperately worried about the care Freddy and Donny are getting during the day when they're alone with Maman. There seems no other option though, save asking Ethel to quit school. I put that away as a last resort. She's clever and loves her lessons and I don't want to take that away from her. There certainly isn't enough money to hire a girl and everyone who can make money is doing what they can. I feel like I am on a runaway train. All I can do is hang on and hope things work out.

We don't hear from Papa. Not a word. His boss stops by one evening looking for him, his attitude a combination of anger and concern. I have to talk to him because Maman refuses to come out of her room. Henry Jr. has already told the man that Papa left but he wonders now if there is new information. Secretly I think he wants to see if perhaps Papa is here, hiding in the shadows. When I tell him there's no news he softens and before he leaves he offers me ten dollars "for the children for Christmas." I'm touched and feel tears welling up to my further humiliation. I don't tell Maman about the money, afraid she'll make me march down and return it. Instead I tuck it away and use it to buy a few things for Christmas dinner.

Aside from a better than usual dinner, Christmas passes with little by way of celebration. There's no happiness in the house and certainly no money for gifts. The older ones seem to understand and the younger ones don't seem to know any better so we get through it. The day after Christmas I pack up Donny and the girls and take them to look at the beautifully decorated shop windows on St. Catharines Street. That ends our Christmas celebrations.

I keep hoping for a letter or a postcard from Papa but nothing comes. There are two or three people claiming they saw him at various locations in Montreal but there is never any verification. As 1914 makes its chilly debut even the rumors dry up. I suppose he's left Montreal. Where he would go I can only guess. Perhaps back to Vermont. His family is there but his relationship with them was always strained and how could he explain a missing wife and six children. Henry Jr. and Martin continue to act oddly and I suspect, again, that they know more than they're telling me.

Weeks and months pass with no word from Papa. Maman recovers a bit and takes a bigger role with the children. At least I feel I can leave the little boys with her during the day and know they'll be cared for. As spring arrives I find a more affordable apartment for all of us on Singer Street. Maman, never one to avoid confrontation, complains because she had no input. The reality is she hasn't been out of the house in weeks and I know she's secretly happy I've taken over decision making. From Maman's point of view, it's easier to criticize a decision than to make one. The apartment is smaller than the first one Maman and Papa had when they came to Montreal but the boys are usually only home for supper and to sleep. I share a room with Ethel, Viola and Leona. Maman has baby Freddy and Donny in the room with her. Henry Jr. and Martin sleep on a mattress in a corner of the sitting room when they're home-which is less and less often as the months roll on.

Trouble is brewing in Europe but it seems very distant to me. I'm occupied keeping my head, and the heads of my family, above water. But in July of 1914 an archduke is assassinated in Europe. It's the culmination of months of posturing and politicizing and before long Britain and most of Europe is at war. Canadian boys rush to volunteer for the British cause, but Montreal is split along English speaking and French speaking lines. The English feel it's their patriotic duty to join the fight. The French feel the Brits can fight their own war. There is a third group, both French and English for whom war has nothing to do with patriotism. It's about excitement, travel and personal challenge. Patriotism is only a veneer, and a thin one at that.

Rosie urges me often to come out with the gang. I almost always refuse, pleading fatigue or an early morning. Really I'm so focused on keeping our little household running and on working to support everyone that the idea of a frivolous night out seems silly and wasteful. Sometimes she stays just to keep me company. Mysteriously, Henry Jr. and Martin almost always come home on those evenings and offer to walk her home later.

There are times, usually when Rosie is particularly persistent in her badgering, that I do join the gang for a walk or just to sit in the park. It's during one of these times that Gus joins the group. He's recently broken things off with his film reel sweetheart (whose name apparently was Matty). It's plain that Gus is still interested but I turn down any suggestion that we date. I'm too busy for a boy right now, I tell him. Still, it's nice to see him, and talk to him, and just have him sit beside me.

That same evening Henry Jr. and Martin also join our group. They've just been to a picture show. I can't help but give them the hard stare. After all, why am I the one making all the sacrifices while they're off to the pictures? They have another boy with them that I don't know. This boy, Jean, invites us to his home since his parents are away visiting relatives in Quebec City. I really just want to go home but Henry Jr. persuades me to go along. Gus declines and goes home. Once at Jean's house Henry proudly produces a flask. I think of the things I could have bought with the money he spent on that flask, not to mention the whiskey he says is in it. I'm exasperated with him but really not angry. That would take more energy than I have. Instead I take the flask when it reaches me and take a tentative swallow. I've tasted alcohol before of course, but only a bit of whiskey in my tea (and, on the day of Papa's departure, quite a lot of whiskey in my tea). I've never had it straight. I'm pretty surprised that, after the initial burn in my throat and stomach, the warmth is quite soothing. Before the flask has made a complete round, a second one appears. I have a few more pulls of the whiskey but the warmth in my stomach is turning to nausea and at some point I begin to pass the flasks along without taking any. Eventually the flasks are empty but a jar of something else has materialized. Henry Jr. and Martin both become quite drunk, paying no heed at all to my big sisterly glowering. I discover that Henry Jr. is a very chatty drunk. Strange, for a lad who rarely speaks in complete sentences at home. At one point he wriggles in to sit beside me, draping an arm companionably over my shoulder.

"You should give Gus a chance, you know. He's crazy about you."

I shrug. "I like Gus. I like him a lot. But there's just no time. When would I even see him? Besides, it couldn't go anywhere. We can't get married. I have to take care of you lot and there's no way I would wish that on him."

Henry Jr. sniffs in boozy indignation. "You don't have to look after me and Martin. We pull our own weight. Don't I give you plenty of money every week to help out with things?"

I nod. "Yes you do. And without it I don't know what we'd do. But, you know what I mean. It's more about time. I just feel like every waking minute is taken up either with work or with doing something for the little ones or for Maman. Maman just lies around feeling sorry for herself and waiting for Papa to come back."

Henry Jr. snorts. "Well he ain't coming back, I can tell you that!"

I grab him by the shoulder and he flinches. I think I actually hurt him. "You rat. You know something. Tell me!"

"Well you have to keep it quiet. It'd kill Ma."

I know my eyes must be as big as dinner plates. I'm not liking the sound of this. But I've been waiting for news and Henry Jr. has some. The liquor has loosened his tongue and I may never have a better chance to grill him. He takes another swallow out of the jar as it comes by, wiping his mouth on the worn and none-too-clean sleeve of his shirt.

"Tell me. I won't say anything to Maman. All I need is for her to get stirred up again."

Henry mimes making a cross over his heart and I nod impatiently.

"Okay. Remember Rachel? Rachel from the quarry office back in Pittsford?" I nod. I vaguely remember a thin, dark haired woman I'd met once or twice on visits to see Owen at the quarry. I remember nothing remarkable about her, except that she was friendly and came to Owen's funeral, along with several of the men he worked with. There was something odd about her eyes, now I come to think of it.

"I sort of remember her. Why?"

"Pa was having a little fling with her. I heard about it when we was still living in Pittsford. A lot of the men were talking about it. It seems they couldn't keep it a secret. The men in that quarry like to gossip worse than a bunch of old housewives."

Henry Jr. leans in a little closer and lowers his voice. His whiskey breath is hot on my face so I have to turn away slightly, unnoticed by Henry who, by now, is heavily invested in his story. "Ma found out about it, see. I mean, it was only a question of time, cuz everyone in town was talking about it. I wasn't home but there was a huge row while you were away in Burlington. That was when they decided we were moving here. I think Ma thought if she got him far enough away from Rachel he'd forget about her. With Ma being pregnant and all, it seems like he just let her have her way. He always did let her walk all over him. Ma's been a bitch since we got here though, and I think Pa just finally had enough. I think he's gone back to Pittsford to be with Rachel."

"You think? You don't know? He didn't tell you?"

"Nope. Never said a word before he left. But he knew me and Martin knew about Rachel. I think he knew we'd figure it out."

"That selfish bastard." I can hear the rasp in my throat and I grab the jar on its next pass and take a huge swig, gasping as it goes down my gullet. I pass it on to Henry.

"I know Min, but I can't say I blame him. Ma isn't easy to live with. Why do you think I'm gone so much?"

I splutter. "Yes, but look who had to move back in with her. Do you think I wanted to do that? I had a life before he left." I feel hot tears starting at the back of my eyes. God damn him. "Nothing changed in your life except you give up a little of your pay check each month. My entire life has been turned upside down. All because he wanted some skinny little office clerk?"

"A wall-eyed preacher's daughter," Henry chuckles. "But really Min. He's been gone for six months. Does it really matter why he left? What did you think he was doing? Ministering to the African heathens?"

I have to admit the reason Papa left matters very little in the grand scheme. He's abandoned us and I'm left to keep the fabric of the family together, helping a mother who has never supported me when I needed support. A mother who has driven Papa away with her incessant complaints.

I get very, very drunk. Henry and Martin walk me home, the three of us singing bawdy French songs at the top of our lungs, causing the occasional resident along our route to yell at us through open bedroom windows. At some point I recall throwing up into a shrub.

HENRY

I know how it all must look. My children must think me the lowest form of scum. Leaving them in Montreal was the hardest thing I've ever done. Like a man planning suicide, I really believed they'd be better off without me. Maybe they were too. But, looking back, I know I laid too much responsibility on the laps of the older children. I knew Jenny was a child herself. She needed care. She was not functioning as a mother by the time I left, nor as a wife either. God knows it was my duty to stick it out with her, to play the dutiful husband. The problem was, I was overwhelmed by a sense of time getting away from me, flowing through my fingers like fine sand. I felt I'd die without ever experiencing real happiness.

Everything I did was wrong in Jenny's eyes. Everything. Eventually I stopped trying. What was the point? She could never accept happiness and made sure no one else felt it either. Rachel was different. She wasn't what you'd call a great looker but she had the most beautiful smile. She was kind to everyone, from the lowest quarry boy to the Italian artists brought in to do the fine carving. I couldn't get her out of my head. I started making excuses to go to the office-questions about my pay mostly-until people began to notice. Then they began to talk. It was nothing but an infatuation but in the minds of the men at the quarry it became a full-blown affair. They'd wink and nudge me and make rude remarks. For all the talk I doubt it would have gone beyond a crush, a flirtation. Eventually, though, to quell the gossip, Rachel had to take me aside and make me promise to stop coming to the office. At the same time she made it known that she had feelings for me and would like to see me from time to time if we could make it work. So I made fewer trips to the office but began to see Rachel away from the quarry, away from prying eyes.

Jenny found out. Of course Jenny found out. No one can keep a secret like that long in a town like Pittsford. I think I can pinpoint the minute she knew, though she never said anything right then. She just got colder, even more distant, more demanding of the children. I knew I should break it off with Rachel, but she was like a drug. I was drawn back to her even as I was telling myself it had to end. Everything was spiraling out of control. I felt like a leaf being carried downstream by the current-thrilled by the ride but dead scared of where I might end up.

It all came to a head one night when I got home from work. Jenny met me at the door and I knew there was going to be a fight. She'd already put the children to bed. Even the boys were in their room. She was like a storm cloud fixing to burst and I hadn't even got my hat hung up before she let loose. She railed on about Rachel and called me and her every name in the book.

We argued most of the night until finally I just gave in. Jenny threatened to leave me and take the children and all the money (though that well was dry and she knew it). She promised she'd make my life a living hell. I believed her though, looking back, my life was not desirable real estate as it was.

Eventually she got to the place she'd been leading up to all along. She said she'd been thinking about things over the last few weeks and the only way we could make it work was if we got away from Pittsford. That was how the move to Montreal came about. A new city in a new country. It would all be okay if we could just start new. Jenny had some folks there. She said it would be like going home.

It broke my heart to part from Rachel. She raged at me but, in the end, said she understood. After that I avoided contact with Rachel until we got ourselves moved to Montreal. I really thought I could do it. I thought once I was away from the draw of Rachel, in a new place, surrounded by new folks, I'd get by alright. But a new city didn't change what was going on with Jenny, nor what was going on between me and Jenny. I'd always lived in quarry towns where a man could always find work if he wasn't too choosy about what it was. Montreal was bigger than other places we'd lived, but I couldn't find work carving stone, not even grave stones. I felt like a fish out of water. Jenny's always been more "French" than me but even she couldn't connect with the Montreal cousins she was so sure would welcome us with open arms. Oh, I got work all right, on the street crew, but I felt like I was drifting. And the more I drifted the more I thought of Rachel. She was home for me. Not Montreal, not Pittsford or Rutland, but Rachel. She felt like my roots.

So, in the end, I left. Saying it makes it sound easy but it wasn't. The part leading up to my going was hell. But once I sat on that train bound for Pittsford I felt like the weight of the world was lifted. Rachel didn't know I was coming. I hadn't wanted to write because I didn't quite know when I would write a letter, or where I should send it, or who might see it at the other end. Instead I just showed up at the quarry at a time when I knew the office would be quiet. I'd like to tell you that Rachel jumped right up into my arms but she was plenty mad at me. She said she wasn't some trout on a line to get reeled in when it suited me. But she got calmed down and finally agreed to have a proper conversation. We talked about a lot of things later that night but about the only thing we could agree on was that we wanted to be together. She wanted me to divorce Jenny but that couldn't happen. Jenny would never go against the church, especially for my convenience. I knew we couldn't stay in Pittsford. It was too close to my family and there were too many people here who knew our situation. Rachel came up with the idea of going to Georgia where her folks lived. To tell the truth the idea made me pretty squeamish. Her Pa was a Baptist minister and I couldn't think of anything good that would come from moving there. But I felt like I had to give Rachel something so I agreed. In the end it worked out all right. She introduced me as her beau and we even had a wedding presided over by her Pa. Both of us knew it wasn't real legal but as long as no one found out about Jenny we were married in the eyes of the State of Georgia. More importantly we had the blessing of her folks who were happy to have their middle daughter home and safely married.

CHAPTER THIRTY

Martin comes home one day in August of 1915 with word he's signed up for the British army, lying about his age to do it. He's two months short of eighteen. Maman takes the news with cold acceptance. She's always left the boys to their own devices more so than we girls, but I expected more resistance about Martin going off to Europe. She doesn't act like a mother who might lose her son, but like a mother whose son is personally insulting her. She flips a dismissive hand at him and tells him to do whatever he thinks he needs to do-that it's none of her business. Then, in October, Henry Jr. enlists as well. Both assure me, at the time of their enlistment, that the pay is good in the army. They'll continue to send money so we won't be short. But neither of them account for how long it takes to get their first pay from the army. For several weeks we're living on my salary alone. Even with the boys now being fed by the army, things are tight. I do extra sewing and Madame Berneau gives me extra hours on the shop floor when she can. With the war though, people are worrying less about dresses and more about shutting down the Germans. Business at the shop is slow. People who previously didn't pay much attention to the upheaval in Europe now devour every bit of news. Every mother with a son fighting overseas waits for a letter to tell her that her son is still alive, and dreads a telegram that tells her he isn't. Among French Montrealers there's a growing rumble of unrest. There's talk of a forced conscription to make up for heavy losses in Europe and anti-British sentiment is coming to a head. English speakers are quick to point out that part of France is occupied by the Germans, making it their war too.

Martin finishes his basic training in Valcartier and is sent to England to finish his training before deployment. Henry Jr. is still at Valcartier but his infrequent letters indicate his eagerness for battle.

One evening in 1916 Gus comes to visit. I've seen him only periodically over the last two years. There were words between Martin, who believes it is the patriotic duty of all healthy males to enlist in the cause against the

Hun, and Gus who feels strongly that the French have no stake in the war. I have no feelings either way, but Gus seems to feel I might be angry with him. He tells me this now, as we sit together in the tiny living room with Maman listening from her room. I assure him I haven't been angry with him and our friendship doesn't rest on whether he enlists. He leaves seeming relieved.

We're all surprised by a knock on the door one crisp fall evening. Gus again stands at the door, hat in hand. He asks me if I want to go for a walk. I turn the job of finishing up the supper dishes over to Ethel and shrug on my old coat with a nod to Maman. She looks up from her darning, brows knit in her signature look of disapproval, but says nothing. Gus and I walk. The sky is brilliant with stars and our words sparkle in front of our faces. It's small talk. We talk about the war, people we know, deaths and marriages. I know something is on Gus's mind. He's nervous, distracted. We pass a small cafe that's still open and Gus steers me inside. It will be easier to talk here, and warmer too. The place is nearly empty, an elderly couple the only other occupants. Gus guides me to the opposite end of the tiny space. He offers to help me with my coat but the cafe is cold and I want to keep it on. When the waitress arrives we both order coffee. She slides the steaming cups onto the table in front of us and I wrap my hands around the cup, allowing the warmth to thaw my fingers.

"What is it you really want to talk about Gus? You're as nervous as a hen in a fox den."

"I'm going to enlist," he says simply.

"What? You? I thought you didn't approve of the war?"

"Whether I approve or not the war is happening. I've lost some very good friends while I sit here wondering what's the right thing. Men are dying by the thousands in Europe. The government will soon put in conscription and force us to go. I think things will be easier for those that enlist voluntarily. Oh Min. I'm not like Martin and Henry. They were so full of fire. They were itching for a fight with the Hun. I just want to stay home and mind my own business. And, and I'm scared. But I don't see any way out. The thing is, I wanted to talk to you first. I'm crazy about you Min. I always have been. I know things have been tough for you since your pa left but I hope when I get home, maybe I could help you. You know. Maybe we could get married and start a family of our own. I'll get my car and I'll have my business. Or maybe I can just drive for someone else. But I can help you Min. I just need to know that you'll be waiting for me when I get home. I need that."

He falls silent. Deflates, almost. It's clear he's rehearsed this speech and now he's spent. The rest is up to me. "Gus, I care for you. I really do. But you don't want to be saddled with my crazy mother and a bunch of half-grown kids. I don't want you to dread coming home from Europe because you've committed to taking on the Menard horde."

He smiles sadly. "Erminie, you might be the only thing that gets me home from Europe. Besides you've been using your family to hold me off for years now. The boys are gone. Ethel and Viola are almost done their schooling. They'll be looking for their own husbands soon. Look, you don't have to say you'll marry me. Not right now. But tell me you won't hook up with any other guy 'til I get home."

"That's not very likely Gus. I don't have energy for a man. It's why I told you I couldn't see you before. It wouldn't be fair."

"I know Min. But it'll be easier. With two of us to share the load it will be easier. Please say yes."

I look at Gus, his eyes are glistening. I'm afraid he might cry.

"Yes, Gus. I promise I won't see anyone else while you're gone. And we can talk about the rest when you get home. Maybe the war will be over before you have to go."

"That would be nice but I ain't counting on it." He reaches out and takes both my hands in his. "Thank you Min. You have no idea how much this means to me."

We finish our coffee. The rest of the conversation is about Henry Jr. and Martin and their letters-always too short on news-and about others of our acquaintance who've enlisted. Three haven't come home but we don't mention those. Gus walks me home. At the door he kisses me deeply. It's not like the chaste kisses we've shared in the past. There's longing in this kiss. If I did not know that Maman was pacing just inside the door, I'd invite him in and perhaps give him a proper send-off. It seems more and more that old rules no longer apply.

Gus goes to the recruiting office the next day to fill out his paperwork. I see him on two more occasions before he leaves for basic training. He gets a few days before he ships off to Europe and we spend as much of that time together as we can. He looks good in his uniform and the intense physical training has made him leaner. I persuade him to go with me to a photography studio on St. Catherines to have his portrait taken. It's something that Henry Jr. and Martin both had done. I tell him jokingly that I want it so I'll remember what he looks like. The real reason-that it might be all I have of him if he never comes back-is too morose to put into words.

In 1917 the Canadian government institutes a conscription program designed to plump up the ranks of men, seriously depleted since the start of the war by death, injury and illness. Though we all know it's coming, the proclamation is met with riots in the streets of Montreal as old French/English rivalries surface. Amid all the chaos of the conscription crises, Maman receives a telegram from the war office in Ottawa. I'm working at the shop when it arrives. When I return home from work at the end of the day she's sitting on the sofa, clutching the unread telegram in her hand. "Open it please," she orders, her voice gravelly. I unfold the sheet and read it quickly to myself.

"He's coming home," I yell. "Henry Jr. is coming home. He's been shot but he's being sent to a hospital in England. When he can travel they're sending him home." I watch the tension drain out of my mother's shoulders.

"Was he badly injured?"

"It just says he was shot by enemy fire-no details. But he's alive and he's coming home." I reach over and put my arms around Maman. Contact is not usual between the two of us but there may never be a better time to share an embrace. To my surprise Maman begins to cry. It seems unusual for her to be so concerned about someone not herself; I stuff the thought. It seems ungracious to think ill of her at this moment. Only now do the younger children peek out of the bedroom. I've not, until this moment, noticed their absence and I'm not sure whether Maman sent them there or if they fled in fear of one of her tempers. They timidly approach and I smile encouragingly at them. I repeat the news to the three excited faces but it's clear they've been listening at the door and already know what the telegram says. There's nervous jubilation, with the children keeping an eye on Maman to see if she might yet turn on them. Freddy is too young to understand what's going on but he's excited because everyone else is excited.

"What about Martin?" Leona asks.

"I don't know. I'm sure he's fine but this telegram is only about Henry. For now we just have to be happy he's coming home and hope his injuries aren't too bad."

It's six months before Henry makes it home. He has a lengthy convalescence at a military hospital outside of London and then has to endure the sea voyage home. The war has taught him that he's susceptible to sea sickness. The misery in his belly, combined with the pain of his leg wound makes his journey home memorable for all the wrong reasons. We all go down to the train station to meet him. I take the day off work and the only one missing is Ethel who has just started a new job and doesn't want to take time off, and of course Martin who's still in Europe. The long train trip from Halifax leaves Henry tired but recovering from the horrid retching of the sea voyage. He hops off the train using a crutch propped under his arm, looking thin and drawn. We have a special dinner for him. I've gotten a nice piece of pork at considerable expense and with no small amount of cajoling of the local butcher. Maman offers to cook it, a surprise since Maman has scarcely done any cooking since Papa left. I'm reluctant to leave the precious pork in her care. In the end though, I decide it's a good sign that Maman is showing interest in day-to-day things again. I needn't have worried. The pork is cooked to perfection. Henry has a bottle of wine and some sweets for the children and everyone is in fine spirits. It's the first time I've seen Maman laugh since Papa left. It's also the first time I've felt the warmth of having a real family in a very long time.

Just two days later the mood is shattered by the arrival of an envelope. Once again, it arrives while I'm at work, but this time Maman opens the letter. It's from Papa. It's brief but he proclaims his love for all of us. He says he knows he left us in a bad way and hopes to make it up to us. He has enclosed a bank note for five thousand dollars. It is, he says, everything he has been able to save over the past five years. There's no return address on the letter, but a smudged postmark indicates it was mailed in Georgia. The name of the town is undecipherable.

The money will be a huge help, no doubt, but the coming of the letter sends Maman into another spiral. It would have been better if he had just left us alone after all these years, I confide to Henry.

"He's with her, you know."

"Rachel?"

"Uh-huh."

"How do you know?"

"She was from Georgia. I remember the men at the quarry poking fun at her accent and calling her a Georgia peach." Henry explains.

"Well, we'll just keep that bit of information to ourselves, shall we?" Henry shrugs but says nothing.

Any bit of ground Maman has gained in climbing out of her depression is lost. She withdraws again, spending most of the time in her bedroom. Again, I begin to worry about leaving the younger children alone with her. I don't think Maman would hurt them, but I'm not sure how, or if, she would respond in an emergency. Donnie is eight and in school during the day, leaving Maman alone with four-year-old Freddie most of the day. Fred is quiet and introspective and in many ways I'm grateful. He's not likely to get into trouble sitting and reading his books or pretending to drive imaginary cars. But I worry about him too. He spends so much time alone with a mother who is really no mother at all. I try to make it up to him when I'm home, lavishing extra attention on him. But he smiles rarely and it's rarer still to hear him laugh. It's a sad life for a little boy.

Henry finds a job quickly. With so many men off in Europe there are plenty of vacancies. He learned to drive in the army and gets a job delivering produce from a wholesaler to several local shops. It's hard work but his leg has healed well. So well he wonders if he should re-enlist. I think he's crazy for even thinking about it and tell him so. I tell him the army doesn't need a crazy man with a limp. Within a few weeks Henry is seeing a pretty blond girl named Jane and there's no more talk of re-enlisting. In the meantime, he pilfers a bit of over-ripe produce when he can and supplements the family's sparse diet. We still have most of the money Papa sent but I'm miserly with it, trying to stretch it out as long as I can. Even with money, many things are rationed or hard to find.

I have a couple of letters from Gus but they're brief and appear to be hastily written. I confess to being a little hurt. When I complain to Henry he describes the conditions in which the letters are probably written, sometimes in trenches with bullets tearing into the sandbags nearby. This makes me feel better about the length of the letters but does nothing for my confidence in Gus's safety. While agreeing to wait for Gus was partly to make him feel better about going, I now find I'm longing for his return. I want the war to be over. I want to marry Gus. I want to have another child—lots of children. I'm not sure if Gus is the one but I am willing to make it work. I just want a normal life.

CHAPTER THIRTY-ONE

The war ends, finally. I haven't heard from Gus or Martin for an eternity but I keep my fingers crossed. No news is good news. Finally I get a telegram that Gus is on his way home and is well. Within a week Maman receives a telegram from Martin. He's being treated for a respiratory illness but once cleared he'll be on a ship headed home. Martin's news makes me uneasy. Influenza is taking down returning soldiers faster than the German bullets. Montreal has been hit particularly hard by the outbreak-so much so that the city has refitted streetcars to transport bodies because the hearses can't keep up. These deaths frighten me more than the distant war did. This is something no one volunteers for and there's no glory in dying with blood crusted on your lips. And the children. I have to keep the children safe. I become fanatical about having them wash their hands, something I learned at Wells as a way to prevent disease. We stop going to church and I keep the children home from school, though eventually the schools close anyway. In fact, no one goes out any more than they have to. People still need food so Henry keeps hauling his produce, though two of the shopkeepers he regularly delivers to are taken by what people are calling the Spanish Flu. People creep through the streets clutching scarves to their mouths to prevent inhaling the virus. Business at the shop dries up so I no longer work down in the shop on Saturday mornings, though I do continue sewing during the week. I enjoy these days. It's the only time I get to visit with Rosie.

Rosie takes the illness just before Christmas and is sick for several days, recovering with no lingering effect. Genevieve, Madame Berneau's former shop girl, now married with two little girls grows ill with aches and fever on Christmas eve and is dead the following morning. That's how it goes. No way to tell who will be taken, but those who succumb are often in the prime of life. The infection comes in waves. Just when we think it's winding down, a new wave of illness hits. It's so unfair that people make it through this ghastly war, only to be cut down by the flu. And those soldiers! They have endured so much in the trenches. I ache for the families who feel the joy of a returning son, only to learn that he died on the ship on the way home.

Christmas 1918 passes-a bleak affair. Though there is relief that the war is over, no one dares to socialize and there is little money or food. We don't even venture out to mass.

I come home one day to find Maman alone in the apartment. "Where are the children?"

"I sent them outside to play."

"You what?"

"They were getting on each other's last nerve being cooped up in these rooms all day. They need fresh air and sunshine."

"Maman, what if they get sick?" I'm angry. I think it more likely that they were getting on Maman's nerves, not each others.

"They'll be fine. I told them to stay together and Leona is with them." She brushes away my concern. "They should be home soon. I told them to be back when they hear the five o'clock bell."

I bite my tongue. Minutes later Leona and the boys come clattering up the stairs. Their cheeks are red from hard play and I have to admit, to myself, they look healthier than they have in weeks. No doubt some fresh air will be good for them.

"We played ball," Donnie chirps. "Look, I got a shiner. The ball hit me-whap!" He turns the left side of his face dramatically toward me for inspection. I see nothing but it seems appropriate to ooh and aww over his "shiner".

"Where did you get a ball?" I ask, trying to sound casual.

"There were some kids down on the street. They had a bat and ball so we went with them to the school yard. It's OK, Min. We know them from school. And we stayed in the school yard." he adds quickly, trolling for a phrase that will make me relax.

"Go and wash up," I tell them. "Use lots of soap. Wash right up to your elbows. Leona you make sure they do it. Anything you picked up out there, I want it going right down the drain, understand?" Leona looks suitably concerned and I know I can trust her to wash everyone's hands twice, just to be sure.

Ethel, Viola and Henry all come in within minutes of each other, all demanding to know what there is to eat. I sigh and wash my own hands at the kitchen sink before boiling potatoes and slicing some cold meat salvaged from last night's dinner. Having four people contribute to the family dinner certainly helps but food is still short due to the war. I am sick to death of rationing and making do.

Three days later, after dinner, Ethel and Viola are cleaning up the dishes while I catch Donnie up on some of his school lessons. His cheeks are flushed but he seems otherwise fine. He's a bright boy and eagerly reads lines for me and recites his multiplication tables. It's only as he gets ready for bed that he complains of a headache and says his bones hurt. I try not to show concern. I finish getting him ready for bed. By the time I tuck him in his skin feels dry and hot. It's when Leona complains of similar symptoms I have to face the fact the flu is in our house and there's nothing to do now but deal with it as best we can. I put Leona to bed in the same room as Donnie and give strict instructions that no one is to go in. I make everyone wash their hands again and stand over them while they do it. No one argues. They must feel my tension because, for once, they do as they're told without argument.

By ten that night both children are burning with fever and I send Henry for the doctor. He comes back with word that the doctor will come when he can, but the illness is spreading like wildfire through our neighborhood. He's out on a call and his wife isn't sure how long he'll be. She has suggested taking the children to Gray Nun's hospital, but to be forewarned that they will be overwhelmed as well. I wrap a tea towel around my mouth and tend to the children with cool cloths and reassurances. When Maman begins to complain of a headache, my first reaction is that she wants some of the attention. But it becomes clear she has a fever. I make up a bed for her on the floor of what we now call the sick room.

I become a general on a battlefield. I do the nursing duties and keep Henry, Ethel and Viola busy washing compresses and doing whatever needs to be done. Henry bristles at his captivity and defies me by going out that evening to see his girlfriend. I'm furious with him and scream, as he slams the door, that I hope he dies. But Henry never does get the illness and I live to regret those horrible words.

CHAPTER THIRTY-TWO

Martin arrives home, unannounced, in time for the funerals. He doesn't send a telegraph because he doesn't want us to worry. He taps at the door then rushes in, arms wide to receive his welcome. He quickly realizes something is terribly wrong. The tiny sitting room is crowded, our family, but also a couple of neighbors and some of Maman's extended family, here looking for free food, I don't doubt. Only those who have already survived the flu dare to come out, but it's still enough people to fill our space. Martin can see through to the kitchen where two shrouded bodies are supported, each on boards slung across two kitchen chairs. I see his eyes dance over the room but before he can take it all in Ethel is in his arms, wailing uncontrollably. Viola and I rush to him and soon he is the center of a crush of bodies, all welcoming him home. Through Ethel's tears he's finally made to understand that Donnie and Leona are gone. Maman is sick but on the mend. I also contracted a mild version and for two days had to turn over nursing duties to Ethel. As with Maman, though, I am weak but well enough to be out of bed. This is hardly the homecoming Martin has hoped for. He tells us how, all through the months in Europe, huddled in muddy trenches, dodging bullets and shrapnel, he missed us. It's an odd thing to hear him tell us how much he missed us in front of all these people. Both Henry and Martin have grown up so much during the war that I hardly know them. In a private moment with Martin he tells me he has seen so much loss and sadness he wonders if there will ever be an end to it.

In fact there is an end, at least to the illness. We mourn for and bury our two babies. The loss of Leona and little Donnie has torn a great hole in our family, but the Spanish Flu finally runs it's course. There is one more wave of the sickness, but we lose no more family members. It's the last major outbreak of the disease in Montreal. Gus returns safely from Europe, delayed in his return by a serious shoulder injury. I meet him at the station and, with his good arm he wraps me in a bear hug. I find myself in tears, not of joy but of profound relief. This man will help me. I won't have to do everything alone any more.

Maman recovers her physical strength but is not the same. She has rarely taken responsibility for anything in her life, but now she embraces the guilt of having sent the children out to play and wraps it around her like a tired old quilt. The depression that has always been a part of her, deepening after Papa left, worsens. She stays in bed for days on end, eating almost nothing and refusing to bathe or take care of her most basic needs. I hear her crooning to her lost children; not just to Leona and Donnie but to Louis, dead many years now. The days of deepest depression are often followed by three or four days of restlessness. She paces and rants and sometimes strikes out at anyone in her way. I'm at my wit's end. Each of the girls must take turns staying home from work to care for Freddy which puts all of our jobs in jeopardy.

One night Maman is in a high rage about a strange smell that she says is "sticking to her brain." She keeps striking herself in the head with the heel of her hand and suddenly, before any of us can stop her, she storms out of the apartment. Henry and I run after her but, just outside our building, she meets an elderly couple out for a stroll. Maman is on them before they know what's happening. She knocks the woman to the ground and starts choking her. All the while the vilest obscenities pour from her mouth. Henry will later confide he'd only heard language like that in Europe during the war and where on earth had Maman even learned those words? We pull Maman off the woman and try to smooth things over with the couple as best we can. They won't be mollified though. The woman hit her head on the sidewalk and is dazed and bleeding. The old gentleman is badly frightened and worried about his wife. Others on the street have witnessed the attack and run to fetch the police. When the police arrive they have to restrain a seething, frothing Maman. It's an ugly, ugly scene.

In the end the court decides Maman is too ill to stand trial. Instead she's committed to St. Jean's Hospital for the Insane. There she's under the care of the Sisters of Providence. I'm sick with guilt because my first response, when I learn my mother will be locked up, is relief.

The girls visit Maman when they can but it's a long trek to the hospital by streetcar. Occasionally Gus is able to drive us in his brand new auto, a Ford of which he is exceedingly proud. By now, though, Gus is working for a cab company and isn't always available. Henry and Martin never visit Maman despite repeated requests from all of us girls. They simply decline and, when asked why, they shrug. As much as they have grown to men, Maman always brings out the unresponsive teen-aged boy in both of them. I envy their ability to feel no guilt. They simply do what they like.

Not that I blame them, really. Visits with Maman are a horror. In spite of the best efforts of the Sisters, the dark hallways are full of people who appear either catatonic or who cry out constantly. The whole building smells of urine and feces and other smells that seem just out of reach of recognition. Maman has moments of clarity but often seems to be somewhere else. Occasionally she is angry and sometimes even tries to kick or bite us. On these occasions the staff restrains her and we are asked to leave. It's a horrible existence and I feel sorry for her in spite of our checkered history together.

CHAPTER THIRTY-THREE

Gus and I are married in 1919 in a small ceremony in Sacred Heart Church. Henry and Martin are there with their girl friends Jane and Willi. Ethel and Viola also attend and Rosie, dear Rosie, is my maid of honor. Gus's practical joking friend Arthur is our best man, meaning I spend the entire day waiting for him to do something to embarrass us. He never does. It's another sign that we've all changed so much since the war started. No one from Gus's family attends the wedding. They say it's too far to travel but we know they don't approve of Gus's choice of career and probably not of his choice of wife, though they've never met me.

I wear an ankle-length, tiered dress designed by Madame Berneau, with a little beaded cap and veil. Gus wears his regimental uniform which surprises me since he never wanted to go to war and still will not talk about his experience. After the ceremony we sit for a wedding portrait and he looks so tall and proud that I can never quite look at the photo without a little flutter of pride.

When they took Maman away I stayed in her apartment with Freddy and the two girls. Now we have a family meeting and agree that little Freddy, now six, will live with Gus and I. It's the logical choice. The boys have plans that will take them off in different directions and Ethel and Viola are both considering joining the Sisters, though I can't see it actually happening. Gus and I have an apartment on Boyer and can give him a more stable environment than any of the others. Freddy has remained a small child, never as vital as his older brothers were at his age. Because he is the same age as Dorothy, I'm constantly reminded of my daughter. Each milestone-the start of school or losing a baby tooth-reminds me that Dorothy will be going through the same stage. During my time in Montreal I've written to St. Joseph's Orphanage a total of six times asking for information. That first letter was answered very curtly by the matron. The second and third letters are answered by a different woman, perhaps marking a changing of the guard at the orphanage. These letters are nearly identical in content but much softer in tone. They are terribly sorry but can't provide any information on Dorothy, or any adoption, due to state regulations. Letters four through six generate no response at all.

I stay in touch with Mary Armstrong in Pittsford, and I'm eager for each of her letters, wanting to hear all about her children, then later, of her new husband. I know Mary and Lottie are good friends so I even stoop to asking Mary if she can get information on Dorothy through Lottie. But nothing comes through that avenue either. It seems no matter where I turn the walls separating me from my daughter are impenetrable. I still have my dreams though. In them Dorothy is a beautiful girl with a doting family who send her off to school each day where she is adored by the other children and is academically superior to them all. Please God, just don't let her have a life like mine.

Much to my surprise Ethel and Viola don't forget about joining the Sisters of Providence. Their visits with Maman have convinced them they want careers in nursing. Ethel joins the sisters as a novice and Viola follows soon after. I see little of them after that. Though I know they're training as nurses, neither are at St. Jean's. When I do see them they seem happy enough with the path they've chosen. I have to accept that, while it isn't my way, it isn't my choice to make. These two beautiful young women, who I hoped would give me many nieces and nephews to dote on, have chosen a life with God.

Gus has gone through some very difficult experiences in the war. He refuses to talk about them but he is a changed man. In that he's no different from the other hundreds of thousands of men who fought in, and survived, the European campaign. He bottles his feelings up and tries to move on with his life. But his drinking, always a big part of his life, becomes a crutch he depends on to get him through the day. He's been broken as a young boy and now he's in danger of shattering. He loves me though. And he treats me well. Freddy is his special buddy and he treats him like his own son. He often speaks of the uncle who took him in when no one wanted him. He wants to be that person for Freddy. I understand that Gus is broken but I think maybe I am too. At 26 I feel I've lived several lifetimes, all of them bad. It's sadly true that reform school was one of the happier sustained periods in my life, even considering Wyre and the abuse I suffered there. But now, finally, I'm in a position I've strived for my entire life. I have my own home, a husband who loves me, a small one to care for and I'm no longer under my mother's thumb. None of that looks quite like it did in my imagination back when I was 16, but I'm willing to accept it and make it work. Especially when I realize I'm expecting a baby.

My beautiful Dorothee is born in 1923 and she is perfect. Freddy is a proud big brother and Gus cries like a baby when he holds her for the first time. I love her with all my heart but each time I look into her blue eyes I am reminded of my other Dorothy. I always wonder what became of her and say a little prayer that she is well.

Henry made a trip to Georgia in 1921 and located Papa. He found him happily married to Rachel, the love of his life. Henry and Papa stayed in touch over the next year and Rachel sent him a note when Papa died in 1922. All of this Henry passes on in letters, as spare of written words as he is in person. I wonder how Papa could have married again since he was, inconveniently, still married to Maman, but Henry believes the marriage was necessary to appease Rachel's father, some sort of fire-breathing Baptist minister. And so I learn that my father is not just a cad but a bigamist. I can't find it in my heart to be angry with him anymore, though, and I never tell Maman about his new life. His decision turned many lives upside down but I can't hate him for reaching out for happiness.

HENRY

For all our trying Rachel has never conceived a child. I can't say I'm too sad about that but I know it wears heavy on Rachel. She's always wanted to be a mother and it doesn't look like it will ever happen. I've never held much of a belief in God but I sometimes feel like maybe he's punishing Rachel and I for our many sins. I think that Rachel believes that too. All that aside, we've been happy.

One morning not so long ago I was out throwing some hay to the cattle when I saw a man walking up the drive. We don't get many visitors out our way so I walked out to meet him. It took me getting right up close before I realized it was my oldest boy, Henry Jr. You could have knocked me over with a feather, I was that surprised to set eyes on him after all these years. I thought he might be angry with me-had every right to be-but we had a right nice visit. He stayed over in our guest room and we sat up into the early hours drinking whiskey and catching up.

Talking to Henry Jr. made me realize how much I miss all my children. Since his visit, I've been toying with the idea of a trip back to Montreal to see them. I'm not sure what Rachel will think of the idea though. And Henry told me Minnie was pretty sour with me. In any case I've not been well the last few weeks. When I'm feeling better I'll sit down with Rachel and see what she thinks of a trip north. Maybe I can mend some fences after all these years.

CHAPTER THIRTY-FOUR

Maman dies, still in St. Jean's Hospital, in 1948 at the age of 75. Henry, Martin, Freddy, and Dorothee are all married by the time she passes. Dorothee and her husband, Laurent, have given me three delightful grandchildren. Martin is married to Willi, the girl he met after the war. He went to the States briefly to work on the railroad but they've recently returned to Canada and are living in Toronto. Freddy, or Fred as he prefers to be called, is also living in Toronto with his wife, Tressa and two rambunctious boys. Henry has returned to the States and is living in Michigan with his wife.

St. Jean's has a cemetery attached to the property and I arrange to have Maman buried there. Rosie sends a telegram of condolence from Quebec City where she's living with her husband and four children. None of the boys come to their mother's funeral. Ethel and Viola get permission to attend, though, and on a cold blustery day in November we lay her to rest. Gus, Ethel, Viola, Dorothee, Laurent, myself and a woman Maman befriended in the hospital are the only mourners. A representative of the hospital says a few words about what a caring woman Jenny was. I wonder, uncharitably, if the woman actually ever met my mother. The burial is presided over by the hospital's priest, a young, raw-boned fellow who wants nothing so much as to get out of the rain. An underling holds an umbrella over his head to keep his prayer book dry, but the wind tugs at it and I can see the pages curling with the wet. It's all over in a few minutes and, flanked by my daughter and sisters, I watch as two workers lower Maman's casket into the ground. In spite of all that has passed between us I grieve for my mother. It may be my grief is for the mother I always wanted, not the one I had. I can't read my own emotions at that moment, but I know I'm sad. The four of us stand beside the grave with bowed heads. By now the rain is streaming off our umbrellas. Gus stands nearby and, from the corner of my eye, I can see him shifting impatiently from one foot to the other. He is, no doubt, anxious about how much water we'll track into his immaculate cab.

Still he gives us time to say our goodbyes without comment and I love him for that.

As the cold rain falls I think back on Maman's life and the way mine was so often at odds with hers. I longed to be on my own, free of Maman's suffocating influence. Now I'm free. I'm fifty-five years old and finally free to live my own life. What now? Strangely I feel empty. I turn and take Gus's arm on one side and Dorothee's on the other. Gus guides us back to his taxi, wet and gleaming on the parking lot. Ethel, Viola and Laurent trail behind.

"Take us home, Gus."

"Sure thing, Min."

MARCH 1913

Mary Armstrong poured herself a cup of tea, sat herself down at her kitchen table and opened the letter from her friend Lottie in Burlington. She and Lottie were friends at nursing school and stayed in touch over the years. Mary savored Lottie's newsy letters, full of gossip about mutual friends and stories about the girls staying in the Home for Friendless Women where Lottie worked. Some of Lottie's tales were funny, some gut-wrenchingly sad but Lottie's letters were never dull. This one started out in the usual way, asking Mary about the children, her new beau, their new home and lamenting about the terrible winter.

With a start, Mary sat her tea down and squinted at the third paragraph.

"You'll recall your friend Erminie, the girl who worked for you for a time? You'll know she stayed with us for a time and had a baby girl she named Dorothy. The poor wee thing was never well and our Dr. Fennimore took some pains in dissuading her from keeping the child. Baby Dorothy was in St. Joseph's as there was no one willing to take such a sickly baby. She couldn't digest her food properly and could not put on weight. I never saw her but my friends who tended her from time to time at the hospital said she was naught but a rail, with not a speck of fat on her little body. Always in pain too. It was a sad situation. I aught not to be telling you this but the wee thing died Friday last. She was just a few days short of her first birthday. Very tragic. Everyone did what they could for her but all agree it was a blessing for the child. My friend at the hospital said she heard the mother had been writing asking after the welfare of her daughter but, of course, they could tell her nothing. I'm not sure how you feel about her knowing, and of course this would have to be held in the utmost confidence. But I pass the information on to you to decide the best course of action."

Lottie's letter went on but Mary couldn't concentrate. She too had received a letter from Erminie, now living in Montreal with her family, asking if she might be able to learn anything from the orphanage. Mary had tried but had no luck through official channels at the orphanage. It had not occurred to her that Lottie would have connections through the hospital and might be able to find something out. Now she wished she didn't know. How could she make such a decision? Could she tell Erminie her baby was dead and crush any dreams she may have had for the child?

Mary carefully folded the letter and put it back into the envelope. She tucked the envelope into a book she was reading and finished her tea. When her friend David came calling that evening she debated telling him about the letter. But she couldn't seem to find the right time and in the end she was silent. She spent a sleepless night. The next day she sat down and wrote a response to Lottie, saying how sad she was to learn of Erminie's baby and that she was still undecided about whether or not to tell her. In any case, she assured Lottie, she would handle it with the utmost discretion. Once she had crafted her response she took the letter from Lottie to the stove, lifted the cover plate and dropped it in, whispering a little prayer for the soul of baby Dorothy as she watched the paper catch and burn.

(p. 7) - Calisthenics are in the square at half past ten for one hour.

(p. 19) ... for half an hour of calisthenics

(p. 16) Jessie / Jesse

use of — instead of comma
needs space before & after
reads like a compound word
i.e., p. 127 pen-gnawing

p 129 "Now," he says reasonably, "how about...

p. 148 - missing space
St. Zotique

Manufactured by Amazon.ca
Bolton, ON